# MADE OR BROKEN:
## FOOTBALL AND SURVIVAL IN THE GEORGIA WOODS

BY
BILL LIGHTLE

Made or Broken

Copyright© 2004 by Bill Lightle

Cover photo by Bill Lightle
Players in photo (from left) DeWitt Williams, Bill Lightle and David McClung

Printed and bound in the United States of America. All rights reserved. No part of this book may be reproduced in any form or by any electronic or mechanical means including information storage and retrieval systems without permission in writing from the copyright holder, except by a reviewer, who may quote brief passages in review.

ISBN: 0-9744668-7-5

Published by

2525 W Anderson Lane, Suite 540
Austin, Texas 78757

Tel: 512.407.8876
Fax: 512.478.2117

E-mail: info@turnkeypress.com
Web: www.turnkeypress.com

*This book is dedicated to my father. He was the first to show me the beauties of team sports.*

Song credits:

**ASCAP** – www.ascap.com
*Alabama* (Performed by Neil Young), Young, Neil, Silver Fiddle Music, ASCAP Title Code: 310126191

*Stairway to Heaven*, (Performed by Led Zeppelin), Page, James Patrick & Plant, R. A., Superhype Publishing, Inc., ASCAP Title Code: 490294198

*Thick as a Brick* (Performed by Jethro Tull), Anderson, Ian, Chrysalis Music, ASCAP Title Code: 500212639

*Jesus Just Left Chicago* (Performed by ZZ Top), Beard, Frank Lee, Gibbons, Billy F. & Hill, Joe Michael, Hamstein Music Company, BMI Title Code: 400062820

**BMI** – www.bmi.com
*Indian Sunset* (Performed by Elton John), John, Elton & Taupin, Bernard, Universal Songs of Polygram Inc., BMI Work #724698

*Whipping Post* (Performed by Allman Brothers Band), Allman, Gregory L., Elijah Blue Music, BMI Work #1659149

# Contents

Foreword ................................................................ 7
Acknowledgements ................................................ 8
Introduction ........................................................ 10
Chapter One - Natural Men ................................ 13
Chapter Two - A Beautiful Sight ........................ 103
Chapter Three - A Group of Husky Youngsters ... 157
Conclusion - Shoot Man, That Cat was Tough .... 217
Author's Note .................................................... 228

# FOREWORD

Bill Lightle has given us a splendid book reminding us of the great passion of high school football in the Deep South. Further, his reminiscences from Albany High's pre-season football camp at Graves Springs reinforce my long-held belief that coaches, especially at the high school level, have a profound effect on shaping the lives of young people under their guidance, teaching them the importance of lifelong lessons learned such as "paying the price," and "working together," and establishing special bonds that last a lifetime.

Perhaps even more important, Mr. Lightle reminds us that it was football, more than any other single reason, which was responsible for integration being accepted in the South better than any other section of the country.

*Made or Broken* will not only be enjoyed by those who were part of high school football in the Deep South, but will keep alive for generations to come all those stories that were told by fathers and grandfathers of how they played and survived the game in the old days.

Vince Dooley
Athletic Director University of Georgia
**June 2003**

# ACKNOWLEDGEMENTS

Over the years, I have camped several times along the Muckalee Creek near Graves Springs Football Camp. Each time I drove down Graves Springs Road, my mind raced back to when I was a player there nearly thirty years ago. Initially, I had considered writing an article for the *Journal of Southwest Georgia History* that would chronicle the camp during the mid-1960s as it underwent racial integration. But the more I thought about the camp and talked with both the coaches and players who went there, I knew that the full story had to be told.

This book consists of three major sections. The first one covers the years I played at Graves Springs, from 1972 through 1974. Here I relied on the memory of my own experiences and also personal interviews with players and coaches who were at Graves Springs during those years.

The second section covers the racial integration of the camp. Again, I interviewed several players and coaches, including Grady Caldwell, the first black to attend the camp in August 1965. I believe that what I learned through these many interviews will lead to a greater understanding of Albany, both today and during the civil rights movement. This section—and the other two to a compelling degree—suggest how sports in our society determines much about who we are and what we become.

The third part chronicles the camp's inception through the mid-1960s. In addition to interviews, I found helpful sources through the *Albany Herald*, school board documents, and the family histories of the players and coaches. In doing the research and writing, I had much help along the way. Special thanks goes out to Bobby Stanford, who not only shared family scrapbooks and documents, but also pointed me in the right direction in terms of who to interview for a historical perspective of the camp. Stanford played at Graves Springs and his father, Hollis Stanford, coached there.

I want to thank my editors, Arlene and Terry Robinson of Buford, Georgia. They gave me invaluable guidance and encouragement. Thanks also to Kathleen Caldwell of Albany State University. Kathleen, who is Grady Caldwell's wife, spoke candidly with me about many of her personal experiences. She also helped me find others whose stories became part of this book.

Thanks goes out to Terri Carroll, Vic Miller and Roger Marietta, who read earlier drafts, caught mistakes and offered important suggestions.

Lee Formwalt, the executive director of the Organization of American Historians, helped immensely with the section concerning the camp's integration.

Special thanks to my wife, Susan, who read earlier drafts and often said during the writing of the book: "Daddy has disappeared again." She told this to our two boys, David and Dylan, because I often "disappeared" upstairs to the boys' playroom where I used the family's computer to write. Thanks, boys.

Bill Lightle
April 2002

# INTRODUCTION

Thirty years later it's almost unbelievable, if not mean and cruel, what high school coaches put us through for two weeks in the backwoods of Georgia during football camp. I remember feeling scared because I knew what had happened to other boys who went to the woods to be on the team. Graves Springs Football Camp hovered over me like a blood-sucking creature ready to swoop down and swallow me whole. But if I wanted to play football for Albany High School, and I did, I had to go.

Southwest Georgia rolls with crimson soil nourished by the region's sun-shaded creeks and rivers. Summers there are as extreme as the winters are in Central Indiana, where I was born. In the summer of 1966, my father accepted a job in Albany, Georgia, and I moved there with the rest of the family: my mother, brother, and two sisters. As a boy in the Midwest, I had played only baseball and basketball. Football was just for the older boys. But in Albany I learned that Southerners had a deep passion for football. Here, football was a game in which nine-year-olds like me could play on organized teams.

Growing up in Albany, I met new friends through sports, particularly football, which I first played in the fall of 1966. In the early 1970s I attended the Graves Springs Camp, Albany High School's preseason football camp. The camp, located outside of Albany along the Muckalee Creek (a tributary of the Flint River), would remain in operation for nearly half a century, having opened during the Great Depression. Over the years, hundreds of local teenagers lived along the creek for two weeks in grueling conditions, practicing football three times a day while the August sun warmed the waters of the creek. Players bathed in the creek and slept in two barracks—one for the varsity, the other for underclassmen—and relieved themselves in the woods. Through the Great Depression, World War II and the civil rights movement, the camp instilled in players the discipline needed to play Southern-style football, a game that captivated the region before the mid-century.

Players who attended the camp transferred the discipline they learned there into other aspects of their lives as they came of age. Some of the players went on to play at the collegiate and professional levels, and all of the ones I interviewed said that no other football camp was as demanding as what Albany High coaches put them through along the Muckalee Creek. Even players who went from high school to the military found life tougher at Graves Springs than during the Army's basic training. Many of the camp's attendees went on to enjoy success in business, politics, education, and other careers, saying that the discipline and sacrifice—especially the "mental toughness" of Graves Springs—helped them into adulthood.

Memories of camp life rested gently in the spirits of many former players and coaches. Players who were teenage buddies remained close into adulthood, while friendships were both made and enhanced by the camp experience. Over the years, the coaches befriended the same players they worked unmercifully under the scorching Georgia sun. This classic experience of sacrifice and suffering created longstanding bonds among players and coaches alike.

By the mid-1960s, the camp itself would undergo the same dramatic cultural transformation that was then underway throughout the South. Integration was being mandated by the federal government onto a Southern culture that had long waved the banner of white supremacy. Graves Springs represented one of the few aspects of Albany's culture where whites and blacks were able to live and work together with a sense of equality. Blacks who integrated Graves Springs went there to compete with white athletes and earn positions on the traditionally all-white team—most thought little of contributing to the civil rights struggle. For these players, it was not until years after they left Graves Springs that they began to fully understand just how monumental it was for them to be the first: not only to integrate the team, but to live with "white guys" at camp.

Many white players grew up in a segregated society where racist attitudes and epithets were as common as the Southern pines and crimson soil. Yet at Graves Springs Camp, what the coaches established was a racial acceptance that put hard work and winning football games above racism.

For those players who attended Graves Springs, there was indeed a contradictory element at work about how the players perceived life there. For nearly five decades, players dreaded the drudgery of the three daily practices and the hard-nosed discipline of coaches who made them practice football in the middle of the woods. At the same time, swimming naked in the creek, poker games, music from eight-track tape players and rites of initiation bound players together in friendship. Still, some players simply left camp, finding it too tough to endure. Others like Tom Giddens and Tommy Ussery left camp after the first day of practice, only to return the following day after being pressured by parents and coaches to do so.

The very players who survived the camp through friendships with their teammates called it, among other things: "hell," "barbaric," "that damn environment," and "that tough son-of-a-bitch."

My memories of Graves Springs remain forever true, like the morning mist rising above the Muckalee Creek. I hope you enjoy this book.

# CHAPTER ONE

# NATURAL MEN

# ONE

**A**UGUST 1972
Throughout that summer I played baseball, slept late and dreamed of the major leagues, but as August approached I was mentally preparing myself for Graves Springs. Sometimes at night I couldn't sleep just thinking about football camp; it scared the hell out of me.

Growing up I had always played sports, and at Albany Junior High School my basketball coach was Jere Tillman, who was as uncompromising as steel and could be as mean as a bucketful of nails. Tillman wouldn't tolerate players not hustling and working hard every minute. I played guard along with Donnie Spence, who later played football with me at Albany High. During one basketball loss, Spence and I played poorly and feared what Tillman was going to say to us. Afterwards in the locker room, we waited along with the team for Tillman's traditional post-game talk.

When Tillman entered the room, his face swollen with anger, I was sitting next to Spence. Tillman moved directly over to the two of us. He looked down, shaking his clenched fist, and spoke with the power of Yahweh. "We lost this game because of you two sumbitches!"

"Yes sir, Coach," I said.

He stared into the blue eyes of Donnie Spence. "Yes sir, Coach Tillman," Spence said, "we're sorry we let the team down. We'll play better next game . . . I promise."

Tillman was right; we *had* played like "sumbitches." The next game, wanting no more fire from Tillman's mouth, Spence and I played much better and we won.

Tillman was a good football as well as basketball coach. He worked the team hard through the fall of 1971; but what he put us through during our daily practice sessions didn't prepare us for Graves Springs in August of 1972. Nothing could prepare you for Graves Springs.

\* \* \*

One Sunday afternoon in mid-August, my parents took me to the high school parking lot to board two beaten-up yellow school buses with other players who were going to Graves Springs. Built in the 1950s, the school in the following decade included about 2,000 students. By the early 1970s, however, the draw of other public and private schools had cut enrollment in half. On our bus we loaded ice chests, football uniforms, and electric fans, which would give us some comfort from the heat.

Assistant varsity coach Ronnie Archer, who drove one of the two buses, waited for the final player to board, turned around in his seat, looked at us and said, "Boys, ain't no turnin' back now." He shifted the gears slowly, making his way out of the school's back parking lot as we began the ride to camp. "Next stop Graves Springs Resort," Archer said with a devilish laugh.

The bus pulled past Hugh Mills Stadium where we would soon play our games in front of thousands of people. Hugh Mills had coached at Graves Springs years earlier. The ride took us down Second Avenue, lined with tall proud oak trees covered with Spanish moss. The bus rambled past rows of houses. We turned off Second Avenue onto Jefferson Street, passing Albany Junior High.

Adjacent to the school was Phoebe Putney Memorial Hospital. The hospital was named after a New Englander, whose son, Francis Putney, was quite a political figure in the area, having come down after the Civil War. Many local Democrats despised Putney—a white man—for aligning himself with the growing Republican Party, which included former slaves. In 1868, Putney led a political procession to Camilla in Mitchell County, about twenty miles south of Albany. As the group of Republicans approached the county courthouse, armed Democrats awaited them. The Democrats fired rifles repeatedly into the throng of a few whites and several blacks who were trying to express their newly won political freedom. About ten black Republicans were killed and several others wounded, although Putney was not hurt. The incident received national attention. Newspapers in the North referred to it as the "Camilla Massacre."

Stopping at Jefferson Street and Philema Road, or Georgia State Road 91, the bus turned right and rumbled a few miles into Lee County. Next, on to the intersection with Graves Springs Road. At Graves Springs Road we turned left, and after about a mile and a half took another left on a dirt road that led directly to the camp along the Muckalee Creek. All the while, we spoke to one another in whispers laced with anxiety.

The fifteen-minute ride itself had been ominous, a harbinger of the unknown that scared me and the other upcoming tenth-graders who were going to camp for the first time. What were the seniors going to do to us? We had heard the terrible stories of hazing, and we believed every word. Just the fact that we were going to be in the woods in the August heat and practice football three times a day was unnerving to me. The coaches, I believed, were just as mean as the cottonmouths in the creek. I was scared of every one of them. I was scared of the varsity players, too. They might as well have been twenty years older than me instead of one or two. Could I survive at all? If we could make it through the first week the coaches would let us go home for the weekend, but we had to return Sunday for another week of camp.

Donnie Spence and I were sitting together, just as we had the time Coach Tillman called us "sumbitches" after a basketball game. "This is gonna be fun, boys," Donnie said, almost in a whisper, as the bus took us closer and closer to camp.

"Yeah, I can't wait," I whispered back to him as the bus rolled along the dirt road that led to camp, the woods so thick with oak, pine, and other trees they seemed to hide some mystery capable of both redemption and destruction.

As the bus got closer to the camp and finally stopped near the creek, two barracks and a dining hall came into full view. The three buildings were all clustered about one hundred yards or so from a practice field that had been carved out of thick pine trees. We filed out of the bus and claimed our bunks in the weathered wooden barracks with a tin roof and no indoor plumbing. The bunks were stacked two-high; each had wooden slats that supported a simple mattress. Covering the walls were names and dates written by previous players who had slept there since the early 1930s. There were [...] the sides of the barracks where streams of light filte[red...] racks had about ten screened windows, each four fee[t...]

I had played in the woods and fished the creeks [...] where I lived as a kid. But the woods along this part of the Muckalee Creek were something much different than what I had ever experienced before. Along the Muckalee where players swam, poisonous snakes and alligators made their homes. Unlike the innocuous woods of Indiana, the landscape was almost tropical with its palm-like plants that covered both banks of the creek and beyond. Spanish moss hung still and straight from the oak trees clustered around the barracks. In the August heat, a breeze was a boon generally not delivered by the gods of football. Sophomores, by decree from the seniors who even refused to give us toilet paper, were not allowed to use the bathrooms in the varsity barracks. So we relieved ourselves in the woods or upstream in the creek, away from the swimming hole, always on the lookout for rattlesnakes, cottonmouths, and other animals of the piney woods.

\* \* \*

My first night at camp, I lay awake fearing that the seniors were coming to pull me out of bed and do things to me that I would be too embarrassed to tell my parents. A few of them walked by my barracks laughing and talking as if they were about to carry out their evil scheme, and I thought, *Oh hell, here they come!* But nothing happened to me. Later, a varsity player threw a carton of chocolate milk through a window, soaking one of my teammates. But that was it.

I didn't sleep much that first night. I listened to the fans humming and the crickets chirping along the creek. It was still dark when B-team Coach Willie Magwood began shaking us in our beds and blowing a whistle. *Is this a dream?* I thought. *Do we really get up before daylight to practice football?*

Yes, we do at Graves Springs. We dressed only in shorts, shoulder pads, helmets, and cleats. The first week of camp was for conditioning; full dress and contact would come the second week.

We carried our helmets as we walked to the mess hall for a cup of rotten-tasting orange juice and a salt-tablet, which made some of us vomit during practice. Then we walked to the practice field under the light of the morning stars.

"Can you believe this crap?" I asked Donnie Spence.

"Yeah, I can believe," he replied. "We're doin' it, ain't we?"

"I guess we are," I said. "I just can't believe it."

When all of us, B-team and varsity players alike, were on the field, the sun was about to slither through the pine trees that surrounded us. For a moment it was serene and beautiful watching the sun appear and illuminate the field. Then the coaches took over.

"Move it! Move it! Move it, boys!" said the head coach, Ferrell Henry. There was a sense of guttural authority tempered by joy in his voice now that the first practice of camp had begun.

First we jogged around the field just inside the pines. The seniors took the lead. At the far end of the field, we were supposed to touch a metal sign as we were running the lap. The sign said something about the merits of hard work, determination, and "Indian Pride." Henry watched every player closely to make sure we ran the correct route. If he saw a player or two try to shave off fifteen or twenty yards of the lap by not touching the sign, he would holler, "You're only cheatin' your-self! You're only cheatin' yourself!" If the "cheatin' " was too obvious and if Henry was in a foul mood, he'd sometimes make the entire team run another lap.

Trying to save a few yards on the initial lap didn't mean much by the end of practice anyway. We probably jogged and sprinted two or three miles during the course of each practice at Graves Springs. We never walked on the football field. Henry wouldn't allow it. After running the first lap, we formed lines and were led by varsity players for about twenty minutes of stretching, push-ups, leg lifts, and other exercises. B-team players then split from the varsity as each group went through fundamental drills lasting about two hours.

"All right, good mens, we're gonna work hard today and every day. You're gonna be the best you can be," Willie Magwood said. "Y'all are gonna love Graves Springs . . . work hard, good mens!" Magwood frequently said "good mens"; it was his favorite coaching phrase. Soon, we would be saying it, too.

He worked us hard, but he didn't intimidate us as did the varsity coaches. Magwood's character was not as high-voltage as the other coaches. Even on the field we could relax some around him: the only black coach at Graves Springs that year, and the first one in the history of Albany High. He told us that, as a boy in South Georgia, he used to pick cotton all day for two and a-half dollars. Magwood had a calming smile and an easy disposition that all who played for him quickly came to appreciate. We liked Magwood, and we knew he liked us.

At practice that morning we ran drill after drill, including the "monkey roll," whereby players jumped over and over one another on the ground while getting covered with sandspurs.

"These things are all over me!" I said after hitting the ground hard a few times.

"They're in my butt . . . they're everywhere!" Spence exclaimed. The sandspurs, sharp and prickly, were part of a weed-like plant common to South Georgia; they felt like tiny pins sticking all over my body.

Red fire ants built their mounds in the field and bit us repeatedly throughout practice. For such a small insect, they had a terrible bite. After the drills that first morning we were beyond the point of exhaustion, so of course the coaches made us run hundred-yard wind sprints. After the first few sprints my gut was about to burst.

"I want some good mens to push it now!" Magwood said.

Some of the players had run off the field to vomit in the woods. We called them "bird feeders." In other eras at Graves Springs, the phrase "the bear got him" was used to refer to players who threw up in the woods. I don't remember throwing up during my three years at camp, but my teammates did.

"Life ain't a bowl of cherries!" assistant varsity coach Darrell Willett bellowed so loudly you could hear it all over the field. He said it a thousand times every season: he said it in the morning, when we put on our sweat-soaked uniforms; during practice, when the sun beat down on bodies battered and bloodied and covered with sandspurs; during the games when things weren't going well.

Every time I heard him say it at camp I thought *Hell no, life ain't a bowl of cherries!*

"That's the difference between chicken salad and chicken shit!" Ferrell Henry said countless times. He exclaimed it when a smaller player made a crushing tackle on a bigger player, or when the offensive unit executed a play to perfection, all eleven players doing their part and helping one another. He said it when watching game films as he praised a player making a key block or tackle. Sometimes, Henry became so excited over a hard hit he'd take his hat off, wave it in the air and then put it back on his head sideways. "Boys, that a lick!" he'd holler. "Hot-dang that's a lick!"

Henry had been a tough linebacker at Florida State University. As a coach, he remained thick-armed and beer-barrel-chested, just a bit over six feet tall. I first met Henry when I was in the ninth grade, and he came to Albany Junior High to recognize our school's top athletes. I was asked to introduce him to the teachers and student body. I couldn't stop shaking; I was in awe of Henry then, and would remain so when I played under him.

When Henry got angry, his eyes evoked the power of a Greek god angered by the foibles of man. He became agitated if we didn't try as hard as we could on every play. His football philosophy was straight-on, physical, and hard. Nothing fancy. "Run it again! Run it again!" he'd say, making the offensive unit run the same play until they got it exactly the way he wanted it. On offense he believed more in the run than the pass. "We're on your time now! We're on your time now!" he'd holler after two hours of practice, indicating that the reason we were still at it was because we weren't running the play correctly or hustling hard enough. We were unquestionably Henry's team.

I felt hesitant around him, respectful and always trying to please him. But like any good coach, he was a hard man to please. He was hard but fair, and he loved to say just that: "Boys, football is hard, but it's fair." No one among us would ever cross him. "Boys, you got to have pride to play Albany High football," he told us as we gathered around him after practice.

We, about fifty to sixty players, were all silent when he spoke. To speak or whisper to a teammate when Henry was talking would be foolhardy. His stare was piercing. Worse yet was his leather strap, which blistered players for being late for practice.

"Look around you, boys . . . y'all are Albany High!"

"Yes sir!" we shouted together. "Yes sir!"

"Dang, it boys, you gotta want it more than anything. Do you want it more than anything?"

"Yes sir!" we shouted again, even louder than before.

"All those other people, they don't mean nothin'," Henry said. Those "other people" were boys walking the halls of Albany High who didn't have the guts to be at Graves Springs. According to Henry, being a part of the team said something strong about your character. It set us apart and made us better than the others, he told us. We believed him. We all knew kids who thought about playing football but weren't willing to make the sacrifices at Graves Springs.

Henry said other things about sacrifice, hard work, and the unwillingness to quit, especially when an opposing player had delivered a crushing blow and you were unable to get up from the ground unless helped by your teammates.

"It's not the size of the dog in the fight," he would say, "it's the size of fight in the dog!"

"Yes sir! Yes sir!" we would respond, huddled around him like warriors in some Paleolithic ritual designed to ensure a successful hunt.

When we encircled Henry he hollered "Breakdown!" and we jumped to a ready-football position, arms extended and fists clenched and shouted back, "YEAH! YEAH! YEAH!" We repeated this until the veins in our necks were straining with every response.

"Breakdown!"

"Yeah!"

"Breakdown!" he commanded.

"Yeah!"

The first practice ended around nine o'clock, and the sun was already beginning to bear down, the temperature past eighty degrees and heading toward a hundred. Walking off the field, I smelled bacon drifting up from the mess hall. It was satisfying. I was covered in sweat, dirt, and sandspurs. I stopped on the way back to the barracks to pick sandspurs from my aching body. My mouth was dry. It was the "cottonmouth." Less than halfway through each session, I became so dry my tongue would stick to the roof of my mouth. At Graves Springs I daydreamed of water . . . of cold, cold water, and plenty of it. All of us did. We prayed for water during practice.

But the coaching philosophy at camp was that water was for sissies, and it would make you cramp. Coaches did not give us water during practice no matter how hot it got or how long and hard we worked. When I got back to the barracks after each session, I drank all the water and Gatorade I could physically hold. It was amazing how water made us so happy. Some guys would drink so much after practice, they would have little appetite for food. They lost weight. Some got sick and went home. But I always ate a lot at camp, and the food was always good.

It was a good feeling to have the first practice over . . . until I realized the next session would start in three hours.

"I am glad that's over," I said to Leonard Lawless.

"Over?" Lawless replied. "The way I got it figured, we have twenty-nine more practices out here the next two weeks."

Lawless and I had grown up in the same neighborhood, fished and slept under the stars together. His parents saw more of me than they wanted to during summers and weekends. I had always called Leonard Lawless "Law." The nickname had stuck, following him through high school. I convinced him to come to Graves Springs and play high school ball.

"I was trying not to think about that," I said. "Let's hit the creek."

"I'll tell you, these sandspurs are killin' me," he replied.

Leaving the field, we walked the trail that led back to the barracks. Now we smelled bacon *and* eggs from the mess hall. We walked up the cracked wooden steps of the barracks, went inside and took off our shorts, shoulder pads, and helmets, hanging them over our bunks to dry before the next practice. We each grabbed a bar of soap and a towel and walked to the creek. Other naked players from both barracks emerged, heading toward the water.

Players were swinging into the water from a rope tied to a large oak tree. Upstream, cottonmouths were bathing in the sun as they lay coiled on top of rocks. The snakes weren't interested in what we were doing.

"Look at those pretty sophomores! Ain't they cute," said Jim Young, a varsity offensive lineman. "Dang, I just wanna grab one by the butt!" Young had a sly smile, and he didn't grab either one of us.

"Ahhh, this is it," I said, easing into the slow-moving, brown water. It was the best I had felt all morning. Submerged in the creek, with my teammates all around me swimming and relaxing, I forgot about football. After a few minutes, I got out of the water to bathe myself in soap and then re-entered the creek. Soon the waters along that bank were covered with thick suds. I was brought back to life by the creek. Players were smiling again, laughing in the water, taunting and dunking one another.

After several more minutes in the water, I went back to the barracks to dress and go to breakfast. At the mess hall there were eggs, bacon, grits, cereal, pancakes, and lots of cold, fresh milk. There were so many gnats that I peppered my food so I couldn't tell if I was eating gnats or pepper. Other players did the same. There wasn't any way to keep the gnats off you unless you were directly in front of a fan blowing on high. After a few days of practice, the cuts and scrapes all over our bodies became covered with tiny black gnats living off the blood and pus. It was futile trying to keep the gnats off once you were bleeding; we just let them eat. At least the gnats didn't bite like the fire ants.

Feeling much cleaner but still exhausted, I returned to my bunk and stared at the cracked wooden walls before drifting off to sleep. By noon our second practice had begun, and I was back on the field with the sun straight up. This session lasted for about ninety minutes, focusing on the kicking and passing games. Some of the linemen lifted weights that had been moved from school to camp.

The final practice, another two-hour plus session, started about four-thirty, when the heat was unbearable and close to a hundred degrees. That was it at Graves Springs: practice, swim, eat, rest and more practice, in the heat, the sandspurs, and the gnats.

That year I considered varsity players to be mythological heroes I wasn't worthy to be around. I was as intimidated by them as I was by the varsity coaches. These players had survived Graves Springs; they had played before thousands of fans against some of the best teams in the state and country. Some were giants like Nathaniel Henderson, the six-foot-five, two hundred and forty pound black lineman who went on to play at Florida State University. We called him "Big Nate." I was afraid, during the times that I did practice with the varsity, that Big Nate might rip one of my arms off and throw it through the goal post.

Johnny "Mule" Coleman was a dark-skinned black senior linebacker. I thought if he ever hit me as hard as he could, I would not live. I was scared by the way he hit people. Mule looked distinguished, like some conquering general in a war for liberation. He left his fury on the field. He wasn't arrogant, nor do I remember him ever doing mean things to sophomores. That year he was selected as the team's Most Valuable Player.

Varsity players carried themselves with confidence, and a bit of cockiness at times. Ferrell Henry wouldn't allow any player to become too cocky; it was the team that you sacrificed for. Henry made sure of that. Sophomores like me were too young and scared to have a lot of confidence—we had yet to make it through Graves Springs. Henry reminded the juniors and seniors that they had a special responsibility to lead, to set the example for the rest of the new players at camp such as myself.

"Let's go, little braves. Let's go, little braves. Move it! Move it!" older players barked at my fellow tenth-graders and I as we went through our drills at practice. "Don't you just love Graves Springs?"

After the first day at camp, home seemed a million miles away, and I longed to be there. Friday certainly would never come, I thought. My body hurt everywhere. I was so tired at the end of the day that I lay motionless in my bunk reading the names of the players on the walls; some had been written forty years earlier. I already hated the intensity of Graves Springs, but I wanted to be with my friends. I wanted to be a part of the team. I was determined not to quit.

At night there was more football, with Coach Henry calling "skull sessions," or team meetings, in order to go over plays or watch game films from the previous season. Some nights, football officials came to camp to discuss the rules of the game. When we did have free time at night we played cards, told jokes, and looked at *Playboy* magazine.

Magwood walked through the barracks to check on us before lights went out after the first day of practice. We had eaten the last meal of the day and so had Magwood, who loved fried chicken and everything that came with it. His orange coaching shirt stretched tight over his stomach, atop his green shorts and white socks pulled up just below the knees. He wore a green cap, always cocked to one side or the other. His white teeth were a sharp contrast to his dark skin, further blackened by the sun. "Good mens—good day, good mens," he said. "It was a good day." Magwood grinned as he went from bunk to bunk checking on us. We were glad to see him.

"Hobbs, how are you doin'?" Magwood asked James Harpe. Magwood always pronounced Harpe as "Hobbs," so we referred to him as "Hobbs" as well. He was a fast and powerful player who had played junior high ball with me. He played wingback or slotback on offense, and was both a tough runner and a good receiver. Harpe was a black whose family some years earlier had received death threats, probably from the Ku Klux Klan, in Baker County, Georgia, just south of

Albany. He would later accept a football scholarship to Springfield College in Massachusetts.

"Coach Magwood, you're killin' me," Harpe said. "But I'll make it out here."

"Hobbs, you're gonna be a great player before you leave Albany High," Magwood said. "A great player!"

"Yeah, Hobbs you're gonna be the best . . . if you live," I interjected.

"Maybe so, Coach, but right now I'm sore all over," Harpe said.

"Well, Hobbs, you're gonna be sore, boy, for the first few days," Magwood said. "After that you'll love it here."

Magwood turned to me. "How's my quarterback doin'?" He lifted his right arm to throw an imaginary pass.

Before I responded, Wes Westbrook spoke. "Coach Magwood, your quarterback's a sissy. He got hot and dirty today." I had played ball with Wes in junior high, and he developed into one of the best all-round athletes at high school. He could hit a baseball out of sight and throw one like it had been fired from a cannon. He went on to play baseball at the University of South Carolina.

Magwood continued to talk with us for a few minutes, and left our barracks only to return later to make sure the lights were out and we were in our bunks by ten o'clock. All the coaches slept together in a small room that was connected to the varsity barracks.

Talk of girls and playing cards helped us forget the drudgery of camp and how badly we all wanted to go home. Throughout the barracks, electric fans blew hard as sweaty, smelly uniforms hung everywhere. We wore little or no clothing to stay as cool as possible. After the card games ended and the lights went out, we could hear rats running over the dusty floor, but we were too tired to care.

"Who wants to play Tonk?" Michael Perry asked. Perry was a black boy whose nickname was "Hamburger." I'm not quite sure exactly how he got that nickname, but the boy did like to eat. Perry was a lineman who played for three years. "Tonk" was a card game that only the blacks knew. Hamburger and other blacks, however, taught their white teammates how to play.

While Hamburger was organizing Tonk, Ray Macolly was calling out for a poker game. "All right boys, y'all ante up," he said. Some of us took positions around Macolly's bunk, using it for a poker table.

We threw our dimes on the middle of the bed.

"I'm in, Ray," said Mike Trotter, a linebacker.

"Count me in," said Harpe, wearing a ball cap, mesh jersey, and sandals.

"Ohhh, Hobbs, I know I'll beat your tail," Macolly said.

"Yeah, boy, we'll see about that," Hobbs replied.

"Here's my dime," I said. "I'm in."

* * *

# TWO

At ten every night, lights were turned out by the coaches, who then walked through the barracks ensuring that everyone was in their bunks. They were always concerned that we would leave. It was a ten-mile walk to town or a long, hard swim upstream. Sometimes late at night or early in the morning I would awake chilled, sleeping only with a sheet, with my fan blowing directly on me. It was so hot during the day I never anticipated the nights cooling down at all, but they did. Besides, I would soon be awakened by Magwood and be miserable again in the sandspurs on the hot practice field. I wished the morning would never come. If it did, let me be back home in my own bed sleeping late in an air-conditioned house, like the other boys of summer.

That first Wednesday, my parents came out for the traditional weekly visitation. Before our families arrived, we cleaned up and swept the wooden floors that after three days were covered with sand, dirt, pieces of food, and other trash. The coaches made us remove pictures of naked women taped to our bunks. We removed from view dirty and nasty clothes; we even made our beds. We had our evening meal of roast beef, mashed potatoes, peas, pears, hot rolls, lots of milk, and ice cream.

"How's it going out here, son?" my dad, Bill Lightle, asked. "Are they treatin' you okay?"

"It's hot and hard," I replied. "I'm surviving. But I can't wait until Friday . . . at least we get to go home for the weekend."

My mother, Joan Lightle, was concerned about what was happening to me. "Are you eating? Are you sleeping?" she asked. "It's hot out here isn't it? I don't see how you stand it out here."

"Mom, it's real hot out here and there's plenty of food, but I'd love to go home."

"What do you do when you're not practicing?" she asked.

"Swim, sleep, that's about it," I replied. "Not much else to do."

"Now, I don't want you swimming in that nasty creek. I know there's snakes in there."

"Mom, everybody swims in the creek," I said. "Besides, the varsity players won't let us in their barracks where the showers are. Anyway, that's where the snakes bathe."

"Oh, that's terrible! Please stay away from the snakes!"

"It's not that bad," I said. "The creek is a lot of fun, and we get to swim naked."

"Where do you go to the bathroom?" she asked

I pointed to the woods and said, "Everyone's too scared to use the varsity bathroom, and we don't have one in our barracks."

"Oh, I can't believe this. It's just terrible out here," she said. "I don't even know why you'd want to come out here."

I complained about the practices and conditions. But I was proud of myself for making it through the first few days of camp. My father hadn't played organized football while growing up in Indiana. He played a lot of basketball and baseball; as a young man he played on a semi-professional baseball team in Gas City, Indiana. I remember my dad and other men clearing land and building the field they played on. They loved baseball so much that when it rained they used gasoline to burn the water off the field to be able to play. I knew he was proud of me for coming to Graves Springs. It pleased him the last few years watching me develop into a pretty good quarterback. I was playing for coaches who loved football as much as Dad loved baseball. I wanted my parents to know, especially my father, that I could make it through this ordeal.

Dad talked with Coach Willie Magwood, who told all the junior varsity parents about how hard their sons were practicing each day. Their kids were having fun, too, Magwood said.

*Some fun*, I thought.

Magwood smiled a lot as he talked about his "good mens." The fathers, more so than the mothers, were excited to learn how things were going and that their boys would one day be a part of the varsity.

"Coach, how's my boy doin' out here?" Dad asked him.

"Mr. Lightle, he's doin' good. He's gonna be a good quarterback. He works hard."

"Coach Magwood, thanks for everything your doin' for him and the rest of these boys."

"They're some good mens out here—they have to be," Magwood said. "They're gonna do good this season. These are some tough mens."

As Magwood walked away, my dad said to me, "He's a good guy. You listen to what he says. I like him."

"I like him, too, Dad." He didn't have to worry. My father knew I was going to follow what Magwood or any other coach said; that was the way he had taught me.

At the same time, Coach Ferrell Henry was smiling and complimenting the varsity players. He told the fathers that all the hard work was going to lead to a winning season. Further, he told them to be proud because their boys were growing in strength of character. They were becoming men. Surviving Graves Springs would make them better football players and better young men. It ain't easy out here, he said.

Damn right about that, Coach. Graves Springs was the hardest thing we had ever done.

Henry, like Magwood, looked content, like some little boy who had just done a good thing, thereby winning the approval of *his* parents. All the fathers were certainly proud that their boys played under Coach Henry. It was good that the mothers, especially, didn't see what the conditions were really like at Graves Springs. It wouldn't be good for their sensibilities. It was easier for fathers, however, to know how their sons were constantly being pushed so hard both mentally and physically each day at camp just to be a part of the team. Fathers understand there's suffering through sports. We weren't being pushed this way to win a war or save the world from some evil. And we weren't trying to make a college or professional team. We were just teenagers who wanted to play football—and to be with one another and wear the orange and green of Albany High.

Henry was talking to Bud Shemwell, president of the team's booster club. "Now these boys are working hard, Bud," Henry said. "And Tom so far has done a good job. He's working real hard."

Bud's son, Tom, was an upcoming senior who played center. Years earlier, Bud had two other sons who played at Graves Springs. Bud himself had played football for Albany High in the early 1930s, before

Graves Springs opened. Back then, the team had trained at Cordrays Mill, about twenty miles west of Albany.

"Coach, I know you'll do what it takes to get these boys ready to play," Bud Shemwell said.

"Yes sir, Bud, I will. This team'll be ready."

\* \* \*

All of us, varsity and junior varsity alike, were at ease and happy that visitation had finally come. Those first three days at camp seemed like three months. We felt good for having made it so far. We knew Friday was near, and we would be allowed to go home for the weekend.

"Thanks for comin' out and thanks for the drinks," I said to my parents, who had brought me plenty of fruit, snacks, and drinks.

"We'll meet you at the school on Friday," Dad said as I walked them to their car.

Before it was dark, they were gone. I returned to the barracks and went to sleep . . . only to be awakened in the morning darkness by the coaches' whistles. There was never enough sleep at camp. Every morning came too soon.

\* \* \*

Seniors claimed individual sophomores for indentured servitude during the first few days at Graves Springs. We didn't endure any of the hazing—such as having our testicles covered with a gel called Atomic Bomb, a muscle relaxer—that sophomores went through just a few years earlier. At Graves Springs, tenth-graders had been made to swallow tobacco juice, perform comedy skits in the nude, and roll a grape over and over on the ground with their noses while they were naked. The varsity also used the dreaded "belt-line" to initiate the sophomores, making them walk between two lines of upperclassmen who hit them with their belts. I was lucky the coaches had stopped that form of hazing by August 1972.

I was chosen by Tom Shemwell, the varsity center who was selected the team's Most Improved Player. I grew up knowing Shemwell and his family. We went to the same church, and I played pony league baseball with Tom on a team that his father coached.

The first time I went inside the varsity barracks was to do chores for Shemwell. The barracks was a cinder-block building painted white and shaded by a cluster of oak trees with Spanish moss. Players' names and numbers had been spray painted on the outside of the barracks. Above the screen door the word "**HOME**" had been painted in big black letters. Next to the door there were three names: "Dallas (Jay), Ussery (Jimmy), and Giddens (Tom),"and right above the names it read: "The 3 Stooges." (After the first day of practice, two of the three stooges—Jimmy Ussery and Tom Giddens—quit the team, unwilling to tolerate the harsh conditions. Their parents made them return, however.) Sweaty uniforms were hanging out of the windows of the barracks, while rock'n roll music from eight-track tape players came screaming through the windows, filling up the day.

The humid air was shattered by the sounds of Led Zeppelin, a favorite among many of us. "Stairway to Heaven" was a song we constantly played. The song began slowly, but before it was over electric guitars ignited the adrenaline as if a crushing middle linebacker had knocked a quarterback unconscious.

> There's a lady who sure all that
> Glitters is gold
> And she's buying a stairway to heaven.
> And when she gets there she knows
> If the stores are all closed
> With a word she can get what she came for . . .
> There's a feeling I get when I look
> To the west
> And my spirit is crying for leaving.
> In my thoughts I have seen rings of smoke
> Through the trees
> And the voice of those who stand looking . . .

Another song from a British band, Jethro Tull, was being played. "Thick As A Brick" was the kind of song that generated so much criticism from adults:

> I've come down from the upper
> Class to mend your rotten ways.

*My father was a man-of-power*
*Whom everyone obeyed.*

There was a lot of rock'n roll played loudly at camp. In between practices, with the music pulsating, players who wanted to sleep were so tired they slept despite the music. The lyrics to some of our favorite songs were critical of existing social authority, but it was the guitars and drums that energized us. Most of it was hard and mean, just like football. Our parents hated it, but we loved it. Most of us wore our hair much longer than players of earlier eras. Leonard Lawless had so much hair it was often hard to find his neck or face. We weren't political, and few of us had any thoughtful views on pressing social and political issues.

Our music may have been rebellious, but we were not; our very presence at Graves Springs indicated our conformity. At camp we knew the authority of the coaches was not to be challenged, and we believed in their authority, and in the fact that it would help us win games. It was the same kind of uncompromising authority we got from our fathers, backed up by a leather strap or belt lashed across our backsides. Both parental and coaching figures were to be obeyed.

The musicians we listened to could also be rebellious in their excessive use of drugs. During the weekends we had parties with our girlfriends and listened to rock'n roll. We drank beer and did foolish things, but for most of us these were our only drugs. We knew the coaches didn't like our music, but they tolerated it.

I was standing outside the varsity barracks, listening to the music. I didn't want to go inside. I knew what had happened in the past to tenth-graders at Graves Springs, but I wanted to believe Shemwell wouldn't let these guys beat me up; I just wasn't quite certain.

As I walked slowly inside, trying not to look at them directly, I noticed their barracks weren't a whole lot different from mine. Names, numbers, and messages had been written on the wooden walls and ceiling. There were short stories about Amanda, Bridgett, and Monica telling how happy they made some of the players feel. Electric fans buzzed throughout, drying uniforms and keeping the gnats off of the players. Naked players walked around the barracks, some with jock itch so bad they hurt with every step they took. Others were sleeping, and some were laying flat on their bunks holding up the foldouts of the latest *Playboy* and *Penthouse* magazines. The smell inside was a combination of sweat, heat, and something worse. The varsity barracks, unlike the one for sophomores, had toilets and showers. Most of the time, though, the toilets didn't flush, and the putrid odors would rise quickly through the sleeping quarters, which was not separated from the bathroom.

As I walked to Shemwell's bunk, some of the players took notice of me. "There's that little Brave quarterback . . . we're gonna bust his butt," a player said. I didn't look around to see who it was. I smiled and was trying not to look concerned, but I was scared. I knew on the field they would eventually "bust my butt." I was what they called "fresh meat."

"Leave the boy alone. He's a pansy quarterback," Jeff "Bodine" Sinyard said.

"Sinyard, I'm here to clean up for T-Bone," I said. Shemwell weighed over two hundred pounds. His nickname was "T-Bone."

"Yeah, good luck with that pig," Bodine replied.

Shemwell's bunk and the area around it was a mess so I made his bed, picked up trash, and hung his uniform on the bunk to dry. Then I put his cleats and helmet out of the way. I found a broom and swept.

"Looks good, Bill. That helps a lot," Shemwell said. He went easy on me. He knew I was catching hell from nearly everyone else in the varsity barracks.

"What else you need, Tom?" I asked.

"That's all right now, but I do want you back tonight to give me a rubdown," Shemwell said.

While walking back to my barracks, I saw a monkey chained to a tree. The monkey was playing in the shade eating peanuts and scratching himself. I stopped to look at him for a few moments. He looked up at me and then back down at what he was eating. There were gnats and flies all around him, but he didn't care. The monkey always seemed happy at Graves Springs, and not worried about a thing.

I found out that the monkey's name was Sam, and he belonged to Bruce Hicks, an upcoming senior. Hicks played offensive end and worked part-time at a local funeral home where, his teammates said, he took naps in the coffins. Hicks was the only boy I ever knew who had a pet monkey.

"Sam, what did I tell you about talkin' to those tenth graders?"

Hicks said. "Those boys can't make it at Graves Springs. They're just a bunch of sissies. I don't want you talkin' to them."

Then Hicks smiled and looked at me. "Hey, boy, how's it going?"

"It's okay," I replied. "I'm gonna make it."

"Hell, yeah, you'll make it out here. If Sam can survive this, you can too," Hicks said.

I said goodbye to Hicks and his monkey and walked back to the sophomore barracks to rest before the next practice. My teammates wanted badly to know what happened to me.

"Lightle, what'd they do to you? Are you all right, man?" Leonard Lawless immediately asked as I entered the barracks.

"Man, they tore me up. It was awful," I said. "They hit me with Ferrell's strap. I am leaving this place tonight. I'm walkin' home. Who's comin' with me?"

For a few moments Lawless and the others were so scared they couldn't breathe. "That's a bunch a crap," Westbrook finally said. "They ain't done nothin' to you, boy. Ferrell ain't gonna let the varsity boys hurt us . . . now don't give us any more of that crap." Westbrook concluded his statement by slapping me across the back and saying: "You sissy quarterback."

"All right, all right they didn't touch me," I said. "Nothin' happened to me."

"Don't do that to me!" Lawless exclaimed, trying to sound agitated, but more so he was relieved that I came out of that place unscathed. It was a good sign for him and the rest of the sophomores.

"No big deal," I said. "Those guys ain't gonna hurt us."

Taking care of Shemwell would be the extent of my initiation. My teammates in the sophomore barracks were relieved to hear there likely would be no humiliating hazing; but our struggles would be with the heat, three daily practices, and the relentless pushing of the coaches

After I finished answering all their questions, I climbed onto my bunk and slept for thirty minutes before the afternoon practice. Thank God for Tom Shemwell.

\* \* \*

Shemwell was an excellent blocker on the football field, attacking defensive linemen below the knees and rooting them off the line of scrimmage. He was a fine first baseman on the diamond as well. We would go on to play high school and college baseball together. His family included seven children and a father who for nearly half a century had been intimately involved in sports in Albany and throughout Southwest Georgia.

When I was about thirteen, I joined a pony league baseball team coached by Bud Shemwell. His two youngest sons, Tom and David, both played on the team. David, whose nickname was "Bubba," graduated from Albany High in 1975. Bud knew baseball and how to teach it. Unlike other coaches, he demonstrated for us the proper way to slide when running the bases. During practice, he had a load of sand delivered to the field so we could work on sliding. But before we did, he slid so we could see the proper technique. He loved to win, and our team finished in first place that year with a seventeen and one record.

Bud was feisty, a fighter as a coach. He worked me and other young players hard, taught us the fundamentals of baseball, and did not tolerate players who wouldn't hustle. Bud was short and had thick gray hair he combed straight over his head. He had a wonderful smile and penetrating dark eyes. Bud constantly chewed Red Man tobacco on the ball field, and juice from his chew dripped down the sides of his mouth when he became excited during a game. When this happened, it was hard to clearly understand his instructions. Nevertheless, with a mouth full of tobacco, when Bud told one of us something, his emotions conveyed meaning.

Bud worked more then forty years in the insurance business in Albany while coaching little league and pony league baseball. Before his death, he was honored for five decades of service to the Georgia High School Athletic Association, during which he officiated high school football games all over Southwest Georgia. At his funeral, family members and those he coached over the years spoke of his love of sports and how he helped so many boys. And I was lucky to have been one of them.

Three of Bud's sons went to Graves Springs: First Mott in the 1950s, Chip in the following decade, and Tom, my teammate. Tom had heard the "horror stories" of camp from his two older brothers and knew his father expected him to play. He told me he was "scared to death" as a tenth grader when he went to Graves Springs in 1970. He played for three years.

"I knew Bud would kick my ass if I quit," Tom recalled as one of a dozen sophomores who reported to Graves Springs that year. "It was just something I knew I had to do if I wanted to play football. You had to survive it, and you knew others had to do it too."

Years later, Tom said, "I don't think you could get by with this today," referring to the way players were treated—or mistreated—at Graves Springs. School officials and parents wouldn't allow such treatment today, especially the fact that we weren't given water during the practice. "I can remember just dying for water," Tom said. "You wondered why nobody ever died. It always amazed me why nobody ever died."

Today Shemwell lives in Americus, Georgia, and works in human relations at a nearby manufacturing plant. For years he has officiated high school football games, just like his father before him.

\* \* \*

After I first entered the varsity barracks that afternoon, I went back that night to bring T-Bone Shemwell ice cream and chocolate milk. It was almost nine o'clock, and the last light was fading from the day. I heard the crickets along the creek harmonizing with the sounds of water cascading over the rocks in the creek. The music of ZZ Top, and of course "Stairway to Heaven" hit me hard as I walked under the oak trees toward the cinder-block barracks. Because of all the running and exercises that day, my legs hurt with every step I took. *I hope they don't feel this way in the morning when we have to practice again,* I thought. As I got closer to the barracks, I wasn't as scared as I was earlier in the day when I had to clean up T-Bone's bunk. I was looking for Sam the monkey, but I didn't see him.

"T-Bone, here comes your boy," said Ricky Spence, whose teammates called him "Blue." Girls loved Blue because he was muscular, over six feet tall, and had dark hair and blue eyes. I wasn't worried about Blue making me do anything disgusting. I had been friends with his younger brother, Donnie, for a few years. I knew his parents too.

"Hey, Ricky. How's it going?" I said.

"How's it goin' for you, boy? Are you gonna make it out here, or are you gonna run home?" Blue said.

"I'll make it."

"It's gonna be tough on your ass," he said. "I'm watchin' you. You're doin' okay out here. But this is a tough . . . crazy place."

"I'm finding that out." It was reassuring for me to hear Ricky talk that way. He was one of the best ball players in Albany, and a leader on his team.

"Bill, over here, bring it over here," T-Bone said. He was playing poker with Jeff "Bodine" Sinyard and a few other players. "Thanks, man," T-Bone said as he took the ice cream and chocolate milk and quickly devoured both treats as if afraid someone was going to steal them.

"Tom, did you taste that ice cream or just suck it down your throat?" Sinyard said.

"Hey, Shorty, why don't you mind your own business?" Shemwell replied. Both were around five-eight.

I gave Shemwell the rubdown and watched a few minutes of the poker game.

As I left the varsity barracks for the second time that day, I could see the monkey hanging from one of the wooden beams. He pulled himself upright to sit, and was scratching himself and picking insects off his thick, gray fur. He looked content, like he had been earlier in the day when I saw him chained to the tree. Sam seemed to be watching over all the activity in the barracks, as if proud that the boys had survived another day at Graves Springs, and now were relaxing and laughing.

"Sam, don't you fall from there and get hurt," said Bruce Hicks. "And relax, I'm not gonna let Sinyard date you. You can do a lot better than him."

\* \* \*

# THREE

During the first week, I became worried about Donnie Spence. Spence was being worked on both the defensive and offensive B-team units as well as the kicking teams; occasionally he even practiced with the varsity. He was a tough and valuable player, but the coaches seemed intent on crushing him.

After each practice, Spence slowly walked to the barracks, drank copious amounts of water and Gatorade, jumped into the creek for a minute or two, maybe ate some food and slept until the next practice session. He had no energy or desire to swim, play cards, or tell dirty jokes between practices. No one was worked as hard by the coaches as Donnie Spence was that year, and none of us slept as much as he did between practices.

"Donnie, let's go. It's time to get dressed," I said awakening him for the next practice.

"I don't know if I can do this any more," Donnie said, wiping the sleep from his eyes.

"Spence, are you all right?"

"They're killin' me out here," he replied.

He slowly get out of bed, put on his uniform and headed to the practice field. Once there he found the desire to play hard—just what the coaches wanted. He wasn't going to disappoint the coaches.

His older brother, Ricky, regularly came over to our barracks to check on him. "Boy, you can make it out here. Don't let'em get you down," Ricky said.

"They've already got me down—they're gonna kill me next," Donnie replied.

As Ricky Spence left our barracks, I followed him down the steps and out under the blazing sun.

"Ricky, these coaches are pushing him too hard," I said. "All he does is sleep. He can barely take his uniform off after practice."

"He'll be all right," Ricky replied. "They won't kill'im."

"Has anybody ever died out here, man?"

"I'm not sure," he said. "But keep an eye out for Donnie."

"I've been doin' that."

Ricky Spence was a senior offensive lineman and captain of the varsity during the 1972 season, and he was selected that year as his team's Best Offensive Lineman. Coaches were determined that Donnie was going to be as good a football player as his older brother was, and they were willing to work Donnie unmercifully to prove themselves right. For the next three years, Donnie Spence was a tenacious player, never weighing more than one hundred and eighty pounds. As a senior he played offensive guard, and he regularly blocked defensive linemen who might out weigh him by thirty or forty pounds.

* * *

Ricky Spence went to Graves Springs for three years beginning in August 1970. The Spence family had moved several times as the brothers were growing up. Their father, James R. Spence Sr., had served in the military, and at one point the family even lived in Brazil. Ricky attended Merry Acres Junior High School in Albany, where he played ninth-grade football. He had anticipated going to newly built Westover High School in Albany and playing football there . . . until he was rezoned for Albany High. After learning about this change, Ricky decided he wasn't going to play for Albany High.

"I had heard about Graves Springs," he recalled. "I didn't want that much football." Being isolated in the woods for two weeks at Graves Springs, enduring the hazing from upperclassmen and forgoing the comforts of air-conditioning did not appeal to the oldest Spence brother. Westover conducted its preseason camp at the school, allowing players to sleep in its air-conditioned gym.

Coach Ferrell Henry visited Ricky at his home in the summer of 1970 to persuade him to come to Graves Springs. It worked. Ricky was one of a dozen or so tenth-graders who reported to camp that year.

The turnout for underclassmen was low compared to other years, probably because of a shift in school zones in efforts to further integration; plus the intense hazing of the late 1960's had discouraged boys from coming to Graves Springs, Spence said.

In the beginning, Ricky Spence regretted his decision to go to Graves Springs. "I remember laying in my bunk at night and listening to the fans and thinking 'what in the f— am I doing here?'"

Ricky and the other tenth-graders endured the rites of passage at camp as seniors took them on the field at midnight to do practice drills and perform comedy skits while wearing only their athletic supporters. Upperclassmen "would sneak up on us and beat our asses up while we were sleeping," he said. They would use paddles, leather straps, or anything that would leave a red mark. One morning, as Ricky was dressing before daylight, he put on his athletic supporter but suddenly jumped out of it, screaming in pain. The night before, while the sophomores were sleeping, the varsity slipped into their barracks and put "Atomic Bomb" in their athletic supporters. Atomic Bomb was a muscle relaxer that elicits concentrated heat, but was not to be applied to the testicles. "It burned like hell," Ricky recalled years later.

According to Ricky Spence and the few other sophomores who endured the rites of initiation that year, their constant refrain was "wait until next year," when they would be the ones to initiate new players. But by August 1971, coaches made the varsity stop its practice of hazing and humiliating underclassmen.

Ricky, who earned a degree in political science from Georgia Southwestern College in Americus, developed into one of the city's best high school linemen during the early 1970s. For the past several years, he has worked with a heating and air-conditioning company in Albany. The coaches who worked him hard at Graves Springs taught him lessons of discipline that he still carries with him, he said. Once, during a high school dance, offensive line coach Darrell Willett caught Ricky drinking a beer. Every day for the next five weeks, Ricky had to run up and down steep stadium steps for nearly an hour. If he didn't, he would be kicked off the team. "He [Willett] gave me a choice: run or quit," he said. "Willett taught me damn discipline. He made me hard headed—like I am today."

* * *

Leonard Lawless, like teammate Donnie Spence, was having his own share of struggles with the coaches at Graves Springs in August 1972. Lawless had gone to Albany Junior High School with me, but didn't play football there. He played with the city recreation league while myself, Donnie Spence and several other junior varsity players had been on the same ninth-grade team.

During the first day at camp, Lawless was being challenged by coach Willie Magwood, who claimed Lawless didn't have the determination to survive Graves Springs and play for Albany High—because he hadn't played junior high ball.

"Coach Magwood was all over me," Lawless said. "I remember going down to the creek after the first day of practice thinking 'What in the hell am I doing here?' I was already thinkin' about quitting."

Lawless was staring into the murky, steady-moving waters of the Muckalee Creek considering whether to quit. He was exhausted from the day's three practice sessions, and dejected because Magwood was challenging his character. He looked up from the water and saw the head varsity coach, Ferrell Henry, approaching him.

"What's the matter, son?" Henry said.

Lawless told Henry that he didn't know if he could make it through another day at Graves Springs.

"Coach Henry—and I'll never forget this—put his arm around me," Lawless remembered years later. "Then he said, 'Son, football is tough and it's not for everyone, but if was me, I'd give it a few more days before deciding what to do.'"

Football's not for everyone, yes sir, Coach. It's mean and nasty . . . meaner still at Graves Springs.

"He spoke to me like a father," said Lawless, who kept playing that year, and the next two. During Lawless' senior year in 1974, he was selected as the Best Offensive Back on our team, which finished third out of ten teams in the region. Lawless weighed about one hundred and eighty pounds at about five-foot-eight; he played fullback like the fury of demons released from a cage. By that year, Coach Willie Magwood called him "one of the hardest hitting" football players he had ever coached at Albany High.

"But he [Magwood] gave me hell my first year," Lawless recalled.

\* \* \*

At one afternoon practice session, some of us were involved in fundamental blocking drills with the varsity. It was a scorching day, and much of the grass on the field already was worn away leaving mostly sand and sandspurs. The sand was not only hard to run on, but during the afternoons, it was hot to the touch as well.

Donald Alley was holding a tackling dummy that was being hit by varsity players. Alley was a sophomore lineman who weighed more than two hundred pounds.

"Hit it, boys! Hit it, boys!" Coach Ferrell Henry barked, then blew his whistle as a varsity players smacked into the dummy that Alley was holding. "That's a football lick, son! Hot-dang, that's a lick! Boys, that's how it's done!" We all loved to be praised by Henry. The player who had just made the hit hustled to the end of the line formed by other players waiting to strike the dummy.

"Next! Next! Give me another one!" Henry said.

As each player hit the dummy, Alley had to regain his grip before the drill could continue. Alley was struggling just to hang on to the dummy after each hit.

"Lock those arms when you hit, son!" Henry said to the next player, who was in a four-point stance awaiting the whistle.

"Yes sir, Coach! Yes sir!" came the reply from that player, who then bit down hard on his mouthpiece. Henry slapped him on his butt, blew his whistle and that boy flew into the dummy making a perfect block.

"That's football, son!" Henry said. "Hot-dang, that's football, boys!"

As players slammed into the tackling dummy, Alley grimaced and moved his football cleats up and down as if he was doing a dance routine. Henry stopped the drill after he saw that Alley was having problems.

"Son, what's wrong with you?" Henry asked.

"Coach, my feet . . . my feet are on fire!" Alley responded, now almost in tears.

"Your feet!"

"Yes sir, Coach. My feet are burning up!" Alley said.

It was a hundred degrees that day, Alley had been standing in the same spot in the sand, and his feet had become unbearably hot.

"Son, take a break," Henry said. "Go take a knee in the shade."

"Thanks, Coach," Alley said. He ran off the field to rest a few moments under the trees that surround the field. That day, I learned that just standing up at Graves Springs was a challenge.

\* \* \*

# FOUR

Tom Giddens and Jimmy Ussery were two seniors who quit the team and left camp after the first day of practice, unwilling to endure the grueling conditions of Graves Springs. They were friends who had played the previous two seasons for Westover High School in northwest Albany. During preseason camp at Westover, the team slept in an air-conditioned gym and had indoor plumbing. The school was located in a middle-class neighborhood, not in the middle of the woods like Graves Springs. Because of redrawn school zones in connection with court-ordered desegregation, Ussery and Giddens, both white, were reassigned to Albany High.

Giddens played offensive guard and weighed about one hundred and sixty-five pounds, while Ussery played defensive back and quarterback, and was about the same size as Giddens. Like the rest of us, they were required to take salt tablets before each practice.

"I threw up after each practice during the first day of camp," Giddens recalled, placing most of the blame on the salt tablets he was made to take. "I was just not prepared for anything like Graves Springs," he said. No one ever was.

After the day's third practice, Ussery told Giddens that he wanted no more of Albany High football and was quitting, even if he had to walk the nearly ten miles to get back to his house in Albany. "I told Jimmy, 'Hell I am with you—I hate this shit too,'" Giddens said.

Leaving their uniforms and the other few belongings they had brought to camp, they left about sundown. Giddens was carrying a sock containing money he had won playing poker. They slipped out of camp at the same time they were supposed to be in a team meeting.

Coach Henry had called the meeting to study a game film from the previous year. As the other players were watching the film, Giddens and Ussery were secretly walking down the dirt road that runs about one-quarter of a mile before reaching the paved Graves Springs Road.

The muggy August night was still as crickets chirped along the creek, and the dust rose gently as they walked away from camp. As they passed the trailer where the camp's caretaker lived, they tried to walk quietly in order not to be noticed by either the caretaker or his pack of dogs. They made it past the trailer unseen.

Meanwhile, back at camp, Henry was showing the film and quizzing his players about what they were seeing. "All right, Ussery, what's happening on this play?" Henry asked. There was silence. "Ussery, I said what's happening on this play, son?" Henry repeated. Still there was no answer. "Where is Ussery?" Henry said.

By then, Giddens and Ussery were walking down Graves Springs Road to Philema Road, which runs west for about five miles before crossing into Albany. But after the two players had walked for about two miles, they waved to a friend of theirs who was driving into Albany. The friend stopped and picked them up. Ussery and Giddens lived in the same neighborhood in Albany; both were nervous about how they were going to explain their sudden departures from football camp to their fathers. Fathers don't like quitters. "We talked for more than a hour before we both went inside" their respective homes, Giddens said.

Both players slept in their own beds that night, but by the next day they were being pressured by their parents to return to Graves Springs. Jimmy Ussery was the first to break. His father drove him back to camp before the first practice Tuesday morning.

Giddens was determined not to return to Graves Springs. "I just wasn't going to go back to that damn environment even though Jimmy did," recalled Giddens, years later.

Giddens' father, who was the purchasing agent for the Dougherty County Schools, tried but was unable to convince his son to return to camp. That morning, former Albany High head football coach Harold Dean Cook took Giddens out to lunch to talk football. Cook knew the Giddens family well; he spoke of pride, commitment, and the glory of being a part of Albany High football. Still, Tom Giddens refused to rejoin the team. He told Cook he wouldn't go back; he was tired of vomiting and sick of the overall conditions of the camp. More pressure came from offensive line coach Darrell Willett, who also visited Giddens in efforts to convince him to return to Graves Springs. Giddens refused Willett's overtures.

Finally, by Tuesday afternoon, Jimmy Ussery's father came to visit Giddens and took him for a car ride. "I had no idea where we were going when Mr. Ussery came over to get me,." Giddens said. "He never told me where we were going."

The two rode and talked for more than an hour, starting in northwest Albany several miles from camp. The ride, however, took Giddens further east, closer and closer to Graves Springs, which was where they finally stopped.

"At this point, I was beaten down," Giddens recalled, having listened to his father, a former coach, a current coach and the father of one his best friends, all of them imploring Giddens, for the good of the team and himself, to return to Graves Springs. By late Tuesday afternoon, having been gone from Graves Springs less then twenty-four hours, Giddens was back at camp, ready for the day's final practice.

Coach Henry talked with Giddens before he rejoined the team. "Son, a lot of people think about leaving," Henry said as he put his arm around Giddens' shoulders. "You never would've left by yourself."

Henry may have been understanding; nevertheless, Ussery and Giddens were punished for leaving in order to send a message to the rest of us that the coaches' authority must be obeyed. For the remainder of camp, both Ussery and Giddens, who quit taking salt tablets and did not throw up again, had to run thirty minutes extra before and after each practice.

It was during these running sessions though, that Giddens developed "a good relationship" with Willett, his offensive line coach, as well as winning the coach's admiration. Giddens, as did Ussery, completed camp and the regular season. Because of Giddens' outstanding hustle and determination, he received the team's Sportsmanship Award.

It was easy for Giddens to walk away from camp with Jimmy Ussery, but it was the right decision to return, Giddens said. By his early forties, Giddens had become a successful insurance executive in Atlanta, and over the years I have seen him work hard in the business world while remaining close to his teammates from Graves Springs. The lessons he learned at Graves Springs—hard work, discipline, and getting back on your feet after an opposing player has just knocked you to the ground—have served him well throughout his professional life. "I give playing ball almost all the credit in terms of the success I have had in business," he said.

* * *

A few days after Giddens and Ussery returned to Graves Springs, two more seniors, Don Fowler and Jeff Sinyard, decided to quit the team and walked away from camp. "I was just glad to get away from that place," Fowler said. "Nobody in their right mind would say that camp was fun. It was hot and miserable and I was out of shape."

When Fowler and Sinyard did leave, their teammates who earlier said they were walking away too, decided not to go. "There was four or five of us who were supposed to leave but when it came down to it, it was just me and Jeff," Fowler recalled. Like Giddens and Ussery, Fowler and Sinyard walked down Graves Springs Road and began hitchhiking. Soon a motorist picked them up and drove them to the McDonald's Restaurant, a favorite hangout among teenagers in Albany. They weren't there long when Coach Darrell Willett appeared. "I think Willett was in town taking someone from camp to the doctor, but I'm not sure," Fowler said. Regardless of why Willett walked into McDonald's that night, he talked to Fowler and Sinyard and convinced both of them to return to Graves Springs.

Back at camp, Sinyard and Fowler had extra running to do as punishment for their departure. They both finished camp, and were defensive starters during the regular season, Fowler at end and Bodine at cornerback.

Don Fowler had grown up in Albany and played football at Merry Acres Junior High School, but in 1970, his upcoming sophomore year at Albany High, he didn't go to Graves Springs. "I was more interested in music," he said. "I just didn't want to practice football that much." But when school started, the coaches convinced him to join the B-team. In 1971, he went to Graves Springs.

Throughout high school and afterwards, Fowler stayed with his music having formed a band called Sunshine Revolution. The band's playlist included songs from Jimi Hendrix, Grand Funk Railroad, and Creedence Clearwater Revival. His group played for local clubs, such as the Jolly Fox, the Library and others, where there was lots of dancing and beer drinking on the weekends. His teammates were among the crowds cheering for Fowler and his music at the local clubs. "We'd load up all the equipment in my van, and I'd have to lay a brick on the gas pedal to go uphill," he said. "I loved playing music."

Fowler loved football enough to go to Graves Springs for two years, and continued playing despite getting stitches in his head on more than one occasion, and having two teeth knocked out. He hated Graves Springs, and said that one year there Coach Henry "made us practice in our underwear at three o'clock in the morning" because some of the boys in the barracks wouldn't stop talking. "We got those damn sandspurs everywhere," he remembered. Early during his senior season, he had stitches at the top of his nose to close a bloody cut. The injury bothered him most of the year and Fowler said, "I went to the emergency room four or five times" to have the wound re-stitched. Today there's a half-inch, clearly noticeable scar at the top of his nose between the eyebrows. "It seemed like every time I'd hit somebody it would open up," Fowler said.

Fowler survived Graves Springs and returned after walking away because he "loved football." But more than the game itself, his best friends were at camp, and he wanted to be with them. "We had a tight group out there," he said. "Everybody got along."

Fowler lives in Albany today, where he owns a home improvement business and watches his two sons, Dustin and Brady, play football at Terrell Academy, about twenty miles from Albany. I saw him at a game where his boys were playing, and the intensity of his playing days at Albany High is still there. "I have to pace the sidelines when my boys play," he said. We talked about how "miserable" we both were at Graves Springs and finally, Fowler said, "The only fun part was the swimming hole."

\* \* \*

# FIVE

"Sixty-five naked football players . . . you have to mention that," former head coach Ferrell Henry said to me twenty-five years after we left Graves Springs. He was referring to the fact that once practice ended, players immediately stripped and went swimming naked. Joey Bateman, a former player who later coached at Graves Springs, described it as a "nudist colony." A standout player from the late 1960s who didn't want to be quoted said that being naked with the other players while swimming was symbolic of "hiding nothing" from your teammates; whereby developing a sense of unity necessary for team success.

Sometimes while swimming naked, it wasn't just the eyes of the animals in the woods that were watching. Martha Glenn Riley and Donna McDaniel Gray were close friends and classmates at Albany High in the 1960s. Martha Glenn's father, Earl "Rat" Riley, had played at Graves Springs years earlier. As she was growing up, her family had a cabin along the Muckalee Creek not far from Graves Springs football camp. The girls sometimes visited the camp when they were not supposed to. Once, when camp wasn't in session, they went downstream to paint their names on the varsity barracks; other times, they went downstream while naked players were swimming.

"I am not going to admit to seeing them, but we did go down there," recalled Donna McDaniel Gray, who was employed with the *Albany Herald* by the late 1990s. Both Donna and Martha Glenn, more than three decades after they graduated in 1968, live in Albany and remain close friends. Going "down there" in between practices meant that one could likely hide behind the brush, on the opposite side of the creek from the camp, and see sixty-five naked players in the creek.

At camp we had a saying that we were living like "Natural Men." While the coaches were trying to break us physically and mentally through sweat and blood, players were living as close to the earth—in its gospel of dying and rebirth—as we had ever done before. For me, that experience, which becomes more profound with each passing year, was one of self-purification. The daily cycle of work, heat, and exhaustion was ritualized. The coaches were the high priests, and as in all rituals, this cycle served to bring us up in accord with the ideals of the existing social structure. This social structure was about winning football games; in order to do so you had to suffer. Natural men, of course, were naked men too. Nakedness was the ultimate expression of the freedom afforded to us at camp. In between practices, we always meandered around the camp without clothes on. We swam naked, and as we did the sweat and blood on our bodies flowed freely into the Muckalee, and in turn the Muckalee connected with the Flint River that joined the Chattahoochee River on the way to Florida and the Gulf of Mexico. From there the waters become universal, salt of sweat and salt of the oceans.

Swimming in the creek was just plain fun, and about the only way to get any relief from the heat. We climbed up the giant oak tree, along the bank, in order to swing out into the creek from a rope that had been tied to one of the tree's branches. We showed off and taunted one another as we swung through the air and crashed into the brown, refreshing water. There, we experienced the redemptive, primordial voices of the creek and the land around it.

That year we had a junior linebacker, Carl Smith, who had long, flamboyant red hair and loved the music of Led Zeppelin. Like the driving rock'n roll he listened to, Smith played recklessly on the football field. The coaches at Graves Springs touted Smith's aggressive play by saying: "He'd put a helmet on you," when describing his play. The phrase, "He'd put a helmet on you," was one of the most praiseworthy accolades a coach could bestow. Saying this about a player meant, above all, that the player simply loved to hit. Smith himself was not big physically, but he played that way because he hit opposing players so hard. "Hot-dang what a lick, son!" Henry said after Smith crashed into another player full speed. One of the functions of Graves Springs was to take players like Smith, Leonard Lawless, Donnie Spence and others who were not exceptionally fast or big, and toughen them to the point where they could compete with physically superior players—at this, Graves Springs succeeded many times.

Carl Smith swung naked from the rope after each practice, extending as far out over the water as he could and then releasing his hold on the rope. He was usually the first one on the rope after each practice; as he flew through the air holding his legs under his chin, he taunted his teammates.

"This one's for you, Red Rob!" Smith said, calling out to Paul "Red" Robertson, whose hair was just as fiery red as Smith's. Red Rob was a senior offensive guard and the son of school superintendent Paul "Mr. Rob" Robertson, who had coached at Graves Springs thirty years earlier. After taunting Red Rob, Smith hit the water hard and stayed under for a minute.

"I'll kick your tail, Smith!" Red Rob said as he jumped into the water swimming after Smith, who was still submerged. The two fought, dunked one another, and finally when they were both exhausted, they dragged their bodies out of the water.

* * *

# SIX

After the first two days at Graves Springs, our uniforms smelled so bad that Donnie Spence, Leonard Lawless, James Harpe, David McClung, myself and others would take them about fifty yards upstream to wash them. At that point, several large rocks appeared in the middle of the current. This was where we usually saw the poisonous cottonmouths sunning their cold-blooded bodies. These snakes have mouths that are as pure white as Georgia cotton; their bite is deadly, and they are as aggressive as a charging fullback. Every year at camp we killed one or two cottonmouths that visited the barracks.

Carrying our socks, athletic supporters, T-shirts, and jerseys, we would wade upstream to the rocks, those ancient washing machines. The snakes slithered away as we approached the island of rocks, and we took pieces of our uniforms, wrung them out hard in the water and beat them against the rocks.

To McClung, it was "just like momma at home."

\* \* \*

On the first day of school in our sophomore year, David McClung, who lived just a few blocks away, overturned his Volkswagen on his way to school. McClung wasn't seriously hurt in the wreck, but the car was beaten up pretty badly. "I knew I was destined for great things," he said of his survival.

McClung played center and offensive guard, and before our senior season began he broke his hand during practice. He convinced the coaches to allow the team doctors to fashion a plastic cast that would give him enough mobility to play while giving the broken bone some protection. He wore the plastic cast all year, but played so well he was selected the team's Best Offensive Lineman.

McClung's past and future were connected to Graves Springs. His father played there during the Great Depression, and his father-in-law would later coach there. After David McClung graduated from high school he married Nancy Field, whose father, Pat Field, was Albany High's head coach in the early 1960s. Field was born in Pennsylvania and served in the military in Europe at the end of World War II. After the war, he accepted a scholarship to play for the University of Georgia; in 1950 he was named the team's Most Outstanding Back. He married Anita Johnson, a "Georgia girl," and they came to Albany after his college career ended.

Field was a hard coach, like Graves Springs itself. "We did give'em no water" during practice, but "we let'em wipe their faces with a wet towel," he said of his players. His underclassmen went through the beltline. Field made his teams run wind sprints at midnight in full uniform when they misbehaved in the barracks. "When the lights went out usually you heard something fly across the room," indicating players were throwing pieces of fruit or other objects at one another, Field recalled. He delighted in the meanness of it all, believing Graves Springs made his players tougher than their opponents.

\* \* \*

"Clean them socks boys, clean them socks boys!" McClung said. While standing on top of the rocks, we smacked each piece of clothing against them, then dipped each piece into the creek. The sun was high and hot, and shining so hard that the Muckalee glittered like Christmas lights.

"You better scrub your bottom," McClung said to Leonard Lawless, who after high school married David McClung's sister, Nancy McClung. "It's might nasty," he added.

Lawless dropped the socks he was cleaning and jumped on McClung's back, taking him down under the brown water. They fought for a few minutes, but stopped because they were laughing too hard to continue.

"Lawless, you better stay out of the water," Harpe said. "A snake's gonna bite your ass."

"Harpe, let me tell you somethin' boy . . . I'll bite a snake's head off," he replied.

I believed Lawless when he said he'd bite a snake's head off. I once saw him kill a dozen or so large rats, some about a foot long, one Sunday morning when we were working at the Flint River Cotton Mill in Albany. We saw about thirty rats run from a pile of trash at the back of the mill along the railroad tracks. Calling ourselves the "Rat Patrol," we searched the mill looking for the animals. Donnie Spence and David McClung were also part of the mill crew.

Some of the rats ran straight at us, unafraid of our size advantage. Lawless picked up a board and beat to death several of them, blood flying everywhere. He was like a madman during the killings, with his long hair flowing as he whacked the rats, grunting with each death-blow. Any boy like Lawless, who was such a great rat killer, just *might* bite the head off a snake.

After we finished washing our uniforms on the rocks, we placed our athletic supporters over our heads, covering one eye. The gang of "One-Eyed Pirates of the Muckalee" began heading back to the barracks, naked except for our jock straps wrapped around our heads.

"*Hey, hey, who are we!*" McClung sang.

"The one-eyed pirates of the Muckalee!" the rest of us responded. "The one-eyed pirates of the Muckalee!"

"*Hey, hey, who are we!*"

"The one-eyed pirates of the Muckalee!"

We sang for a few moments . . . until Spence stopped us and pointed downstream. "Look, boys, they're back!" he said. "I knew they'd be back!" His blue eyes were lit with excitement.

"White-back dolphins? Here at Graves Springs? I don't believe," I said. "Those are only at Panama City."

"Are you sure?" McClung asked. "Are they really here?"

"If y'all don't believe me . . . just look for yourself," Spence replied. "Six beautiful dolphins. Ain't they pretty?" He told the same story we'd heard many times from him—of how the rare white-back dolphins, seen by so few people of Panama City, Florida, leave the Gulf of Mexico once each year, swimming all the way to the Muckalee Creek. It's a mysterious account of salt-water animals surviving for days in the brackish rivers and creeks of South Georgia.

"Look, that one's a black-back!" Harpe exclaimed.

"No, boy, you're wrong. They're all white-backs," Spence said.

"Donnie, how do you know they're dolphins?" I asked, looking upstream like a lost explorer. "I see something," I added, "but I'm not so sure those are dolphins."

"Can't you tell? Just look at 'em."

"Yeah, I guess you're right. They're the same ones we saw at the beach a few weeks ago," I said, playing along with Spence's story.

Some of our teammates were swimming in unison as their backsides arched out of the water in stark contrast to the dark, brown Muckalee. The dolphins were swimming to recognize the return of the One-Eyed Pirates of the Mucaklee. We felt honored.

"See, there's your white-back dolphins," Spence said, pointing to a handful of our teammates.

"Yeah, that's sure is pretty," McClung said. "It sure is."

\* \* \*

After camp ended in 1972, and school had begun in early September, I was happy knowing there would be only one practice a day. Our season was about to start. No more sleeping in the woods, bathing in the creek, and enduring three practices in the summer heat. It felt great not to get up before daylight to practice, and it was great to be home.

During my junior varsity season, I played quarterback under Coach Willie Magwood. We won five games, tied two, and lost one. I fractured a collarbone that year while scrimmaging with the varsity. (I had suffered the same kind injury the year before—the opposite collarbone.) I was playing quarterback and ran the ball out-of-bounds almost onto a road that ran by the practice field. I stopped running after the coaches blew their whistles, but Jeff Sinyard hit me anyway.

"Why did you do that to me? You knew that play was over before you hit me," I said to Sinyard a few days after it happened.

"You dated my girlfriend," he replied.

"Your girlfriend? That was last year," I said. "She was my girlfriend then. You're datin' her now."

It was true that Sinyard's girlfriend that year had been mine the year before. It didn't matter to him, I guess, that I was no longer interested in her, and she was no longer interested in me. As the seniors had told me the first week of Graves Springs, I was "fresh meat" to them. Sinyard had reminded me of that.

Sinyard was a co-captain and selected the Best Defensive Back for the varsity in 1972. We played American Legion baseball together, and were college roommates in Americus, Georgia. Later he served on the Dougherty County Commission at the same time I was working as a reporter for the *Albany Herald*. Sinyard would go on to own and operate a successful pest control company in Albany, and serve as chairman for the local economic development commission. Years later, he still likes to laugh about the fact that he broke my collarbone at practice. To this day he says, "Hey, you shouldn't have gone out with my girlfriend." I still don't laugh about it.

* * *

In 1972, the varsity finished with six wins and four losses. Once during that season, B-teamers were allowed to wear our uniforms and stand on the sidelines during a game. It was exhilarating just being on the sidelines as nine thousand fans watched the varsity play. Some years after Coach Ferrell Henry retired from coaching, he told me his 1972 team was his favorite because they did so much with players who weren't imposing in size or speed. He had players with character, whose hearts were big. As he liked to say, "It's not the size of the dog in the fight, it's the size of the fight in the dog." Many players were like Sinyard, Tom Giddens, Tom Shemwell, Jay Dallas, Jimmy Ussery, Johnny "Mule" Coleman, and others who were made mentally tough at Graves Springs. Of this Henry said, "That was a good group, they would never quit fightin'."

One local sportswriter said that Henry and his staff built a good football team when "nobody in the region expected [them] to win one game." The writer went on to say, "I guess if anything can be said about the Indians this year it would be that they had plenty of 'GUTS.' They weren't expected to do much of anything this year and everybody wouldn't have been too surprised if they had not done anything at all."

* * *

# SEVEN

AUGUST 1973
I knew what to expect from Graves Springs as an upcoming junior and backup quarterback. I entered camp with confidence after surviving it as a sophomore. I took my place among the upperclassmen in the "fancy" varsity barracks, the one with toilets and showers. Next to our bunks we were given large chests to store our clothes and other belongings. This was a luxury I didn't have the year before. We brought electric fans, and the constant humming fans at night were hymns to the stillness as we slept only to be awakened before daylight by the gentle *tweet-tweet-tweet* of Coach Henry's whistle.

After Coach Henry's wake-up call, offensive line coach Darrell Willett offered his philosophy on life: "Boys, life ain't a bowl of cherries." Willett constantly chewed on grass, pieces of string that held his whistle around his neck, pieces of a chinstrap or anything he could put in his mouth as the intensity of a practice or game mounted. Linemen complained that he even chewed the index cards used to diagram plays, which they had trouble reading during practice because of Willett's teethmarks. He called a two hundred and twenty-five pound lineman "baby," but slapped his players across their helmets when they failed to do their best. Or he patted them on their butts when they did their best. He loved to see his lineman root around on the ground, getting dirty and bloody.

\* \* \*

That year Ray Wallace, an upcoming senior, came to Graves Springs for the first time. He had not played football previously in high school, but Wallace and I played little league baseball together. Over the years he lost interest in organized sports, until his last year in high school.

On the first day at camp, the coaches set out to make or break Wallace.

"We're gonna put you back in Marlboro Country, Wallace!" defensive back coach Ronnie Archer proclaimed during our opening-day drills.

There wasn't much the coaches didn't know about all of us. Wallace was indeed a smoker.

"If you're so tough, boy, why didn't you come out here when you were a sophomore!" Archer hollered. "I don't think you're tough enough to be a Albany High Indian!"

I felt bad for Ray. I didn't believe he would survive camp—the coaches didn't seem to want him there.

"Come on Marlboro Man," Archer continued. "Let's see if you're gonna make it out here. You gotta wanna it, boy." Archer was making the backs run one wind sprint after another. Wallace struggled, and Archer rode him without mercy. "You wanna another cigarette?" Archer said.

"No sir! I don't want a cigarette," Wallace replied.

"Are you sure? I'll find one for you."

"No sir, I don't want a cigarette," said Wallace, who was now coughing as if he had smoked a million.

Archer was a fiery coach with dark hair and sideburns that extended to his earlobes. He instilled into the defensive backs a desire to hit and win and play beyond their own perceived limitations. It was a show watching him put his backs through their fundamental drills.

"Hot-dang boys, when that running back turns the corner you gotta break down in a football position," he commanded. "I mean keep your tail low!" At that point during his instructions, Archer bent his knees, flexed his arms out in front of his body, and clinched his fists all the while he had his butt close to the ground, illustrating the proper football position. "You've gotta hit and lock those arms. Keep drivin' your legs and tail."

The boys who played under Archer respected him, and if they worked hard they won his praise. He disliked players that didn't give everything they had on every play. "Yes sir, Coach Archer! Yes sir, Coach!" his backs responded as they listened to his instructions.

Archer was our school's head baseball coach, too. I played baseball under him, and he was often as emotional on the baseball field as he was at Graves Springs. But at camp that year, he was putting Wallace through the supreme test. I hated seeing it, because it seemed that Archer and the other coaches weren't willing to give Wallace a fair chance.

"Ray, they're workin' you hard out here," I said.

"Yeah, Archer's tryin' to kill me."

"Are you gonna make it?" I asked.

"I hope so," Wallace replied. He didn't look confident.

Wallace did "make it" at camp, and by the end of the second week he had shown enough grit to win the admiration of Archer and the rest of the coaches. He simply refused to be driven away from Graves Springs. Wallace played a lot at cornerback that year, impressing the coaches with how hard he hit running backs, often below the knees and turning them upside down. Wallace even became a model for his teammates, one that Archer looked to during practice.

"Boys, that's some lick!" Archer said after Wallace smashed into a running back during a scrimmage. "Dang it! That's what football's all about. Ray Wallace knows how to use that helmet!"

\* \* \*

While Wallace had been catching it from Archer, I was playing directly under Phil Spooner, offensive back coach. Spooner had been a running back at Florida State University and a teammate there of Ferrell Henry's. The Green Bay Packers had their "Golden Boy" in the glory days, Paul Hornung, the great running back; we had ours at Graves Springs. Spooner was muscular, tanned, and had wavy brown hair. He evoked the image of a California surfer who rides the waves of the Pacific during the day and at night buys the pretty girls piña coladas. We didn't get hellfire motivational talks from Spooner; those came from Henry, Willett, and Archer. I don't remember Spooner ever raising his voice at us. Because of his reserved demeanor, it was possible for me and the offensive backs to relax a bit as we worked on individual drills and ran through plays away from the other coaches and the rest of the team. During practice, Spooner kept a piece of grass in his mouth that stuck out a few inches. He turned it over and over until it became soaked with saliva and had to be replaced with another piece.

"All right, boys, Ferrell wants us to go through these plays before we scrimmage," Spooner said to me and the other backs huddled around him. As we ran the plays, Spooner kneeled on one knee, keeping his eyes on Coach Henry, who was working with the defense, and us. "I guess we better keep running these plays some more," he said, growing impatient waiting for the signal from Henry to begin the scrimmage. We all knew that Spooner hated Graves Springs. Spooner hated getting up before daylight. His tastes were more urbane. I enjoyed playing under Spooner. He was a good football teacher, and his easy coaching style was a reprieve from the Old Testament gods of Graves Springs.

Spooner coached for only a few years leaving the game to enter private business. Years after Spooner had left coaching, Henry told me, "Phil just couldn't stand Graves Springs." On that account, he was like the rest of us.

\* \* \*

After the first few days of camp, I became concerned for Brent Brock, a junior varsity player who lived just a few blocks from me in Albany. We had played baseball together growing up, and my father and his mother worked for the same manufacturing firm. I'd come to know his family pretty well, and was fond of them.

"I heard that Brock fell out," Leonard Lawless said.

"Fell out" was a common expression used at Graves Springs. It meant that one of us had become so exhausted that we were unable to continue to practice. I never fell out at camp, but I saw boys who did. The constant heat, hard practices, and lack of water during practice caused players to fall out.

"So what happened to Brock?" I asked. "Where is he? Is he okay?"

"His mother came to pick him up," Lawless replied. "I think she took him to the doctor."

"I hope he's okay. I hope he doesn't quit," I said.

His mother *had* taken him to see a doctor, and Brock missed the last couple of days of the first week of camp. His body had grown weak at camp because he had eaten little food between practices. Brock consumed so much water and Gatorade that he had little appetite for food. He returned the second week of camp and practiced every day.

"I just gave completely out of energy," recalled Brock.

\* \* \*

During the last night at camp my junior year, two hours after the barracks' lights had been turned off by the coaches, I began to hear talking and laughing. The noise kept getting louder. Soon, fruit and other pieces of food were being thrown throughout the barracks. Finally someone hollered: "You m——f—— need to shut up! Shut up and go to sleep!" I heard a loud pop as something, a Coke bottle maybe, shattered after being thrown against a wall.

"Man, we need to put our helmets on!" said Lawless, whose bunk was near mine. There was just enough light for me to see as he reached for his helmet hanging from his bunk. He put the helmet on his head.

"Yeah, this is gettin' crazy," I said. I found my helmet and put it on, too.

Other players took the same measure of self-protection, including Davey Davis, a junior offensive lineman. "I didn't know what was happening," Davis recalled. "It got crazy that night."

Davis' bunk was near that of Donald Alley's, who had placed a Styrofoam ice chest over his head; the ice chest was hit by something and torn apart. "After that, Alley put his helmet on," Davis said.

A few moments after I had heard the crash against the wall, Coach Henry entered our barracks and turned on the lights. He was mad.

"Y'all don't want to go to sleep—get your helmets, shoes and shorts on," Henry said. "You got two minutes to be on the field! Move it!"

We got dressed and headed to the practice field, and Henry told the other coaches to awaken the sophomores and get them on the field too. It was about midnight, and we had to be up for our regular practice in six hours.

As we walked through the darkness, I heard the crickets along the creek and saw two of the coaches driving pickup trucks toward the practice field. "What are we gonna to do?" I wondered out loud as I ran next to Lawless.

"We'll do whatever he tells us to do," Lawless replied.

Both trucks sped past us while we hustled up the now-dusty trail that led to the field. Henry had instructed his assistants to park the trucks at both ends of the field and keep the headlights on. Now the four beams of light provided Henry all the light he needed.

"All right, all right let's have one line right here! Give me a line right here," Henry said as several of us got into the three-point position across one of the end zones and prepared to run full-speed for a hundred yards. Henry blew his whistle and the first group of players, which included Lawless and me, ran through the sand kicking up dust that filtered hazily through the light beams from the pickup trucks.

"I'll bet y'all will go to sleep when we leave here," Henry said. "Give me another line . . . right here!" The second group lined up, awaiting the sound of the whistle. Like a giant snake weaving its way across the sand, as some parts are out front only to be overtaken by other sections of its slithering body, we pounded the sand while the stars were bright above us.

"How many of these things are we gonna run?" I asked Lawless.

"I don't know," Lawless said, panting. "We'll run until Ferrell tells us to stop."

Ferrell Henry seemed to be in the mood to run us until daybreak.

"Line up! Line up! Keep runnin', keep runnin'!" Henry shouted in a deep, thick guttural voice. On the field his voice was authoritative and tough, but that night he sounded meaner than usual. He was not happy having to get out of bed and make us run. We continued to run sprints, with thirty seconds of rest in between, and each time we stirred up more dust until it became difficult for me to see my teammates.

After about six or seven sprints, as we began to tire and slow down a bit, Henry yelled: "Boys you're slacking off on me. I'll make y'all run until the sun comes up if you stop hustling."

At that point, I knew we would keep running some more, but I was still relatively certain that Henry would let us return to the barracks and get a few hours sleep before our next practice. We continued to run and after a few more sprints, with sixty-five players gasping deep for each breath, Henry sent us back to our beds.

"Now, maybe y'all will go to sleep," he said, pointing to the barracks and blowing his whistle.

We ran off the practice field, and I looked at the pickup trucks that had lighted the field in the morning's darkness. "Ain't we havin' fun, Quarterback?" Donnie Spence said as we jogged off the field on the way back to the barracks. Henry never allowed walking off the field.

"I'm havin' a lot of fun, Spence," I replied, nearly out of breath. "This is a great summer vacation."

Just above the field a cloud of dust was lifting up, first directly over the field and then moving beyond the pine trees that surrounded the field. Further skyward, the dust climbed until it meshed with the dark sky and the light from distant stars. Returning to the barracks, we quietly undressed, hung our clothes up so the sweat might dry and went to sleep. But we were soon awakened by the soft *tweet, tweet, tweet* of Henry's whistle. It was still dark, but time to practice again.

Years after I graduated from high school, Henry and I laughed together as we recalled that particular midnight practice at Graves Springs. Henry told me that he liked having one or two midnight practices every year at Graves Springs. "Those were all part of the mental toughness" connected with becoming an Albany High player, he said.

Maybe so, but I hated them.

\* \* \*

By September 1973, as I began my junior season as the backup varsity quarterback, the local newspaper had picked us to win eight of ten games. This would be a fine achievement, considering that we played some of the best teams not only in the state but also in the nation. That included Valdosta High School, located about ninety miles south of Albany. Valdosta was winning state championships regularly then; by the 1990s, the Wildcats had won more than twenty titles.

We won our first three games that year, including victories over city rivals Westover and Monroe. Our fourth game was at home against Valdosta, and it attracted about nine thousand spectators. I entered the game after our starting quarterback, David Hitson, injured his knee. Hitson would miss the remainder of the year. I was nervous and intimidated against the powerful Wildcats, who beat us handily. But I started each game after that, and was selected to the All-City Team as we finished the season five and five.

\* \* \*

# EIGHT

AUGUST 1974
In preparation for the 1974 season, we had our traditional four weeks of spring practice and Henry worked us hard, constantly reminding us that another five-and-five season would be unacceptable. I played varsity basketball that winter and baseball in the spring. Some days after school I practiced both football and baseball. But during a football scrimmage at the stadium, I was hit hard on the right knee and had to leave the field. The pain wouldn't go away, so my parents took me to the team doctor, and later I underwent surgery to repair the ligaments and cartilage. The knee was slow to heal, and bothered me throughout the summer as I played American Legion baseball.

That year, we were shocked and hurt after learning Coach Henry had accepted the head coaching position at Crisp County High School in Cordele, Georgia, about thirty-five miles from Albany. Henry had worked us hard at Graves Springs and during spring practice, and it was difficult for us to accept his departure. Henry, during January and February, worked some of the players, making them lift weights and run the steep stadium steps after school each day. This was done before our regular spring practice. Because I was playing basketball, I wasn't required to be a part of his program. Players like Leonard Lawless, David McClung, Donnie Spence and others called themselves "Bird Feeders" because Henry made them run the steps to the point of not only exhaustion, but also until they threw up their lunches, providing meals for the pigeons that made their homes in the stadium.

Years later, Henry told me he resigned after meeting with superintendent, Paul Robertson, who, according to Henry, said Albany High's enrollment would likely continue to fall because of changing school zones. From the late 1960s to the early 1970s, the school's enrollment had gone from about 2,000 to less than half that number. Henry came to believe that his chances of winning the region were better at Crisp County, a school with a larger enrollment and the only public school in that county.

Henry and his assistants were gone. There would be new coaches at Graves Springs.

\* \* \*

Throughout the summer of 1974, as August neared along with the first day of Graves Springs, I was thinking seriously about quitting the team. I was simply tired of being hurt. Over the last few years I had fractured both collarbones and undergone knee surgery. The knee was still not at full strength. Plus, like my teammates, I was hurt emotionally and even bitter about losing Henry. A couple of weeks before camp was scheduled to begin, the local school board hired Cardon Dalley to replace Henry. Dalley had coached at Dougherty High School in Albany, but he had never coached at Graves Springs.

A few days before we were supposed to report to camp, I decided not to quit. To be with my teammates, the energy and emotion of the Friday night crowds, and the sense of accomplishment football had already given me were too powerful to walk away from, bad knee and all. For the third year I went to the "Graves Springs Resort Area," as it was referred to in our football program.

We gathered at the school on a Sunday afternoon in August to begin the first week. As was routine, we loaded our uniforms, electric fans, and drinks on the yellow school buses. There was uncertainty about Dalley and the new group of assistants, but there was a feeling of pride and leadership among myself, Leonard Lawless, Donnie Spence, James Harpe, David McClung, Wes Westbrook and other seniors who had survived Graves Springs.

\* \* \*

After the buses stopped along the creek, we grabbed our belongings, went into the barracks, and began claiming our bunks while bemoaning the start of another preseason camp. The air was motionless and the heat oppressive as thousands of gnats greeted us.

"Home, sweet, home," McClung said. "Don't you just love it here?" McClung slapped me across the back as he walked through the door of the barracks.

Donnie Spence was settling in near my bunk, and was looking into his ice chest as if there was something sacred in there. "Come over here," he said.

"What's up?"

"Look in there," Spence whispered.

"What for?"

"Just look in the very bottom and don't give me any of your crap," he said.

I looked inside the ice chest and saw fruit and soft drinks. "So. What's the big deal, man? What am I lookin' for?"

"Go deeper, man, all the way to the bottom," he insisted.

I moved chunks of ice from side to side and saw on the bottom of the chest, lined up like soldiers standing at attention, six cans of beer.

I looked up at Spence, who by now was directly over me; the only thing brighter than his smile was the glow from his blue eyes. "What in the hell have you done?" I said. "Cardon's gonna bust your butt, Donnie."

"Cardon won't know a thing," he replied with the wry confidence I'd come to expect from him.

"Yeah, remember what Ferrell did to you last year," I reminded him.

"That was last year. This is a new year, new coaches," he said. "These guys won't catch us. Relax, man. You worry too much."

One night the season before, Coach Henry saw Spence leaving a store with a six-pack of beer. Instead of kicking him off the team, Henry allowed Spence to remain only if he ran a mile after each practice. There were several days I thought Spence was going to collapse because of the extra running. I remember leaving practice around seven o'clock one day, and Spence was still running laps around the gravel track in the stadium. I knew he wasn't going to quit, and Henry knew how good a player he was and what he meant to the team.

Spence and I had spent a lot of time together away from the field. We fished and partied and had worked together at the Flint River Cotton Mill. He was great company. He drove a white Monte Carlo that he kept spotless, and his eight-track tape player crooned songs by Al Green, the Spinners and other singers whose vocals were as smooth and confident as he was.

"Boy, you need to relax," he repeated. "We're gonna drink these Wednesday on the field and quit worrying about it. Everything's gonna be all right."

Typical Spence. Very convincing.

"You're the one who should worry," I replied. "But they'll sure taste good, won't they?" I was quickly approving of the plan. With Spence you had no other choice.

"Yeah, they're gonna taste great," he said.

That Wednesday, after our parents and girlfriends left, we sneaked the beers to the practice field right before dark. It was quiet except for the birds. The fading sun cast shades of orange over the sky and trees. A few other players were walking their girlfriends back to the barracks. One more kiss before they left. Spence and I sat among the trees at the edge of where we daydreamed of water during practice, and we drank those beers. They did taste good. We buried the empty beer cans in the sand near the field. By the time Spence was in his forties, he was working as an executive for Miller Brewing Company in Milwaukee.

\* \* \*

Not long after we began settling in the barracks that first Sunday afternoon, our new head coach, Cardon Dally, came to talk with me.

"I didn't think you were gonna play, Lightle. How's the knee?" Dalley asked.

"The knee's all right," I said.

"We'll get you a brace and have Coach Magwood tape it up before each practice," Dalley reassured me.

"Thanks coach."

Dalley was from Nevada, and had played football for Southern Utah University. He was heavyset, balding and had a comforting smile. I always felt at ease around him both on and off the field. He was soft-spoken and generally not as emotional as Ferrell Henry was. Dalley took over with new assistants except for Willie Magwood, who continued coaching the junior varsity and helped with the varsity. I was glad Magwood hadn't left us.

* * *

Although the coaching style had changed, Graves Springs was still miserable and the hottest place on earth. We still had three-a-days. Along with the changes Dalley, unlike Henry, was allowing me more responsibility at practice. This carried over to our games, where I called nearly every offensive play. Dalley put a lot of faith in me, and in doing so helped me gain greater confidence in myself, and in the team.

"All right, Lightle, take'em over there and run some pass routes then go over some running plays," Dalley said after we finished our team exercises. At this point in practice, offensive and defensive units worked separately, going over plays and drills. Later, the two units would come together for a scrimmage. Besides being the head coach, Dalley ran the offensive unit. He knew I would take the backs and receivers and work on our own when he wanted to spend a few minutes with the defense.

"Hobbs, line'em up," I said. "You too, Westbrook, over here on this side." Two lines of backs and receivers formed on both sides of me, each line about ten yards or so from me. I would take an imaginary snap, drop back a few yards, and throw passes, alternating my receivers from line to line. First we would start with short routes, five or ten yards, then slant across the middle, and in a few minutes both lines would be running longer routes.

James Harpe ran the first route. We still called him "Hobbs" like Willie Magwood had started two years ago when we were sophomores.

I fired the ball and Harpe missed it. "Hobbs, catch that ball," I said.

"Hobbs, you can't catch nothin'," said Wes Westbrook, our starting wide receiver.

"Lightle, throw me another one. Throw me another one," Harpe insisted. He ran the same pattern again and caught the ball this time.

Next Lawless ran the same route, turned to catch the ball as I threw it as hard as I could; he was only a few yards from me. Lawless always ran the routes at practice shorter than what I called for. He didn't like catching passes, and he wasn't very good at it. The ball bounced off his shoulder pads, hit the ground, and by the time it got back to me it was covered with sandspurs.

"Lawless, you can't catch a dang thing either," Westbrook said.

"Quit throwin' it so hard, Lightle," Lawless pleaded. "I'm runnin' it again."

Lawless got into a three-point stance again, his long, thick hair flowing out from under his helmet. I dropped back to throw him the ball, and he ran the same short pattern. I threw it about as half as hard as the first pass, but he missed it just the same. We did it a third time. This time, he caught the ball. After he made the catch, the rest of us clapped.

Lawless didn't catch many passes that year during the regular season. He was a grinder, a fearless blocker and runner. His desire to hit hard had no limits.

"You still can't catch," Westbrook said as Lawless came back to line up again. Lawless said nothing, but he did let Westbrook see, up close, the longest finger on his left hand.

After a few minutes of the drill, Dalley returned and we went over some plays. Dalley had watched the defense, which was being worked over pretty well by assistant coach Ray Kinney.

Kinney had graduated from Mars Hill College where he had been an All-American player in 1972. At Graves Springs he coached the defensive line while trying—the wrong way—to make us All Americans.

"I said do it right! This ain't a football team," Kinney bellowed. "I ain't got nobody that wants to do it right!" He hollered a lot at camp and throughout that season. He hollered so much that most of us, particularly on offense where Dalley's style was much different, ignored him. Away from the field, we joked about Kinney's antics.

"Hambone, you got to lock your arms, move your feet. Let's go, boy. You gotta do better than that!" Kinney shouted to Mike "Hambone" Hamilton, a senior linebacker, as he was going through some tackling drills.

*Smack!*

Hamilton made the next tackle harder.

"Hambone, that's not good enough!" Kinney would yell.

It was almost impossible to please him.

The other linebacker Kinney was watching closely was Mike Trotter. Trotter couldn't do anything well enough for Kinney either. He was covered with sandspurs, his sweaty uniform smelled like ammonia, and his face was smeared with sweat, dirt and blood. Moreover, Trotter was mad as hell at Kinney, mad enough that, if he had any strength left in him, he might have taken Kinney to the creek and held him under water the rest of the day. Kinney was a stout man; he'd likely put up quite a fight.

* * *

# NINE

My high school yearbook says this about Graves Springs in 1974:

"Graves Springs once again . . . New Faces, New Coaches . . . Who stole my mattress? Sand and Stickers . . . Long Days and Short Nights, Up at 6, in bed at 10, Card Games, Losing Money, Blaring Tape Players, Baths in the creek. Coaches yelling, Kinney screaming, Root Hogging, Ups and Downs, stretching exercises, Beep Beeps . . ."

"Fried Chicken, rubber pancakes, hot dogs, gnats in potatoes . . . "Living rough, but being Natural Men. Seniors Last Camp. Scrimmages morning and afternoon"

"Run, Run, Run . . . taped hands, arms, ankles, etc . . . Health Clinic, X-Rays, doctors, Traditional Sleep-in, Meetings in the Cafeteria. Learn new plays, forget old plays . . ."

"Hot days and longing for home. A lot of hard work but deep down loved every minute of it."

On the next page, there are a handful of photographs that were taken at Graves Springs that year. One picture shows the varsity barracks where bunks, three high, were adorned with: helmets, shoulder pads, dirty clothes being dried by electric fans, mouthpieces, cleats, and arm pads. The sacred relics covered the altars.

This picture doesn't show the several eight-track tape players we brought to camp to hear rock'n roll. A Georgia band, the Allman Brothers, was a favorite.

> *I'm run down I been lied to I don't know*
> *why I let that mean woman make me a fool.*
> *She took all my money and my new car*
> *Now she's with one of my good-time buddies*
> *Drinkin' in a cross-town bar.*
> *Sometimes I feel like I'm tied to a whipping post*
> *Sometimes I feel like I'm tied to a whipping post*
> *Good Lord I feel like I'm dyin'.*

Every day we were tied to a whipping post along the Muckalee Creek.

\* \* \*

Pictured in that yearbook is Carl Williams, a first-year coach who worked with the defensive linemen. Williams had played at Graves Springs in the 1960s. He had a fiery personality and an enormous passion for Albany High football. And Williams was fun to be around. He worked players hard, but he had a sense of humor, which was a relief from the daily grind at Graves Springs. "Pride, boys! Pride! That's Albany High football!" he told us.

Williams grew up dreaming about playing for Albany High before thousands of people: the marching band playing to push the adrenaline even higher, pretty girls on the sidelines jumping and moving and encouraging strong, brave young men to do things beyond what they had thought possible. Life offers nothing to surpass this, so Williams thought as a young boy and later came to know was true. Williams knew firsthand how hard Graves Springs was, and sometimes he said you had to act like an "animal" just to survive.

"Boys, I remember teammates throwin' up the first day of practice," Williams said.

"I've seen several players do that out here, Coach," I said.

Williams recalled that one of his teammates had eaten several hot dogs the night before their first practice. "One year Sambo Arnold threw up a bunch of hot dogs and ate the vomit so the coaches wouldn't call him a sissy," Williams said.

"I've never seen that happen," I said.

"Boys, sometimes you got to be crazy to make it out here," he said.

\* \* \*

As it had been the previous two years, rock'n roll music was heard daily at camp, pulsating through the hot, sticky air. As you walked through camp and the barracks, the music you heard depended on who was playing his tape player the loudest or which bunk you happened to be closest to. As I walked around camp, I heard these words from ZZ Top, an electric-rock band from Texas that attracted quite a following among my teammates that year:

> *Jesus just left Chicago*
> *And he's bound for New Orleans*
> *Jesus just left Chicago*
> *And he's bound for New Orleans*
> *I took a job in Mississippi*
> *Muddy water turned to wine*
> *I took a job in Mississippi*
> *Muddy water turned to wine*

\* \* \*

Being "Natural Men," as my yearbook reads, was a phrase that we used many times at Graves Springs and during the season. Natural men sweated and bled and lived naked in the woods.

Nineteenth-century writer Henry David Thoreau went to the woods himself in New England, not to practice football but to contemplate, read, and write. Of *Walden* he wrote:

> I went to the woods because I wished to live deliberately, to front only the essential facts of life, and see if I could not learn what it had to teach, and not, when I came to die, discover that I had not lived . . . I wanted to live deep and suck out all the marrow of life, to live so sturdily and Spartan-like as to put to rout all that was not life, to cut a broad swath and shave close, to drive life into a corner, and reduce it to its

lowest terms, and, if it proved to be mean why then to get the whole and genuine meanness of it, and publish its meanness to the world . . .

Anyone who went to Graves Springs recalled the "meanness" of it all. I am certain that Thoreau had a lot more time to relax then we did at Graves Springs, and he wasn't catching hell from football coaches nor having the hell knocked out of him by his teammates.

The call to the woods at Graves Springs was for the team itself, but every player who went there was on the "hero's journey" as described by the late writer Joseph Campbell—the call to adventure, sacrifice, and danger. The classical hero leaves a place of safety and comfort to venture into the wilderness, the desert, the mountaintop, the cave, or any place representing danger and personal challenges. Mental and physical tests await the hero, as with Sir Gawain who challenged the powerful Green Knight. Or like Muhammad in the cave, afraid when he is confronted by the angel Gabriel. Or Isis, who goes in search for the body of her lost husband, Osiris, who was killed by his jealous brother, Seth.

Why the journey for these heroes and heroines? And why the journey to Graves Springs? If one accepts the hero's journey, it is a call that comes from turning inward. The sacrifices and dangers along the way, when they are met head-on by the hero, indicate the ideal of living an authentic life. Thus, by the hero's very actions and commitments, he becomes a model for others to emulate.

At the time I didn't think of Graves Springs in terms of a mythological experience. Intellectually, I wasn't prepared to think in that manner. Every mythology, as Joseph Campbell said, is true in that it seeks to bring children up in accord with the culture. In doing so, myth incorporates rituals that challenge one's own character. These rituals are a reminder that there will be suffering and sacrifice in the lives of everyone. As Campbell said, "When we quit thinking primarily about ourselves and our own self-preservation we undergo a truly heroic transformation of consciousness."

* * *

Coaches at Graves Springs could be extremely hard on players who waited until their senior year to come out for the team. The year before, they tried but failed to run Ray Wallace from Graves Springs. During one late afternoon practice, I saw Larry Hacker "fall out" or collapse on the field.

Hacker was an upcoming senior receiver who hadn't played organized football before coming to Graves Springs in August 1974. He had asthma as a child, and still struggled with the condition. Hacker did play neighborhood ball with guys like Wes Westbrook, who convinced him to come to camp. Hacker was neither fast nor exceptionally big or strong, but he had sure hands, and was catching the ball well during camp, and doing everything to survive and prove his worthiness.

When Hacker collapsed, he was covered in sweat and dirt and was having problems breathing. We'd been practicing for two hours, and the coaches had us running sprints to conclude the session. We hated the sprints. It was hot and my mouth was dry and aching for water. These sprints were killers—a hundred yards at full speed, rest a few seconds and do it again. I was running next to Lawless when I saw Hacker fall down in the sand.

"Lawless, Hacker fell out," I said, trying to catch my breath.

Lawless turned around to look back up the field. "Man, it looks like he can't breathe," Lawless said.

"What's goin' on down there?" I asked.

"I hope he's all right," was Lawless' only reply.

Hacker was trying to regain his footing, but he couldn't. From where I was, about fifty yards away, I could see he was having a hard time. He got up on all fours, but then hit the ground and lay motionless.

Coach Willie Magwood ran to help him. He took Hacker's helmet off and tried by himself to pick Hacker up and carry him off the field, but he was unable to do so. "I need some good mens to help me!" Magwood cried out.

Two players rushed to help Magwood with Hacker. They got him steady on his feet, wrapped both of his arms around their shoulders and hustled as fast as they could down the sandy trail that leads to the barracks.

"What's happening to that boy?" said David McClung, who had grown up with Hacker. McClung was now standing near Lawless and me. The three of us, as did the rest of the team, watched as Hacker was carried to the barracks.

"I don't know what happened to him. It doesn't look good," I said. "Dalley needs to call an ambulance."

"Hacker'll be okay. He just fell out," McClung added. "He don't need no ambulance."

"I don't know," I said. "It doesn't look good."

Magwood used scissors to cut Hacker's uniform off of him and put Hacker in the shower, running cool water all over him. After several minutes under the water, he began to regain his strength. Magwood gave him water and Gatorade to drink.

After practice, I went inside the barracks and saw Magwood standing near Hacker and looking relieved. "Now good mens, take care of Hacker tonight," Magwood said. "I think he's all right now."

"Coach, I'm okay. Thanks for helping me," replied Hacker, now sitting on his bunk.

Several of us gathered around him, including James Harpe. During camp, Harpe had taken a special interest in helping Hacker learn the plays and be a part of the team. During scrimmages, Harpe would fake a minor injury so Hacker could run plays with the first team offense. The two players, one white and one black, developed a friendship at Graves Springs.

"Hacker, I thought you were dead," Harpe said.

"Well, Hobbs, I thought I was dead too," Hacker said.

"If you did die, I was comin' to your funeral and maybe sing a song or two. Like 'Stairway to Heaven' by Zed Lepplin," Harpe said.

"Hobbs, that's *Led Zeppelin*," Hacker said.

"You know what I mean," he replied.

"I'm glad I didn't die. I don't wanna hear you sing at my funeral," Hacker said.

"Hey, butthole you're not dead," said Westbrook, who slapped Hacker across his back. "You're just tryin' to get out of practice."

"That's right, I just don't wanna practice," Hacker said. "But I'm gonna be dead if you keep hittin' me."

David McClung came to see about his fallen teammate. "Boy, now don't fall out again or I'll have to kick your tail."

"Thanks, Mac," Hacker said. "You're always there to help me."

Dalley and the other coaches checked on Hacker, and were satisfied that he was going to be all right. Magwood reminded us to take care of Hacker. "Good mens, Hacker is a tough player," he said. "You take it easy, Hacker. We need you back on the field in the morning."

"Okay, Coach," he said.

We stood near Hacker for several minutes. He seemed to enjoy the attention, but not what it took to get it.

"Larry, we didn't think you were gonna make it," I said.

"For a few minutes, I didn't either," he replied.

The next morning Hacker was back at practice, and he didn't "fall out" at Graves Springs again. The coaches, however, weren't any easier on him because of the asthma attack. No player got special treatment at Graves Springs.

* * *

"Root Hogging, Ups and Downs, and Beep Beeps" were the most dreaded drills and tests we endured at camp and during the regular season. "Root Hogging" involved two players positioned nose-to-nose, low to the ground. At the whistle, the two tried to run over one another. As they were fighting, the rest of us cheered. "Rip his head off!" coaches screamed during the drill.

I hated the drill and usually wasn't made to do it because I played quarterback. This was for the linemen, the boys that did the grunt work. At Graves Springs I saw the best of friends physically assault one another during this drill. But when practice ended, the drill was forgotten and their friendships were re-established. As a ninth-grader, I saw Donnie Spence and David McClung doing a drill similar to "Root Hogging." The drill became so intense that they started swinging, grabbing, and clawing one another and both looked, with fire in their eyes, as if they wanted to kill the other. But when practice ended, all was forgotten.

The other drills were "Ups and Downs" and "Beep, Beeps." During these two, we attacked not one another but the earth itself. While doing "Ups and Downs," we ran in place and then, at the sound of the whistle, threw ourselves flat on the ground, arms extended as if we were trying to fly. We repeated this fifteen times or more if they weren't done well enough to satisfy the coaches.

"Beep, Beeps" were tougher still, and we hated this one more than the other two drills. We formed a line up, ten players or so, and on the whistle we sprinted as fast as we could downfield. But the next time we heard the whistle—it could be after the first ten or fifteen yards—we extended our arms birdlike and flew through the air, landing belly-first on the ground. After hitting the ground we got up as quick as possible and continued sprinting. As soon the whistle blew again, after another ten yards or so, we belly-flopped again. We repeated this a dozen times or more before the drill ended. Afterwards, we were sore all over, covered with sandspurs, and struggling to catch our breaths.

After camp ended and school started, assistant coach Ray Kinney was making the team do "Beep, Beeps" as a form of punishment. Kinney became agitated during practice because of what he said was a lack of hustle and desire. "We're gonna do these damn things the rest of the day!" he barked. "Maybe then some of you boys will start hustling!"

We began running and Kinney blew his whistle, enjoying watching us pound the earth with our bodies. "Get up! Get up! Get up! You sissies, get up!"

This continued for several minutes, until we were so tired that we were barely trotting instead of sprinting, prompting Kinney to yell, "We'll be here until dark!"

During this drill, Head Coach Dalley had been away from the practice field that day. This seemed to be Kinney's way of demonstrating his newfound authority.

As we were running up and down flopping on the field, it was clear that no other previous coach, as tough and demanding as they were, had ever displayed this kind of behavior. Some of us had all we were going to take from Kinney.

"I've had enough of this mess," I said to Leonard Lawless.

"Let's just get out of here," Lawless responded.

"What'd ya mean?"

"I mean let's leave," he said. "Let's just get the hell out of here."

Lawless and I both looked at Donnie Spence and David McClung. They had enough of Kinney, too.

While the upstart Kinney kept blowing his whistle and giving orders Spence, McClung, Lawless, myself, and a few others ran off the field, across the street to Hugh Mills Stadium—all the way to the locker room. We had challenged the coaching authority of Albany High School, something that was unthinkable the previous year under Coach Ferrell Henry and his staff. But Henry and his group never demanded we do such a stupid thing as these Beep, Beeps.

As we ran off the field, Coach Kinney continued screaming at us to come back. But we kept on running. Later, Coach Dalley talked to all of us who had left practice that day. We told him exactly what had happened. Dalley agreed that it was wrong that Kinney made us do so many Beep, Beeps. We weren't punished for leaving practice, and were back on the team the next day.

\* \* \*

When camp ended in late August 1974, I and the other seniors had special reason to rejoice: knowing that never again would we return to Graves Springs—as players anyway. On my last day at Graves Springs, two school buses appeared to take us back to town. What a joy it was to see them arrive.

I sat in the back of the varsity bus surrounded by happy teammates, and as we drove away from the barracks, I looked out the back window and saw the dust rising from the old yellow school bus. In the still of the afternoon with a hundred-degree heat, the Spanish moss was hanging as ornaments, a tribute to our survival at Graves Springs. The steady buzzing of the insects was music in our honor as the barracks began fading from sight. Through the window I took a final look at the Muckalee Creek flowing easily, its brown water clean and confident, making its way to the Flint River. Above the creek, the rope tied to the oak tree from which we swung out into the water was motionless. At Graves Springs, with each baptism in the Muckalee, my salvation had been ensured.

\* \* \*

# TEN

My team finished the season winning six, losing three, and we tied cross-town rival Westover High School. It had been Albany High's best football season since the 1967 team won eight and lost two. We certainly surpassed the expectations of some local sportswriters and others who followed high school football in Southwest Georgia. Some had predicted we'd win only three or four games.

We lost our first two games. The second was a thirty-four to twenty defeat against powerful Thomasville High School, which went on to win the state title that year while being proclaimed one of the best high school teams in the country. Thomasville, about fifty miles south of Albany, traveled to Hugh Mills Stadium, and about eight thousand people saw our game. They had won the state championship the previous year, while allowing only thirteen points during the entire regular season. Again in 1974, they had one of the best players in the state, running back William Andrews. Andrews scored three touchdowns against us that year, and one was on a sixty-three yard run.

"How are we gonna stop that?" I said to David McClung as we watched Andrews score one of his touchdowns. Our defensive players were bouncing off him like silver balls in a pinball machine.

"We ain't," McClung said, looking me straight in the eyes. "We ain't gonna be able to."

McClung was right; we weren't able to stop Andrews.

The day after the game, the *Albany Herald* headline read: "Albany Gives Good Account, But Andrews Makes the Difference." To this day, Andrews was the best high school player I have ever seen. Andrews crushed linemen and linebackers alike as he ran over them only when he chose not to run past them. That year Andrews rushed from more than thirteen hundred yards, averaging more than seven yards a carry.

After he graduated from high school, Andrews played at Auburn University. The Atlanta Falcons later drafted him, and he had an outstanding career with them. As I watched him on television during the 1980s, he seemed to run over defensive backs in the NFL with little difficulty, just like he did against the Albany High Indians.

After our loss to Thomasville and the future NFL standout, head coach Jim Hughes at Thomasville called our team "the best 0-2 team in the state." We played his team a solid game, but we were still without a win. With all the hard work at Graves Springs that year and the previous two, my final season at Albany High had not begun very well.

Our first win was over Dougherty High School, a local rival. Dougherty was the only team that year to beat Thomasville. They were, of course, favored to beat us on September 20, 1974, as about nine thousand fans filled Hugh Mills Stadium. Our halfback, Celious Williams, scored two touchdowns, but after each one Dougherty went on to score. With about two minutes left in the game, trailing by three, our offense drove sixty yards in eight plays to Dougherty's one-yard line. With less than thirty seconds in the game, I ran a quarterback sneak behind the blocking of guard Donnie Spence and center Davie Davis. All the agonies of Graves Springs were erased by that moment of victory. After the final touchdown, we jumped on top of one another in celebration and disbelief.

A week later, again our stadium was packed as we played Monroe High School, the all-black school in Albany. We knew when there was a pile of bodies on the field there would be pinching, hitting, kicking, and lots of cussing. The Monroe Tornadoes would be just that—fast and destructive. Their marching band gyrated in perfect unison, and its music caused an eruption of emotions among the Tornado fans.

The game began poorly for us. In the opening drive, I threw an interception. But in the second quarter we drove the ball forty-two yards with Wes Westbrook catching a seventeen-yard pass from me before he was stopped at Monroe's one-yard line. Lawless scored the touchdown behind Spence's blocking. After Lawless scored, however, we missed the extra point attempt. Monroe would go on to score with two minutes and forty-five seconds left in the game, but they failed to convert the extra point.

With bands playing and fans screaming, Rex Fox returned the Monroe kickoff thirty yards, almost to midfield. Fox was a tough defensive back, and one of our leaders. He was a senior and his younger brother, Kip, played tight end. With the game knotted at six and time running out, our offense took over. We completed three passes moving the ball down to the Monroe ten-yard line with only seven seconds left.

We brought in our field goal kicker, Vince Williams, to win the game. Vince lived in the same neighborhood as I did, and we had grown up playing sports together and fishing at a small neighborhood pond. Vince loved the outdoors; for fun, he and his brother would often wade through the swamps of South Georgia shooting water moccasins with their pistols. "There ain't nothin' better than that," he'd say. "I love shootin' a snake."

Now it was time for him to shoot a field goal.

I held the ball during the field goal attempt, as I had done all year. Our offense was set. The official blew his whistle, indicating that the clock was running now. Those seven seconds began ticking away. The snap came to me crisp from Donnie Spence, who had moved over from his guard position to snap the ball. Usually sure-handed, I fumbled the ball trying to put it in place. Vince missed the field goal because he was unable to kick the ball squarely. Monroe's fans were dancing in their seats, and their cheerleaders were doing flips ten feet off the ground. Our side was quiet. I had lost the chance to win the game.

"I blew it, Vince. It's my fault. I blew it," I said repeatedly.

"Don't worry about it," Vince replied. "It's over now."

I had not seen the yellow flag on the ground. The officials had called Monroe offside during the play, penalizing them and giving us another chance to win the game.

"Dang it, we get another shot now," Vince said. "We'll make this one."

"I can't believe it," I said. "I'll get it right this time."

This time my hold on the ball was true, and Vince made the field goal with three seconds left. We jumped and screamed and hugged one another as we had done a week earlier after beating Dougherty High with only seconds left in that game. Celious Williams, Al Steele (who made six tackles), Dewitt Williams, Jimmy Snead, and the other black players on my team were especially happy to have beaten Monroe and some of their boyhood friends. The next day, the *Albany Herald* ran a picture of me holding the ball and Vince kicking the winning field goal. The photographer caught the ball in flight as it was sailing up over the Monroe defenders. The editors had added a white circle to the picture so readers could find the ball. The ball in the picture is forever suspended in midair, as our emotions were in every game we played. The joy of winning will be forever suspended in the night sky, like that ball in the photograph.

Mike Hamilton was one of our senior linebackers who made several tackles during the Monroe game. He had been a tough, dedicated player for three years. Coach Kinney had been especially hard on Hamilton at Graves Springs. Mike Hamilton's father, Phil Hamilton, was originally from Portland, Maine, where he had been an all-state high school football player. By the 1950s, as part of the Marine Corps, he was sent to its supply depot in Albany. After leaving the Marines he stayed in Albany with his wife, Marjorie, and took a job with the Albany Police Department. He was on the force when Dr. Martin Luther King Jr. was arrested in Albany during the early 1960s. He personally kept a key that was used to lock King's jail cell.

But Phil Hamilton was different from most of the other white officers on the force. After the force began hiring blacks, Hamilton regularly invited them to his house. "Every year blacks came to our house for a Christmas party," recalled David Hamilton, Mike's younger brother. "I didn't know we weren't supposed to eat with or talk to them."

By 1972, with Mike Hamilton at Graves Springs, living and swimming with black teammates along the Muckalee Creek, things had changed in Albany since his father was part of the police force that had arrested Dr. King.

Before we graduated in 1975, Hamilton wrote a note in my yearbook next to a picture of himself taken during one of our games:

*Big Bill,*
*You are a real good friend and all around athlete. I'm very proud and honored that I was on your team. I will always remember you, Bill, for you*

*and Law inspired me greatly. Best of luck in the future. And save me a beer when I come home with bruises from East Texas. Keep on Truckin'.*

*A good friend and loyal fellow player,*
*Mike (Hambone) Hamilton*

Hamilton received a football scholarship from East Texas State University, along with Rex Fox. I didn't see much of Mike Hamilton after high school graduation. He played college ball, got married, had children, and stayed in Texas. But in 1989, Hambone died of smoke inhalation after his house caught on fire. He was a helluva a teammate.

\* \* \*

Our last game of the season was at home against the Cougars of Crisp County High School, who were coached by our former coach, Ferrell Henry. As game day approached, we were charged like firecrackers on the fourth of July: particularly the seniors, who for the last time would run out of the locker room at Hugh Mills Stadium before thousands of screaming fans. The local paper ran a pre-game story in which it listed "the Indians' 22 seniors who would be dressing out for their final time." Most of us had gone to Graves Springs together for three years; in that time of struggle, unbreakable bonds had formed as we helped one another survive the ordeal.

"I am real excited about the game," Henry was quoted as saying before the game. "I am looking forward to seeing some of the boys again."

Meanwhile, the seniors, including me, were especially looking forward to settling the score with our old coach.

Henry's team was five-and-four going into the final game, and they were physically bigger than us. Their roster included Bubba Ivey, a tough middle linebacker who had been a childhood friend of mine. We knew if we were to win, we would have to find a way to block him.

Before the game, Henry told the local paper that we had "an outstanding season" surpassing what many sports observers in South Georgia predicted. "I don't think size will make that much difference in the game," he said. "What they lack in size they will make up for in quickness and agility. This game should be called superbowl '74 because that's what it's going to be." I recalled what he had told us before: *It's not the size of the dog in the fight. It's the size of the fight in the dog.*

Although he had left us, and now was the opposing coach for our last game, a big part of what we were as a team was because for two years, Coach Ferrell Henry instilled in us determination and a strong work ethic at Graves Springs.

I was intercepted three times during the game. There was tremendous energy in the stadium and much concern on our part after Crisp County scored easily on the opening drive, going seventy-four yards in seven plays. The game, however, stalemated until our final possession.

Our offense regained the ball with two minutes and twenty-six seconds left in the game after a Cougar punt went into the end zone for a touchback. Could we drive eighty yards and pull off yet another come-from-behind win during the closing moments?

Celious Williams and Wes Westbrook both caught passes from me, about fifteen yards respectively. Westbrook then made a diving catch at the Crisp County twenty-two yard line, but the play was called back because we had an illegal receiver downfield.

Tackle John Boyette was called for the infraction. "Man, I'm sorry, I'm sorry, I'm sorry!" I remember Boyette saying it over and over as he walked up to me on the field after the penalty had been called.

"Don't worry about it. We'll get it back," I said, trying to reassure him.

I wasn't sure we would, though. The game was growing tighter and time was slipping away.

Boyette repeated: "Man, I'm sorry. I'm sorry, Lightle." John felt awful because his mental mistake appeared to have let the team down at a most crucial time.

John Boyette was a junior with thick, curly brown hair, an infectious smile, and was a great teammate. He would be one of the two hundred or so U.S. Marines to die in the early 1980s after a bomb exploded in their barracks in Beirut, Lebanon.

He was a great kid.

After the penalty, I threw again to Westbrook for twenty-seven yards—no penalty flag this time—and Boyette did his job of blocking well. On the next play, James Harpe caught a thirty-yard pass. A pass interference penalty put us on the eleven-yard line. Lawless ran for eight yards on the first down . . . then we stalled. I missed the first down by inches after a quarterback sneak.

With fourth and just inches for a first down and a yard for touchdown, I gave the ball to Lawless, who scored following a block by guard David McClung, his future brother-in-law.

At that moment we scored both times, and thought seemed to have been suspended. My teammates flopped their bodies on the ground and on top of one another. I grabbed and hugged my teammates, one after another. Some of us looked to the heavens above as if to pay homage to divine intervention. But we were still down by one. We chose to go for the win instead of the tie.

Time was called, and I went to the sidelines to talk to Coach Dalley. I went back to the huddle and called Lawless' number again. From three yards out, he made the two-point conversion. Again our crowd erupted in celebration as my teammates embraced one another on the field.

After we kicked off to Crisp County, Mark Honeyman, our defensive back, intercepted a pass, securing the victory. It was the third game we won by rallying late in the fourth quarter.

Before our last game with Crisp County, *Albany Herald* sports editor Paul McCorvey wrote a column under the headline "Fantastic Year":

> . . . And no matter what happens by this Saturday when Albany High hosts Crisp County in the season's finale at Mills Stadium, it will go down as the best year collectively for local schools in some time.
>
> I know its been the most exciting and rewarding I've had in the six seasons I've spent covering their exploits. Fantastic is the only word for it.
>
> If you're unaware football has been improving here by leaps and bounds, look at the record. With four schools playing in the toughest AAA region in the state, three are apt to finish in the top five in the standings.

\* \* \*

Just as Theseus follows the thread through the labyrinth to slay the Minotaur, the monster of Greek mythology, the hero on the football field accepts the impossible task. Monsters on the football field could be physical in the form of imposing players, or they could be invisible, inward thoughts of trepidation and fear. Many times, they were both. Part of the ordeal of Graves Springs was to toughen players to such a level that we willingly challenged the monsters, both external and internal. It is part of the transformation a player undergoes in athletic competition. This transformation pleases the coaches, who reward their warriors by allowing them into the labyrinth on Friday nights before thousands of spectators, all of whom are cheering for the hero's journey.

In Joseph Campbell's *A Hero With A Thousand Faces*, the story is told of the hero's journey:

> . . . Furthermore, we have not even to risk the adventure alone; for the heroes of all time have gone before us; the labyrinth is thoroughly known; we have only to follow the thread of the hero path. And where we had thought to find an abomination, we shall find a god; where we had thought to slay another, we shall slay ourselves; where we had thought to travel outward, we shall come to the center of our own existence; where we had thought to be alone, we shall be with all the world.

At Graves Springs, Davey Davis, a five feet, eight inch, two hundred pound center for the 1974 team, was determined to prove to the coaches he could play with the best and the biggest. During one practice, the linemen were doing the "board drill," where two of them straddled a board in a four-point football position, nose-to-nose. At the sound of a whistle, the two players blocked, pushed, and forearmed one another until one or both were knocked off the board. Davis volunteered to go against Nathaniel Henderson, "Big Nate," who outweighed Davis by forty pounds.

"I was trying to prove something to the coaches," Davis said. But "he [Henderson] just picked me up and threw me down," causing Davis to severely sprain an ankle. This was his most serious injury during his playing days, keeping him on the sidelines for a couple of weeks.

\* \* \*

According to Campbell, "The agony of breaking through personal limitations is the agony of spiritual growth."

\* \* \*

By the 1974 season, Davis had improved immeasurably, becoming the team's starting center and after the season ended was selected as our Most Improved Player.

After graduating from Albany High in 1975, Davis enrolled at Valdosta State College where he earned a degree four years later. Along the way he married Gay Willis, also an Albany High graduate. The couple moved to Nashville, Tennessee where he worked for Aetna Life and Casualty Insurance Company. Over the years they had three children. At the age of thirty-two Davis enrolled in the Nashville School of Law. He kept working full-time in the insurance business while attending classes at night. Initially his class included one hundred and forty students. A year later there were less than half. "On the first night the professor said his job was to run the weak" students off, he told me. Davis stayed in school, and four years later was awarded a law degree.

"That lesson in endurance from Graves Springs really came through," Davis said. It was during this "difficult period" of his life in which he reflected back on the struggles at Graves Springs. If he could survive Graves Springs for six weeks, he could certainly finish his law degree. "It [camp] taught you that you can endure a helluva lot of hell." By 1994, he had his new degree and a job as staff counselor with Travelers Insurance in Nashville, where he works today.

Over the years, Davis watched both of his sons play football at Lebanon High School in Tennessee. Both boys have had knee surgery as a result of injuries while playing. Their football camp consisted of two practices a day at the high school field, while at night they were in the comforts of their own home.

"Yeah, I told them about Graves Springs," he said. "It's just unbelievable looking back."

\* \* \*

More than anything, Brent Brock grew up wanting to play football for Albany High. As a boy, he went to the stadium and watched the Indians play. If he couldn't attend out-of-town games, he listened to them on the radio. But as a sophomore himself in 1973, Brock didn't survive his first week at Graves Springs. He became sick and his mother, Frances Brock, came to camp and took him to a doctor.

"I got overheated . . . dehydrated," Brock recalled. He missed a couple of days of his first week at Graves Springs. Like the rest of us, he wasn't given any water during practice. Brock, who was six-foot-three and more than two hundred pounds, was normally a hardy eater, but he drank lots of Gatorade and water after each practice, becoming "bloated," and with little appetite for food. His body grew weaker and weaker until, finally, he was unable to practice at all.

I grew up in the same neighborhood with Brock and we played baseball together, but it was football that captivated him. It was special to Brock when Phil Franklin, a standout Albany High player from the 1960s, took the time to talk football with young Brock. Franklin and other high school players were icons to Brock. They were Friday-night heroes; Brock longed to be one himself.

Brock's parents had moved to Albany in the late 1940s from Grady County, which is south of Albany along the Florida border. His father, Eulie, was the personnel director for the city of Albany. Meanwhile, his mother was a nurse at Aerow Commander, a local company that made airplanes: the same place my father worked. Brent's older brother, Brocky, had played football at Westover High School in Albany. Their father was always supportive, but didn't push the two boys into athletics. I remember Eulie watching Brent play baseball and football. During baseball games, Eulie and my father sat together in lawn chairs along the right field fence away from the other fans.

When Brent Brock was attending Merry Acres Junior High in Albany, older players started telling him "horror stories" connected with Graves Springs. "I had a lot of anxiety going out there," he said, along with a sense of "excitement." He got little sleep during his first night there; instead he and his teammates played cards all night in the B-team barracks. Not long after the games ended and Brock was in bed, the coaches entered the barracks. "The whistles went off and it was still dark. That was a shock to me." After that first day of practice in 1973, Brock would be too tired to stay up late again and play cards.

He went to Graves Springs for three years before graduating in

1976 and accepting a scholarship to play at Florida State University under Bobby Bowden. At that time, Bowden was beginning to build a powerful winning program in Tallahassee. Brock played four years there. Preseason camp at college was tough, but not as grinding as Graves Springs. "The first time I ever saw water" was under Bowden, Brock recalled. During practices, Bowden placed ice chests on the field. According to Brock, Bowden told his players, "Get what you need but don't miss any drills."

Brock, who went on to become a high school coach, said that it was during the 1970s when the coaching philosophy was beginning to change in regards to giving players water. Coaches like Bowden were realizing the necessity, in terms of preventing dehydration or heat stroke, of having athletes replenish the fluids they expended while practicing. But at Graves Springs, coaches continued not giving their players water until after practice. They were stuck in the old ways, the ways Graves Springs had been founded upon.

Of the Graves Springs experience, Brock said, "That situation put you in a position where you had to step forward and become a man." For Brock, a self-described "mommy and daddy's boy" while growing up, the camp helped transform him. It was the beginning of his passage into manhood. "It toughened you up" both mentally and physically, he said. There was suffering, but "you saw the older guys and your peers" going through the same ordeal. "It was a time of survival," he added.

After graduating from Florida State, Brock's first high school coaching job was in Thomasville, Georgia. Then he coached for about ten years in Moultrie, another South Georgia town where football still dominates the culture. His first head coaching position was at Worth County High School, just east of Albany. There in the 1990s, he had some successful years; the best was a regular season record of eight and two.

Brock's coaching style was guided by some of the things he had "learned" at Graves Springs. He took his Worth County team away from campus for preseason camp. Brock secured a Methodist Church camp in Ray City, about an hour's drive south of the school. There he housed his players in six cinderblock, air-conditioned buildings.

"It's as close to Graves Springs I've ever been" since leaving Albany High, he said. "You want the kids to rough it a bit."

The living conditions and the treatment from the coaches at Ray City were not as extreme as what Brock himself had struggled through at Graves Springs. His players, of course, were given water during practice. They had indoor plumbing and cool rooms in which to relax and sleep. Unlike coaches at Graves Springs, Brock didn't make players participate in drills that serve only to make them "mentally tough"—like Beep, Beeps—while not necessarily teaching them a particular fundamental.

Players today, according to Brock, are quicker to question authority then those who played at Graves Springs. One reason may be that today's players lack the parental guidance of earlier generations. Divorce and family breakups troubled players who Brock has coached, while players from his and earlier generations came from families that were more stable, families with a strong male-authority figure. Coaches at Graves Springs were "war oriented," according to Brock. The camp was founded in the midst of the Great Depression, a time of extreme hardship, a time when many families didn't have sufficient food. Even without the Depression, South Georgia was and still is one of the poorest parts of the nation. Then came a world war, more suffering and despair. Men and boys who would coach and play football, tempered by these two events, lived through a period of sacrifice and suffering. They followed orders. The coaches throughout the history of Graves Springs were as uncompromising as were the times in which they lived.

Brock, who by 2000 was an assistant coach at Westside High School in Macon, Georgia, is right when he says that as a player at Graves Springs "you just followed instructions and didn't ask why" when a coach told you to do something.

That was how it was for me, Brock or anyone else who went there. We never questioned the coaches. It was easy for me, because I never questioned the authority of my parents. When my father disciplined me, he used his thin leather belt. Those whippings hurt. Coach Ferrell Henry at times used to hide behind the locker room door if we were late—just a few seconds—for practice. As we ran through the doorway into the field, he would yell, "I told you not to be late!" Then *Smack!* that leather strap came thundering down across your backside. That was the price you paid for kissing your girlfriend too many times before practice.

When I played sports, I followed exactly what the coaches said without ever questioning them. Coaching high school is different today. "Now you got to tell them why something is being done" at practice or explain the purpose of a specific drill, according to Brock. "It's tougher today to get all the kids on the same page. But once they're there, they're committed," he added.

If Graves Springs set out to "make or break" players—and it did—today's athletes need not endure such hard physical demands in just two weeks. Many high school football players in South Georgia and elsewhere train almost year-round by running and lifting weights, according to Brock. I remember some of my teammates vomiting during the first few practices at Graves Springs, partly because of the extremely hard workouts, and also because most had done no conditioning before camp began. "From a physical standpoint, today's athlete is stronger and faster" because of better and smarter training, Brock said. Therefore, the intensity of the practice sessions that marked Graves Springs is unnecessary today.

No matter of which era, team sports requires a togetherness among players, a belief that there is something more at work than personal accomplishment. As a coach, Brock took his own team to camp at Ray City, Georgia to recreate the ideal of *team* that he learned at Graves Springs. For his players, there was "bonding" with one another. They learned to struggle together. To win and lose together.

* * *

This is what the varsity barracks looks like today, in the backwoods just outside of Albany. The Muckalee Creek, which is not in view, is behind the barracks. It hasn't been used in twenty years.

Graves Springs encampment in the 1960s. The two buildings to the left, the mess hall and the B-Team barracks, were both destroyed in the 1994 flood. The varsity barracks was made of cinder blocks, and remained standing.

Stretch those legs, boys! Stretch those legs! This was taken at camp my senior year.

David McClung, who played his senior year with a broken hand, at Graves Springs 1974.

The coaching staff in 1974: (from left to right) Cardon Dalley, Tim Goodwin, Ray Kinney, Don Hicks, Willie Magwood, and Carl Williams

Captains Al Steele (left) and Celious "Crab" Williams before the start of a 1974 game.

Coach Ray Kinney charging his troops at Graves Springs in 1974.

Our defense gets ready for a play during the 1974 season against local rival Westover High School.

In between plays I'm talking to Head Coach Cardon Dalley.

I handed the ball off to Celious "Crab" Williams and Leonard "Law" Lawless, number thirty-nine, prepares to block.

The 1974 Albany High Indians. I am not in the picture because of a doctor's appointment. I had knee surgery the previous spring.

Grady Caldwell in the 1967 yearbook.

Kathleen Jones in the 1967 yearbook. She dated and later married Grady Caldwell. And she feared for his safety when he went to Graves Springs.

## A. H. S. Varsity Football Team

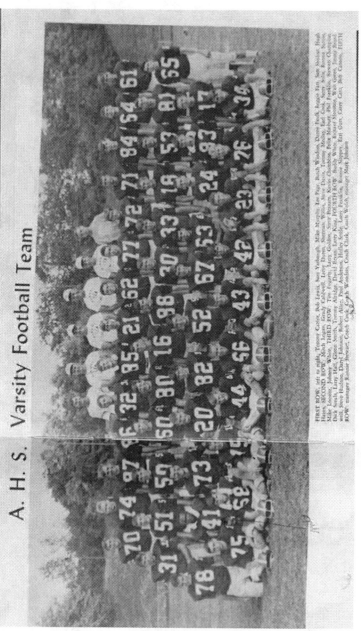

The 1966 team included number forty-one, Grady Caldwell. The year before he became the first black at Graves Springs, and the first to play for Albany High.

# CHAPTER TWO

# A BEAUTIFUL SIGHT

# ONE

Only white boys played at Graves Springs during the first thirty years the camp was in operation. The camp's policy reflected the longstanding racial divide that marked the South and Albany since its inception in the 1830s. By 1965, however, the first black player attended Graves Springs, a move that reflected court-ordered school desegregation and the beginnings of a monumental cultural shift. After the Indians were removed from Southwest Georgia, white planters began pushing into the region to grow cotton, and they brought with them black slaves to do the work. At the outbreak of the Civil War in 1861, Albany's population included about two thousand whites and three times as many slaves.

Before the war, slaves were auctioned in Albany for as much as two thousand dollars. Not long after the war ended in 1865, newly freed blacks began living under a strict system of institutional racism that would not end until a century later. Since its inception, much of Albany's history has been marked by oppression by whites and fear among blacks. Shortly after the Civil War begun in earnest, the *Albany Patriot*, then the daily newspaper, urged white Southern men to guard against possible slave rebellion. Because of the war, blacks in Southwest Georgia would "congregate together contrary to law, *exhibit their weapons*, and no doubt devise their secret and destructive plans," the newspaper reported.

R. H. Warren Sr. said this of Albany's racial strife in 1870:

## Made or Broken

> I remember one night, when our family was sitting on the east porch of my grandfather's house, there was heard the sound of the feet of horses approaching from the north. Soon there rode by, and east into Broad Street, about thirty men, dressed in long white robes, with faces masked. A few days later I heard my parents speak of the Ku Klux Klan having 'operated' that night.

By the late 1800s, writer and teacher W. E. B. DuBois traveled down to Albany from Atlanta. DuBois came to interview black families, and he eventually included these interviews in his classic book *The Souls of Black Folk.*

Among his findings was that extreme poverty and illiteracy was pervasive throughout these families. He recorded the stark racial oppression that permeated Albany and Southwest Georgia. DuBois, an eloquent writer who was the first black to earn a Ph.D. from Harvard, wrote this of Albany: " . . . Below Macon the world grows darker; for now we approach the Black Belt - that strange land of shadows, at which even slaves paled in the past, and whence come now only faint half-intelligible murmurs to the world beyond." He goes on to describe Albany as:

> . . . a wide-streeted, placid, Southern town, with a broad sweep of stores and saloons, and flanking rows of homes - whites usually live to the north, and blacks to the south . . . For a radius of a hundred miles about Albany, stretched a great fertile land, luxuriant with forests of pine, oak, ash, hickory, and poplar; hot with the sun and damp with the rich black swampland; and here the cornerstone of the Cotton Kingdom was laid.

More telling of Albany was the illiteracy of its children and their unfulfilled potential:

> . . . The degree of ignorance cannot be easily expressed. We may say, for instance, that nearly two-thirds of them cannot read or write. This but partially expresses the fact. They are ignorant of the world about them, of modern economic

organization, of the function of government, of individual worth and possibilities - of nearly all the things which slavery in self-defense had to keep them from learning. Much that the white boy imbibes from his earliest social atmosphere forms the puzzling problems of the black boy's mature years. America is not another world of opportunity for all her sons.

The schools in Dougherty County (for blacks) are very poor. I saw only one schoolhouse there that would compare in any way with the worst schoolhouse I ever saw in New England. That was a board house equipped with rude benches, without desks, no glass in the windows, with no sort of furniture except a blackboard and three boards put together for a teacher's desk. Most of the schoolhouses were either old log huts or were churches - colored churches - used as schoolhouses.

Some fifty years after DuBois chronicled illiteracy and the poor conditions of schools in Albany, a state government report was just as bleak in its description of "Negro schools," saying that they "are very badly overcrowded even when all available space, regardless of suitability or safety, is used."

Sam P. Clemons, state supervisor of schoolhouse planning and construction, signed the report, noteworthy for its prose on the wasting of human potential during a time of institutional racism. Most certainly a white man, Clemons detailed the chronic needs of public schools that served minority children:

> To adequately house the anticipated 1946-47 enrollment, there seems to be an immediate need for approximately 6 white classrooms and 22 Negro classrooms. To care for the anticipated increase over the next five or six years will apparently require approximately 16 white classrooms and 30 Negro classrooms. If the 12$^{th}$ grade is added, the needs will be increased proportionally.

Under a section entitled, "The Negro Situation," Clemons is even more reminiscent, presumably not meaning to be so, of Du Bois. Below is the entire first paragraph of that section:

With 27 classrooms, only 13 of which meet minimum standards as to size, lighting, etc., Albany is housing a total enrollment of 1823 Negro children. This is an average of 67 pupils per classroom. At the same time 73 white classrooms, all but two of which meet standards as to size, etc., are used to house 2516 white pupils. This is an average of 34 pupils per classroom. Each Negro classroom is thus accommodating twice as many Negro children as each white classroom is accommodating white children. When the size of the classroom is considered, the Negro classrooms are only approximately one-third as adequate as the white classrooms. The per pupil investment in white school buildings is more than ten times as great as the per pupil investment in Negro buildings in Albany. Under these overcrowded and unhygienic conditions, it is probably impossible to properly develop the Negro human resources of the community.

Clemons was thorough in his findings, including that of poor transportation for black children who in some cases walked more than a mile to school. He includes one of history's most common liberal refrains, at least since the establishment of tax-supported education by the mid-1800s, in his argument to improve "Negro schools":

> The economic, industrial, and moral welfare of a community is dependent upon the educational development of both races. An adequately trained individual is usually an efficient worker who earns and spends in a community a substantially greater sum than an untrained individual. Ignorance, indolence, crime, and disease often are found together. It is the sincere belief of the writer that a reasonable expenditure of funds to provide adequate physical facilities where Negroes may be effectively taught to become healthy, efficient workers would pay dividends to the economic and industrial development of the city far in excess of the capital outlay involved ...

At about the same time Clemons issued his report to the all-white board of education, the members received a petition signed by about forty "colored teachers" requesting equal pay with that of their white counterparts. The teachers were asking for an increase in their local supplement to twenty-five dollars. By September 1946, according to school board records, the supplement was set at twenty dollars for "Negro teachers." White teachers, on the other hand, were paid twenty-five dollars per month. The same kind of pay inequities was then mandated by the State of Georgia. The state salary schedule indicates that, on average, monthly pay for white teachers could be anywhere from ten to twenty-five dollars more than that of minority teachers.

* * *

A few years before Clemons released his report in the mid-1940s, the *Albany Herald* stated that "Negro Leaders" had appeared before the all-white city commission to complain of the over-crowded and deplorable conditions of some "Negro schools." The group's spokesman was Joe Watson, who had lived in Albany for seventy-five years. Watson said that half of black children in the city are "romping the streets, growing up in vice and crime. These will become criminals you will have to contend with in the future."

While blacks in Albany were subjected to fewer educational opportunities than whites, they had reason to cheer for one of their own who was becoming not a criminal but an international sports star. Alice Coachman, one of nine siblings who earned fifty cents for every hundred pounds of cotton she picked as a child, won a gold medal in the high jump during the 1948 Olympic games in London. She was the first black woman to win a gold medal for the United States.

* * *

For the first nine years of my life I lived in an all-white community, Gas City, Indiana, where I had little contact with blacks until my family moved to Albany in the summer of 1966. In Indiana, I had heard the language of bigotry. People I knew used the word "spic" in describing Latin American seasonal farm workers. I sometimes heard the word "coon" used to characterize blacks.

My father, Bill Lightle, was born in 1929 in Cincinnati. He loved baseball, and before moving to Georgia, he played and coached for a semi-professional team called the "Bankers" which was sponsored by a local bank in our hometown. The team traveled throughout central Indiana, and I went along as batboy. It was during one game in Gas City, Indiana that I encountered black people, who played on an opposing team, for the first time. I was asked to be the batboy for their team. I remember how embarrassed I became during the game as I asked the same players more than once if they wanted a cup of water during the same inning. They all looked alike to me. I was born in Marion, Indiana, just a few miles from Gas City, in 1957.

In 1930, a white mob in Marion had beaten and lynched two blacks who had been accused of a crime. Over the years, as I taught both high school and college history classes, I have used as part of my class discussions on racism a photograph of the Marion lynching that later appeared in *Life* magazine. The photo shows the beaten bodies hanging from ropes tied to a tree. This kind of brutality is a reminder of America's racial hatred.

From 1880 to 1930, the Cotton Belt of Southwest Georgia, which includes Dougherty County and the county seat, Albany, had one hundred and ninety-six documented lynchings of blacks. This was the most for any region in the country. From Marion, Indiana to South Georgia, lynchings have epitomized this nation's racial bloodletting. Moreover, from 1961 to 1965, twenty-one civil rights murders were recorded in the Deep South.

\* \* \*

While growing up in northwest Albany in the 1960s, I met neighborhood boys who came to my house to play. In those days, that part of the city was all white. Most whites found intolerable the prospect of an integrated community. It was not uncommon for some of my playmates to use the word "nigger" in the presence of my father. To the shock of the boy who used the racial slur, my father scolded him, demanding that such language never be used again in our house. When I was a child, I was often embarrassed when my father chastised one of my playmates in Albany for using the word "nigger." I was eager to make new friends, and I didn't want his tirades to prevent me from doing so.

My grandfather died when my father was himself a young boy, and my father joined the Air Force at the end of World War II. For most of his working life he was employed by manufacturing firms, and at times worked as a welder. According to him, it was "stupid" to judge people based on skin color. It was a lesson that he instilled in me, and over the years through my own study and reading, I came to understand my father had been correct about the effects of the racial divide in the South. Specifically, how its historical meanness oppressed both working-class whites and blacks alike. He realized that rich white Southerners used the theme of racial hatred to attract the political support of poor whites. In aligning themselves with upperclass whites, lowerclass whites such as sharecroppers, mill workers and others forfeited their chances to improve their social status. Whites, regardless of class, were united politically by their disdain for blacks.

Over the years I have come to know and appreciate the work of David Williams, a professor at Valdosta State University. Williams has written extensively on Southern history. His book, *Rich Man's War: Class, Caste, and Confederate Defeat in the Lower Chattahoochee Valley*, recognizes how elements of racism, nationalism, and religion were used to suppress class conflict hits uncomfortably close to home. Williams states that by "examining the ways in which common folks have historically been manipulated to their own disadvantage reminds us of our own vulnerability."

* * *

By the 1950s, there was change underway nationwide concerning race as the U.S. Supreme Court ruled in *Brown vs. the Board of Education of Topeka, Kansas* that racially segregated schools were unconstitutional. A decade later, this change filtered down to Graves Springs and Albany High School football, while the camp itself was at the forefront of integration. But along the way, blacks were vulnerable to the retaliation from whites who refused to accept racial change.

Violence against blacks in Albany during the civil rights movement included assaulting pregnant women. Mrs. Slater King was visiting a prisoner in the Camilla jail, about twenty miles south of Albany, when she was attacked by a deputy sheriff. As a result, she lost her baby. Mrs. King's brother-in-law was Albany attorney C. B. King. At the time, King was providing legal representation for The Albany Movement, a group seeking to end the city's longstanding segregationist policies. King himself was once caned bloody while seeing clients at the Dougherty

County Jail. Of the assault, Sheriff Cull Campbell said, "Yeah, I knocked the hell out of that son-of-a-bitch, and I'll do it again. I wanted to let him know . . . I'm a white man and he's a damn nigger."

On September 3, 1962, the *U. S. News & World Report* published a story on the ongoing racial unrest in Albany. At that time, whites outnumbered blacks thirty-six thousand to twenty thousand. While whites controlled the local industries, two large federal payrolls—Turner Air Force Base and the Marine Corps Supply Center—were feeding the economy. That same federal government was being petitioned by local blacks to end racial segregation in public facilities. Lawsuits were filed requesting that the U.S. government desegregate bus lines and depots, libraries, parks, playgrounds, swimming pools, theaters, the municipal auditorium, recreation centers for teenagers, toilet facilities, and schools. The story went on to report:

> Before the Negro campaign began last year, Albany was considered a rather moderate Southern city. There had been a minimum of racial trouble. A Negro once held the elective job of coroner. There has been little activity by the Ku Klux Klan or White Citizens Council - even during the recent racial disturbances. The climate of race relations began to heat up early in 1961, when Negroes stepped up demands for desegregation.

One of the community leaders in Albany during this period was James H. Gray Sr., a New Englander by birth who amassed a financial fortune by the 1960s, including ownership of both the local television station and newspaper the *Albany Herald*. Through his editorials, he attacked efforts by The Albany Movement to achieve equal opportunity for all of Albany's citizens. One such editorial claimed that there was a "cell of professional agitators" in town, which included Dr. Martin Luther King, Jr., who had made personal visits to Albany during the movement. Gray even accused the future Nobel Peace Prize winner as trying to make "the fast buck." Of course, Gray never provided details in print of just how King was trying to "get rich" by putting his life in danger while in Albany. It was a dangerous time, even for those first few blacks who attended Graves Springs.

\* \* \*

# TWO

Grady Caldwell was born at home on Corn Avenue in 1949. As a boy, he saw the flaming crosses of white resistance, and he shook the hand of Dr. Martin Luther King Jr. Caldwell later became the first black to attend Graves Springs and wear the orange and green of Albany High.

When he was two years old, Caldwell's father died, leaving him to be reared by his mother Leola Caldwell, a public school teacher. Her only other child was Loretta, who was older than Grady. Growing up in Albany, Grady Caldwell became close friends with Gil Anderson, whose father, Dr. William Anderson, was becoming a leader in the local civil rights movement. The Andersons lived on Cedar Avenue, and Dr. King stayed at their house when he came to Albany.

By 1961 Anderson, an osteopath, had become president of The Albany Movement. Members of this group were involved in efforts to desegregate public facilities and register black voters. The movement took off with the Student Non-Violent Coordinating Committee's voting-rights drive in Southwest Georgia. Anderson's personal telephone call to Dr. King on December 14, 1961 persuaded him to come to Albany and help the movement. By the middle of the month, hundreds of protesters were jailed in Albany while protesting segregation. Some of the conditions for those incarcerated were terrible. For example, fifty-four girls were incarcerated in a cell built to accommodate six people.

On one occasion when Dr. King was staying at Anderson's home and Caldwell was there visiting his friend, Gil, the Ku Klux Klan burned a cross and rallied near the Cedar Avenue house. Concerned for the safety of the children, King and Anderson led them away from the windows to a safer part of the house.

"They had a rally within a couple hundred yards from my house," Anderson said. There were "maybe two hundred" Klansmen in attendance. Some used loudspeakers to threaten Anderson and King, saying they were going to "get those niggers."

No one was hurt that night. After the death of Caldwell's father, Dr. Anderson became a surrogate father to him. Anderson was there to help instill the principles of hard work and commitment. "He [as a boy] was always responsive to the direction I'd give him," Anderson recalled. He tried to shield his own son and Caldwell from the degradation connected with segregation and racism.

Even while driving with the two boys in his automobile, Anderson took alleys and back roads to avoid contact with whites. "We didn't understand then why" Anderson tried to stay away from whites, Caldwell said. But Anderson knew it was safer that way.

As a young boy, Caldwell went shopping with his mother, Leola Caldwell. Once while in a store, he pulled on the dress of a white woman, mistakenly believing that she was his mother. Leola Caldwell intervened, realizing the social taboo her son had just committed. "I remember the fear on my mother's face," when she saw that her son had tugged on the wrong dress.

Without any regular contact with whites and in light of what the young boy was learning about racial segregation, Caldwell was developing an attitude in which he generalized all whites as being "bad," and that they conspired to oppress blacks and used violence in doing so. This held true for him until Graves Springs.

In 1964, Caldwell was a tenth-grader Albany's all-black high school, Monroe High School. He was a good football player in junior high, and he joined the football team at Monroe. During one practice session, when the coach paddled all the players with a wooden board after he became disgruntled with their efforts, Caldwell quit the team, refusing to be paddled. "I played in the band the rest of the year," he said.

Following his sophomore year, Caldwell considered transferring to Albany High School and playing football there. Because of government-ordered desegregation, any black student in Albany could transfer to a school where his or her race was in a minority. By the fall of

1964, only a handful of minority students were attending Albany High, where the total enrollment was more than fifteen hundred. In fact, there were no blacks on any of the school's athletic teams.

Grady Caldwell was about to change all that.

The same year Caldwell was changing sports in Albany, black professional football players were showing their solidarity. In 1965, black players arrived in New Orleans for the American Football Leagues East-West All-Star Game. Because of their race, they weren't allowed into some of the city's social clubs. These players quickly agreed to boycott the game, causing league officials to move the contest to another city. As professional football was changing in regards to race, Albany and Graves Springs were changing, too.

In making his decision to transfer and ultimately attend Graves Springs, Caldwell's family members expressed growing concern for his safety. Ira Bryant, an uncle who lived in nearby Tifton, was against Caldwell's decision to attend the camp. His mother, Leola, didn't necessarily try to stop her son from changing schools, but she worried about what white players might do in an effort to force her son to leave Graves Springs. His girlfriend, Kathleen Jones, who he eventually married, tried unsuccessfully to convince Grady not to go. She argued that there would be danger awaiting Grady at Graves Springs, and she didn't want anything bad to happen to him. Pulling him in another direction, some of his Monroe classmates encouraged him to join Albany's team and break the color barrier.

For Caldwell, the decision was personal, and had little to do (as he viewed it at the time anyway), with cracking the segregationist culture that had defined Albany since its inception. "I wanted the challenge," he said, "and at the time I was as much a supremacist as any white person." Before Graves Springs, Caldwell believed that he wasn't just as good as white athletes, he was better. So, in mid-August 1965, Caldwell and his friend Ernest Jenkins became the first blacks to attend Graves Springs and integrate Albany High's football team.

They both spent the first Sunday night at camp, but by the end of the initial day of practice Monday, Jenkins was gone. Unwilling to tolerate the name-calling and humiliation from white players, Jenkins walked away from camp and caught a ride back to Albany on a garbage truck. Jenkins, who died in the mid-1980s, never returned to Graves Springs.

Grady Caldwell was determined to stay and make the team, even though, after Jenkins left, he remembered several white players saying to him, "'We're gonna make you leave too.'"

"There were deliberate attempts to run me off," he said.

Caldwell was five-foot-seven and weighed around one hundred and thirty pounds, and he played defensive back and running back on offense. At Graves Springs, his teammates tackled him during practice and said, "'Nigger, we're gonna kill you.'"

Caldwell worried the most at night. He could handle the heat and the physical tests on the field, but there was uncertainty at night—as he lay in his bunk—about to what extent players might go to force him to leave the team.

Head Coach Harold Dean Cook became so concerned for his safety that he made Caldwell sleep next to the coaches, away from the players. Cook had moved to Albany in the early 1940s from Miller County, Georgia. He lived on the "fringe" of an all-black neighborhood and had few frills as a child. "We came up pretty tough," he said of growing up in Albany. Cook himself even had black playmates as a child, but he understood that for many of his players at Graves Springs, there would be resistance to Caldwell and this impending racial change.

"It was natural for some of the white kids to have racist attitudes," Cook said. "They were brought up that way."

Cook found himself in a difficult position. On one hand, some whites were pressuring him to maintain an all-white team and not play Caldwell. On the other hand, Cook was determined to guide the team through this period of change, and he showed real concern for Caldwell.

"I admired Coach Cook," Caldwell said. "I knew the kind of pressure he was under from the white people in the community."

During one meal at camp, Caldwell sat at a table where a group of white players were eating. As he sat down, they in turn got up and moved to another table. Upon seeing this, Cook took a seat at the same table with Caldwell. It was a visible sign of support for the team's lone black player . . . offered by a white man who had come of age during the era of Jim Crow.

After that incident in the dining hall, "things got better" according to Caldwell, and players began to accept him. Some players showed signs of animosity to Cook himself after they realized that their coach was not only going to allow Caldwell to stay on the team, but also play during the regular season.

Caldwell, meanwhile, was proving his worthiness on the practice field at Graves Springs. Physically and mentally, he would not be broken, and white teammates were taking notice of Caldwell's resilience.

One such player at Graves Springs was Phil Franklin, a quarterback and defensive back. He was one of the Indians' toughest players during the mid-1960s. Franklin was a leader who earned his teammates' respect, but when Caldwell arrived at camp Franklin felt a sense of "hostility" toward him. Caldwell's presence alone contradicted and challenged Franklin's "Southern upbringing."

"You felt you weren't supposed to like him," Franklin said. "But Grady was such a good guy, you couldn't help but like him."

Franklin was one of the first players to offer Caldwell a sense of "camaraderie." Later, Caldwell found himself being defended by some of the very same teammates who were against him when he first arrived at Graves Springs. After camp had ended and the regular season begun, the Indians were playing a game in which some of the opposing players tried to "bully" Caldwell by calling him a "nigger" and making other derogatory comments throughout the game. It was Franklin, though, and other teammates who "rallied" behind Caldwell as he was being taunted by the opposition.

"Phil and some others supported me," Caldwell said. "I felt a part of the team then."

Years after their playing days had ended at Albany High, Franklin said that the presence of Caldwell at Graves Springs did indeed lead to the changing of perceptions among white players. "I think it [Graves Springs] did lead" to a reassessment among white players concerning racial stereotypes. "You didn't have any association with them before Graves Springs and football," said Franklin, who later became a local bank executive. What some white players learned at camp was that "they're [black players] just like us."

The key for Grady Caldwell and the team was that "once the white kids found out Grady could play, he was accepted," according to Cook.

Not too long after camp's 1965 season began, Caldwell's theory that blacks were superior athletes was disproved. Steve Hudson played linebacker for the Indians then, and several of his former teammates called him the hardest-hitting football player they had ever seen. Bobby

Stanford, who would go on to play for the University of Alabama, was a player who respected Hudson's aggressiveness. "He was one of the toughest guys I ever played with," Stanford said.

Caldwell would come to think likewise. "Steve Hudson hit me so hard in practice that I saw stars," he said. "That let me know that white guys can play. And I couldn't label anyone anymore," as Caldwell had done while growing up in Albany.

Graves Springs "taught me I could do anything I put my mind to," Caldwell said. "It also taught me that white people are not as bad as I perceived them to be. That helped break some of the false beliefs that I'd developed over the years."

After his first year at camp, when the team returned to Albany and the season started, Caldwell still confronted racial harassment. Before each practice session, the Indians changed into their practice uniforms in the locker room at Hugh Mills Stadium. One afternoon as Caldwell was changing clothes, he opened his locker to find a large, dead rattlesnake. He became so agitated that he grabbed his helmet and hit the "first white player" he saw. It happened to be one of the student managers. "I remember feeling bad about what I did," he said. "I was trying to establish boundaries. I was the only black person on the team."

There were other times during the 1965 playing season when Coach Harold Dean Cook openly supported Caldwell. Once, when the team was traveling out of town, they stopped at a restaurant that refused to allow Caldwell to eat in the same dining area with his white teammates. In response, Cook refused the service altogether and took his team elsewhere—a place where all the players could eat together.

During the two years he played for the Indians, Caldwell became a contributing member of the team, which won eight of ten games during his senior year in 1966. At Graves Springs in 1966, his experience was much different from the previous year. He called it "very smooth." He had established himself as a determined athlete, one with the strength of character to survive the humiliation he encountered at camp the previous year. "I had respect [the second year at camp] and I always gave respect," Caldwell said. There were no racial slurs (at least openly) or other efforts to force him to leave Graves Springs. In fact, he had earned the acceptance of most white players by the beginning of his final year at Albany High. At camp that year, it was a white player who taught him how to play chess.

\* \* \*

Grady Caldwell graduated from Albany High in 1967, and it was only after this period that he began to fully understand that what he did at Graves Springs, and as a member of the team, had resonated beyond his own life experiences. Becoming the first black to survive Graves Springs helped both races in Albany come to view one another in more humane ways, he said. In one sense, football, elevated to the realm of mythical images in Southern culture, was becoming at least one way in which the races were finding common ground. Football, and in particular Graves Springs, was doing something that other aspects of Southern culture had failed to do for the most part: Winning high school football games was beginning to take precedent over generations of racial division.

It is unreasonable to expect Caldwell, as a teenager in 1965, to understand the lasting influence that his arrival at Graves Springs would have. It was personally intimidating and dangerous, yet his very survival and his teammates' acceptance of him indicated that barriers that rob one another of a fuller human experience were falling. "I wasn't doing it to be big," he said. "To me it wasn't that big of a deal."

To Dr. William Anderson, it *was* a big deal. Anderson, Caldwell's surrogate father, had moved from Albany by the time Caldwell joined the Indians at Graves Springs. Anderson, however, was kept informed of Caldwell's decision, as well as his progress at Albany High. Anderson, who later became an administrator at St. John's Detroit Regional Hospital, understood what confronted Caldwell, and also the significance of what he had accomplished. "I think athletics played a vital role in the process of integration," Anderson said. High school sports was something that brought the races together. It allowed for personal contact, and team sports, by its very nature, requires common effort. Anderson compared Caldwell to another Georgia-born athlete, Jackie Robinson, who by the late 1940s became the first black to integrate modern major league baseball. But because Caldwell was the one who "broke the barrier" in Albany, Anderson felt that, like Robinson, danger awaited him. "Those who were first in this arena bore the brunt of penned up hostility," Anderson said.

\* \* \*

Grady Caldwell and Kathleen Jones were married in 1969, the year after she graduated from Albany High. "Kat," as her family and friends called her, transferred to Albany High as a junior in 1966. She left Monroe High School after the tenth grade at the urging of her mother. Lois Jones believed that her daughter would be academically challenged at Albany High, more so than she had been at Monroe. Kat's mother was right, but while attending Albany High, Kat had her own odds to beat. She confronted racial animosity from white students, and from at least one white teacher.

There was one particular history teacher who openly used racial epithets toward her and other black students. One year, Kathleen was the only black student in one of the teacher's classes. It wasn't uncommon for him to use the word "negra" in front of the class. He also allowed white students to use the word "nigger" in reference to Kathleen.

"I hated that room," she said. "Some days I wanted to quit." She was never physically hit by another student while at Albany High. Instead, the abuse came in the form of being ostracized and verbally attacked by some of the white students. Pennies, symbolic of what some thought a black student was worth, were often tossed at Kathleen as she walked the halls. "On some occasions I felt inadequate about being around white people," she said. "Sometimes I'd rise and stand my ground."

One of the few white classmates at Albany High to befriend Kathleen was Martha Glenn Riley, whose nickname was "Duster." Martha Glenn was brought up in a family that was more "opened minded about race" and integration than some of her white contemporaries, she said. Her view was that the new black students were an overall "asset" to the school—especially athletes like Grady Caldwell, who would certainly help the school's sports program.

Martha Glenn herself played on the girl's basketball team, which by the end of the decade included black players. She was called a "nigger-lover" by some of the white students who resented her association with the minority students. "It was pitiful the way they were treated," Martha Glenn said. "It was like they had some disease."

The relationship between Martha Glenn and Kathleen that was formed at Albany High, often under strained circumstances, endures today. "Even to this day when she sees me . . . she hugs me," Kathleen said.

For Martha Glenn, there is at least one vision that lives on in her to this day concerning Kathleen and Grady, future husband and wife. "The thing that stands out to me is seeing Grady and Kathleen walking down the halls together . . . you'd always see those smiles," she said. "God guided them through and gave them strength."

* * *

During football games, Kathleen watched Grady Caldwell play, along with the thousands of fans who packed into Mills Memorial Stadium for home games. At one game, probably during the 1966 season, Kathleen took her younger brother, Stephen, to watch Grady. He scored a touchdown during the game, and as he carried the ball into the end zone Stephen, about six at the time, jumped from his seat and hollered: "I love to see that little nigger run!"

In embarrassment, Kathleen held her head down after hearing her brother's cheer. Kathleen and Stephen were sitting among a throng of white faces at the stadium. "They had been calling us niggers at school," Kathleen Caldwell said.

* * *

More than thirty years after their wedding, Kathleen and Grady remained married. But it has been a far tougher battle than Grady Caldwell ever fought at Graves Springs. In the beginning things were good. By the early 1970s, both had earned degrees from Albany State College, now Albany State University. Kathleen accepted a job with the college by 1973, and twenty-five years later she became Director of the Recruitment, Admissions, and Financial Aid Departments. Grady worked at Albany State himself as Director of Student Affairs and later Director of Alumni Affairs by the early 1980s. Along the way they had three children.

But in just a few years their lives would turn hellish. Grady Caldwell became dependent on drugs: first marijuana, then cocaine. He was unable to keep a steady job and at times would go on a "binge," leaving the family for two or three days at a time, only to return and act as if he had been gone for ten minutes or so to buy a gallon of milk for the children. His habit became so destructive that he pawned Kathleen's wedding ring in order to get money to buy drugs.

"It's been a struggle for me," Kathleen said of her husband's addiction and his inability over the last several years to be the kind of husband and father he had once been.

She is, however, proud of their three children, and has tried hard to give them her best. Her two daughters, Daphne and Carmen, are both college graduates. The youngest, Grady Caldwell III, who I met while interviewing Kathleen, was attending Albany State University in 1999, doing well academically and playing on the school's basketball team.

Because of his drug abuse through the 1980s and into the following decade, Grady Caldwell had spent nearly three years in jail. By early 2000 he was incarcerated in the Jefferson County Correctional Institution in Louisville, Georgia, a three-hour drive north of Albany.

I spoke with Grady there one Sunday afternoon during visiting hours. He spoke with hopefulness for the future. He said, however, that the drugs and the obsession to get them "was about to kill" him had he not been sentenced to serve time in the Jefferson County prison. "Only time can heal some of the wounds I created," he said.

\* \* \*

As Grady Caldwell was changing local football, five years before he arrived at Graves Springs one professional coach was making a quite statement himself about race and team sports.

In 1960, Green Bay Packers' coach and general manager Vince Lombardi received a letter from Willie Wood, who was a starting quarterback for the University of Southern California. Wood was a fine athlete, with aspirations of playing professionally. But he was black. After not being selected in the National Football League's draft, Wood wrote to a number of teams asking for a tryout. Only Lombardi agreed to give him one.

Lombardi, winner of League championships and the first two Super Bowls in the 1960s, had experienced racial prejudice himself as an Italian-American growing up in New York. According to his biographer, David Maraniss, one of the greatest professional coaches "had gone through life called dago - wop - guinea because of his dark skin and Southern-Italian heritage."

Wood, who got that tryout from Lombardi, eventually became a

Hall of Fame free safety following a spectacular career with Green Bay. Wood called Lombardi "perhaps the fairest man I ever met." Before Wood, there were few black professionals, and Green Bay actually signed its first in 1950—Bob Mann from the University of Michigan.

With just a few blacks on the team in 1959 when Lombardi took over, he likely recalled his own past when he delivered this statement to his new team: "If I ever hear nigger or dago or kike or anything like that around here, regardless of who you are you're through with me - You can't play for me if you have any kind of prejudice."

The Packers played an exhibition game before the start of the 1960 season in New Orleans, which was standing true to the Southern dogma of segregation. Wood and the team's three other black players, therefore, were not allowed to stay in the same hotel with the white players.

After that incident Lombardi never again put his team in a hotel that didn't allow all players to stay together. He said that on his team there were "no barriers"; all things were "equal racially and socially."

Ironically—or maybe not—is that Maraniss reports that Lombardi *was* actually color blind. But when it comes to race, Maraniss concludes, "It has always been easy for whites to claim color blindness in the United States since white is the dominant color in American society, but the claim often serves as a ruse for not recognizing the particular obstacles faced by non-whites."

Caldwell's efforts worked to make high school football and Graves Springs "color blind" in the way that Lombardi had envisioned his Packers of the 1960s. Like other blacks who followed Mann and Wood on the Green Bay Packers, there would be others who followed Caldwell.

* * *

# THREE

Before the start of the 1967 season, local sportswriter Vic Smith wrote this about Graves Springs:

Under the circumstances as far removed from the general concept of football as Stokely Carmichael from George Wallace, the Albany High School Indians are banging away at Graves Springs these days in their first of two weeks annual encampment in preparation for the coming football season - which is just a mere 15 days away.

Smith contrasted Carmichael, a black man advocating civil rights, with Wallace, the white-segregationist governor of Alabama, to illustrate just how strange it might be to sports enthusiasts that teenagers were suffering through Graves Springs not because they were compelled to by a governmental decree, but just to be part of the team. He referred to Ronnie Nelson as a halfback who ran like a "hoss" on the B-team the previous season. Being called a "hoss" in South Georgia is a football compliment of the highest kind. The hoss is a hitter, a destroyer on every play. The hoss, if he does experience fear and trepidation, doesn't show it. Coaches, of course, love the hoss.

On August 24, 1967, the *Albany Herald* published a photograph of the upcoming Albany High football team, saying that it was "rated in many quarters as the favorite for region and state honors." The picture included forty-six white players, a few white student managers, four white coaches, and one black player—number forty-one, Ronnie Nelson.

Nelson was one of nine children in his family, and he was born in Albany in 1951, at home at 710 South Madison Street. His father, Jimmy L. Nelson Sr., was from Terrell County, about twenty miles northwest of Albany. During Jim Crow's reign, Terrell was known as "Terrible Terrell" because of the racial oppression there.

As the civil rights movement got underway in the early 1960s, efforts were made to register black voters in Terrell County. In reaction to this, some whites in the county started a wave of violence aimed to stop blacks from participating in the political process. One worker in the registration drive was wounded by a shotgun blast in Dawson, the county seat. Those who refused to accept living in a society that included equal rights for blacks burned both Mount Olive and Hope Baptist churches. At that time, Terrell County Sheriff Z. T. Mathews met with "disturbed whites" and said: "We want our colored people to go on living like they have for the last hundred years."

As Ronnie Nelson was growing up, his father and other adults told him about lynchings that had occurred in Southwest Georgia. Meanwhile, Nelson Sr., who died in 1984, worked as a house painter, carpenter, and other jobs when Ronnie was young. Nelson Sr. was prone to drink, and at times became abusive to his family. "He was an alcoholic," Ronnie Nelson said of his father. "Me and my daddy didn't get along . . . he used to beat my butt."

"If my daddy was raisin' children today he'd be in jail for child abuse," said Nelson, who during the course of the same conversation used the word "love" to describe his feelings for his father. In addition to physical abuse, Nelson was emotionally hurt by his father, who would not directly praise him for his athletic accomplishments. Once, Nelson did overhear his father telling a group of men how proud he was that his son was developing into a fine football player. But when his father realized that Ronnie was listening to the conversation, Nelson Sr., stopped talking about his son.

Ronnie Nelson grew up a street fighter. He fought some of the "terriblest boys of the black race." That toughness would come to manifest itself on the football field. At Carver Junior High School, he became a quarterback known for his hard-running ability. Carver Junior High was built in 1940 on South Monroe Street, and before the early 1960s it had served as the black high school.

In contrast to his father's persona, Ronnie's mother, Ethel Mae

Nelson, was loving and openly supportive of her son's football success. She had been born in Miller County, southwest of Albany, and also the birthplace of Coach Harold Dean Cook, under whom Ronnie would play at Albany High. Ethel Mae Nelson provided constant encouragement to her son, and told him to his face that he was indeed a good player. After completing the ninth grade at Carver Junior High in 1966, Nelson was considering going to Albany High instead of Monroe. "My momma said I was real good and that I was gonna have to be twice as good as those white boys," he said.

His mother's assessment was correct. Anyone who has seriously looked at race and sports in American history would have to agree that for minorities, because of prejudice from whites, standards were higher when they attempted to integrate team sports. Leonard Koppett, a *New York Times* sportswriter for many years and a 1992 inductee into the writers' wing of the Baseball Hall of Fame, wrote that "the marginal black player, whose talent was on a level with that of a white player competing for the same job, was a nuisance and a threat to some perceived racial imbalance." Therefore, "the black players who made it, had to be better than anyone else." Over the years whites falsely rationalized that "blacks lacked courage under pressure, weren't as quick mentally as whites, were showboats, and they didn't develop enough team loyalty."

What was happening at Graves Springs was disproving long-standing racial prejudices regarding American sports. Friends and family members encouraged Nelson to play for Albany High and "represent black people." In the process of making his decision, Nelson and his mother talked about his safety and what might happen to him at camp. "I was never afraid. I had been a good fighter" while growing up. "My momma told me if one of those white boys hits me to knock the hell out of him and come to her," he said.

Finally, Nelson's decision to go to Graves Springs was primarily based simply on football opportunity. Contrasted with Monroe, Albany High had better athletic facilities, much more financial support, and statewide recognition. So he reported to camp in August 1966, one year after the color line was erased by Grady Caldwell.

Living at Graves Springs and playing with white athletes was a "whole new world" for Nelson. "It was the first time I'd ever seen a sprinkler system," he said. At Albany High itself, he found a first-class weight room. He would be playing in Hugh Mills Stadium, one of the best stadiums in Georgia and able to accommodate up to ten thousand fans. "It was like a dream," Nelson said. "All we had at Carver was a field."

Nelson was even impressed by the food at Graves Springs: three meals a day and as much as a hungry player could eat. "I had never had so much milk and orange juice," he said, "and we ate steak, too. I guess being a black boy from a big family, getting a steak was a blessing."

During his first year at Graves Springs, Nelson generally encountered overt acceptance from white players and coaches. That acceptance was won through his blend of athleticism and humility. But occasionally at camp, Nelson heard players and coaches say: "Look at that monkey run." Nelson was converted into a running back at Albany High, and by his senior year he was one of the best in the region.

Generally throughout his playing days at Albany High, he felt a sense of camaraderie with his teammates and support from the coaches at camp. One former white teammate of his was Glenn Smith, who graduated in 1968 and was a starting linebacker for the team. Smith recalled that there were efforts made by whites to give Nelson hell his first year at Graves Springs and force him off the team. As the team scrimmaged, an offensive lineman would tell the defense exactly where Nelson was going to run the football. Meanwhile, the offensive line would purposely not carry through their blocking assignments, leaving the defense an open and easy shot at Nelson.

"We knew he'd be running up the middle," Smith said. "Then we'd put a helmet on him," meaning that most if not all the defensive players hit Nelson simultaneously. "We made it tough on him," Smith said.

In turn, Nelson was tough himself and "stuck it out" in order to make the team. "If they [blacks] could take it on the field, then we [whites] could accept it," Smith said. But he added, "I don't know why a black boy would want to play with forty white players." But for Nelson, to "play with forty white players" was a chance to play with one of the best football programs in the state with the hopes of later playing college ball. Some thirty years after leaving Albany High, Nelson is philosophical about his decision to go to Graves Springs. "Maybe God chose me to go there at that time." If God had chosen Nelson, it was likely that Coach Harold Dean Cook played the role of World

Redeemer. "Harold Dean was my dream man," Nelson said. "I'd jump off a mountain for that man." Cook treated Nelson hard but fair—the way he did white players. At times Cook boasted of Nelson as he ran the football. Cook referred to Nelson as "Little Jim Brown," referring to the exceptional professional running back during the 1960s. Cook would take time to talk to Nelson, helping him cope with the pressures of being one of the few blacks on the team and at school. "He treated me like a son," Nelson said.

Nelson was one of a handful of black students to graduate from Albany High in 1969. Prior to graduation, there were several fights involving whites and blacks and one of his friends, a black student, was hurt so badly that his jaw was wired shut by doctors in order for it to heal, according to Nelson. There was name-calling among students as well that sometimes precipitated into fights. Nelson himself said that he was never in a fight at school. On one occasion during practice a teammate called him a "nigger." Nelson responded by calling him a "cracker." The two fought, but players and coaches quickly stopped the fight.

Among black students, the athletes were more accepted at school than those who didn't play sports. Nelson, who helped the team win football games, found that white classmates and even some teachers were more willing to tolerate his presence because of that. "School pride" meant winning football games.

But behind this facade Nelson found something else. "I used to see those fake smiles at school," he said. "I used to hate them. Almost nothing was genuine." History's long march of racial divide still haunted the halls of Albany High. Prejudice among white classmates, according to Nelson, was "imbedded," passed down from generation to generation.

At Albany High, Ronnie Nelson was a good football player, but he was not a good student. He didn't work as hard in the classroom as he did on the football field. After graduating from high school, his grades were so poor that he had few options to attend college and play football. During the first two years after leaving Albany High, his life was adrift. He gambled and played pool. He was doing little that was useful to himself; he was also doing things he was later ashamed of.

But he still believed he had the ability to play college ball, and Nelson eventually accepted a scholarship at Albany State College, where he played for three years before being injured and leaving both the team and school. He moved away from Albany by the mid-1970s, beginning a period of personal anguish that included several years of drug addiction. By the mid-1990s, he had returned to South Georgia. Today he sells cars at an Albany dealership, while he and his wife, Brenda, live in nearby Worth County.

Nelson was waiting for me as I drove my car into his driveway for our interview. He came out to the front door to greet me, wearing the dark pants and white shirt he had earlier attended church in. Nelson was slim, muscular, and over six feet tall. His wide hands offered a strong handshake. In response to my comment about that, he said, "Oh, you got a pretty good grip yourself!"

He showed me weights in his backyard that he lifts regularly, and the bench inside his house on which he does sit-ups. "Sometimes, even today, I still think I can play football," he said.

As we talked nearly two hours, his television remained on but the volume off. He had been watching professional football before I arrived. Nelson said, "I gotta have my football."

Nelson had recently attended a class reunion with about twenty or so blacks who had graduated with him from Albany High in 1969. He showed me a glass mug he received during the gathering. The mug was marked with the traditional Albany High emblem, an Indian head in traditional dress. Underneath the emblem was inscribed: "Night to Remember—The class of 1969. We Are Survivors. Love Each Other Always."

"Some of us have had problems since then," Nelson said referring to his own past drug addiction. "But we made it through Albany High. It was hard." Nelson attributes his well-being today to his faith in God and his wife's love and patience. "I never would've made it without her," he said. "I'm happy again."

\* \* \*

# FOUR

In 1965, John Murphy joined a few other blacks by becoming the first to enroll at the all-white Albany Junior High on North Jefferson Street. Murphy was originally from nearby Lee County, just north of Albany, where his parents had been farmers. Lee County had witnessed racial violence in the early 1960s, as blacks there began conducting civil rights meetings in churches. Whites attacked these houses of God, including Shady Grove Baptist Church, which was firebombed and burned to the ground. Nightriders riddled with bullets the homes of four black families in Lee County. Murphy's family eventually left Lee County and moved to Albany, where he attended all-black Southside Junior High. Academically, he was one of the top students there, but by 1965, as he was entering the eighth grade, he chose to come to Albany Junior High and "compete" with white students in both sports and academics.

A few of Murphy's friends were critical of his decision to leave Southside. "I was ridiculed by some black folks for moving to Albany Junior High," Murphy said. "They thought I was trying to suck-up to white folks . . . I just wanted to compete." Of those who were critical then, Murphy responded: "I would say to them that you're not here [Albany Junior] because you're scared."

It was hard on Murphy in the beginning, as school got underway in 1965. He often felt "a lot of fear" during school, and one day a white student who became agitated by his very presence confronted him. The white student stopped Murphy in the hallway and said, "'I heard you wanted to whip my ass.'"

Murphy replied, "I am not here to fight you or anyone else."

Following the exchange of words between Murphy and the white boy, a crowd of students gathered around the two, anticipating a fight. "It was just madness . . ." Murphy told me. "I found myself in a defensive posture with this guy." Tensions escalated before a teacher broke through the throng of students, grabbed Murphy by the hand, and led him away from danger.

Not long after that confrontation in the hallway, one of the football coaches asked Murphy to come out for the eighth-grade team. Murphy agreed, and later reported to the gym to pick up his uniform before the first practice. As white players watched Murphy collect his equipment, they looked on in disdain. He was the only black on the team.

Through football, Murphy found the acceptance that had eluded him during the regular school day. After school during football season, players changed into their uniforms in the tiny school gym and then walked for ten minutes down Third Avenue, past the local hospital, to the practice field known as the "Limesink." Along the journey, players walked underneath mammoth oak trees planted methodically years before on both sides of the avenue. Spanish moss dripped from the trees, waving slightly in the autumn breeze. During these walks, some white players like Johnny Fordham befriended Murphy, making him feel a part of the team, Murphy said.

Things were changing at Albany Junior High School. Once during class that fall, Murphy left his desk to sharpen a pencil. When he returned, a white student (who was not on the football team) had taken his seat. After seeing this, his teammate James Cleveland intervened, and insisted that the white student allow Murphy back into his desk. "Once I gained acceptance by the football team," Murphy said, "I didn't have any more racial encounters at school."

Murphy played football his ninth-grade year at Albany Junior, and by August 1967, as an upcoming sophomore at Albany High, he reported to Graves Springs. He was the only black player on the B-Team that year. He was strong and weighed about one hundred and seventy-five pounds, but was "scared to death" about what could happen to him at Graves Springs—not so much about racial confrontations, but about the hazing which the upperclassmen had been known to put all the younger players through.

"I had no concept of what was going to happen out there," he said, and remembers wondering, "Are the older guys going to tear our butts up?" Murphy, who later played football at Florida State University and earned a degree there, endured the same kind of initiation rites at Graves Springs as his white teammates. Varsity players, for instance, made Murphy and the other sophomores strip naked and roll a grape over and over on the ground with their noses.

Murphy survived the hazing, the heat, and the hard work on the football field. He loved playing football. He felt he had found a team in which the coaches and most of the players were judging him not by race, but how hard he played football. A strong and quick defensive lineman, Murphy played football as hard as anyone else, and he attended Graves Springs for three years before graduating in 1970. Graves Springs was a "much tougher" camp than what Murphy experienced in Tallahassee where he played college football for Florida State University, referring to FSU as "a piece of cake" contrasted with the encampment along the Muckalee.

Harold Dean Cook, at Albany High, was the most demanding coach Murphy ever played under. Murphy had known Cook before he went to Graves Springs. Cook and Murphy's father worked together as brick masons. Like the other blacks who played under Cook, Murphy has fond memories of him and how he handled the tenuous relationship between the white and black players. "Harold Dean Cook was almost like an extended father to me," Murphy said.

It was another white coach, assistant Ferrell Henry, who himself had played at Florida State and helped Murphy get an athletic scholarship there. At Tallahassee, Murphy played under Bill Parcells, who later coached in the NFL.

In August 1968, David "Tex" Wall joined the Indian encampment at Graves Springs and befriended John Murphy. Wall was a white player who had just moved to Albany from Texas. But Wall was born in Lumberton, North Carolina where his father, Mal Wall, had been a traveling salesman. Mal Wall's job had taken the family from Lumberton to Charlotte, North Carolina, to Irving Texas and on to Albany. Tex played linebacker at Graves Springs so he and Murphy, also on defense, worked together on the field, and socialized at night in the barracks.

Someone brought a guitar to camp that year and Tex often played it, including songs by the Chad Mitchell Trio, a folk group of the

1960s whose songs espoused racial equality. "They were pretty esoteric," Tex said of the songs he and Murphy sang together. "John and I were very close friends."

Murphy said they were "ice-breaking songs" that dealt with racial issues and how American society must begin to live up to its ideals of equality. "Tex and I sang together. We became friends," he said, remembering those days.

David Wall grew up in the rural South, but he didn't bring to Graves Springs any deep feelings of racial prejudice. He attributed this to his parents, Mal and Faye Wall. "I don't ever remember my father saying anything derogatory about race," he said. But there was at least one instance where racist remarks from David Wall were clearly heard by his black friend and teammate, John Murphy.

After their senior season ended in 1969, Murphy, along with Wall and a few other white players were riding in a car together during a recruiting trip to the University of Florida in Gainesville. (Wall would eventually sign a scholarship with the University of North Carolina at Chapel Hill.) During this particular road trip, a song came on the radio sung by a black musical group. Wall couldn't recall the name of the song, but he clearly remembered what he said when he heard it on the radio. "I said out loud, 'GET THAT NIGGER SHIT OFF THE RADIO!'"

After Wall's epithet, the car was filled with silence. "I remember later trying to apologize to John. I was horrified," Wall said. Wall made the comment without thinking, as he put it, "It just came out." He referred to what he said as being the "indoctrination" of racial slurs he had heard all his life.

"That's still a vivid memory for me today," Wall said.

Thirty years after leaving Graves Springs, Murphy, who now works in employee relations for Procter & Gamble Corporation in Albany, said the camp represented "whites and blacks reaching out . . . you wouldn't find it any other way in the community" during that period. Over the years, he has come to fully appreciate that what occurred at Grave Springs between the races was "monumental" and he remains nourished by his experiences there. "It [Graves Springs] has been really sustaining to me over the years," he said. "Even today if I experience overt racism I go back to football lessons."

\* \* \*

What John Murphy, Ronnie Nelson, and Grady Caldwell represented at Graves Springs, in one sense, has been occurring in professional sports in America since the nineteenth century. When major league baseball was in its infancy in the early 1870s, some of the teams included both white and black players. By the late 1880s, there was growing resistance among some white players toward allowing black athletes in the league. Southern-born players in particular were becoming openly hostile as they found themselves on the same teams with blacks. Two white players on the Syracuse Stars refused to sit for a team picture because the team included a black pitcher, Robert Higgins. One of the white players told a reporter: "I am a Southerner by birth and I tell you I would rather have my heart cut out before I would consent to have my picture in the group."

By 1887, owners of major league teams had agreed informally to hire no more black ballplayers. Some fans and members of the press objected. The *Newark Call* published this:

> If anywhere in this world the social barriers are broken down it is on the ball field. There, many men of low birth and poor breeding are the idols of the rich and cultured; the best man is he who plays the best. Even men of churlish disposition and coarse habits are tolerated on the field. In view of these facts the objection to colored men is ridiculous. If social distinctions are to be made, half the players in the country will be shut out. Better make character and personal habits the test.

The few blacks who had integrated Graves Springs by the late 1960s were proving, at least in Albany, that character and work ethics meant much more that the color of skin.

\* \* \*

By the time sophomore Larry West arrived at Graves Springs in August 1968, the camp was beginning to foster an environment that the historical culture of white Albany had fought to resist. At camp, white and black players, if still only a few, were living and practicing football together with a sense of equality rarely found during the city's past. Racial differences were overlooked; what mattered was ability and effort.

West, a black player, attended Graves Springs for three years before graduating in 1971. "I don't remember any mistreatment at camp," West said. "I found that when you have a job to do, and when you do the job, people tend to lower barriers."

The *Albany Herald* quoted Coach Harold Dean Cook referring to West as the "best sophomore in the county and a potentially really great player."

In the same story, sports columnist Vic Smith referred to West as that "brilliant sophomore." He played defensive back and ran the forty-yard dash in four and a-half seconds. West was a fast, determined athlete who loved football. Once, because of an injury, he couldn't play as his team battled Robert E. Lee High School. Watching from the sidelines, West became so upset that he cried because he was unable to play. West was so good that he was one of the first blacks to be given a football scholarship to the University of Georgia, where he earned a degree. By the late 1990s, West was a Baptist minister living with his family in Washington, DC.

Yet when he joined the Indians at Graves Springs in 1968, he was more concerned with football than with race relations. "I never thought about black and white," West said. "I thought about winning a position on the football team."

* * *

If West wasn't thinking about "black and white," some of his family members were. Because of the legacy of violence connected with segregation, there was concern for West's safety at camp. One of his supporters in his decision to attend Graves Springs was his aunt, McCree Harris. Miss Harris was born in 1934 as one of eight children of the Reverend Isaiah and Katie Harris. Her father had been a pastor at both Mount Zion and Mount Calvary Baptist Churches. Her mother, a graduate of Albany State College, taught school for more than thirty years at Jackson Heights Elementary. "We were very close knitted," Miss Harris said. "We looked after one another."

Miss Harris would do the same for her nephew, Larry West. Reverend Harris tried to shelter his children from the realities and dangers of the segregated society they were growing up in, but as McCree Harris came of age she was determined to change the very culture her father had tried to protect her from. Rev. Harris didn't allow his children to attend the Albany Theater, where blacks were made to sit in the balcony away from white patrons, feeling it unwise to put children in a position of vulnerability.

"He always reminded us that we were living in the South," she said, and that the family shouldn't take unnecessary risks.

After graduating from high school, Miss Harris left Albany to earn two college degrees, including a master's in French from Columbia University. She returned to Albany and began a thirty-six year teaching career at Monroe High School.

With the civil rights movement gathering steam in Albany and throughout the South by the early 1960s, she became an active member of the local chapter of the National Association for the Advancement of Colored People. She, too, became involved in events in Albany that were making national news, participating in rallies and meetings, and getting to know Dr. King when he came to Albany to speak and protest. But her involvement in the Albany Movement clearly irritated school superintendent J. J. Cordell, and according to Miss Harris, she was told by Cordell that if she did get arrested while protesting, she would lose her job.

In order to protect her career, she was very cautious during the movement and was never arrested in Albany, but "I got arrested [while marching] in St. Augustine with Dr. King," she said.

\* \* \*

During the midst of the civil rights movement in Albany, McCree Harris realized that an opportunity to further the cause lay along the banks of the Muckalee at Graves Springs. The color barrier was broken there in 1965, and three years later her own nephew, Larry West, was struggling with the idea of going to Graves Springs and Albany High instead of Monroe.

Before reaching his decision to attend camp, West was a student at Merry Acres Junior High, located in the northwest part of Albany and composed mainly of white students. When West was a boy, Miss Harris took him downtown to a dime store and while they were shopping, West told her that he needed to use the restroom. She in turn told him that these bathrooms were for whites only. "Larry didn't like that," she said. "Nor did he understand it."

Although concerned about his safety, Miss Harris encouraged West to go to Graves Springs, believing that his presence there would help break racial barriers throughout the community. During this period she counseled other black players such as Grady Caldwell, John Murphy, and Ronnie Nelson, supporting them in their decision to play ball at Albany High.

"McCree was a big help to me—then and now," Nelson said.

Miss Harris said that she wanted West to go the Albany High because he would likely get a better education there as opposed to Monroe, where she was teaching. "It wasn't easy for me teaching at Monroe and sending Larry to Albany High," she said. "I wasn't sure what was going to happen to him. But we had to believe he was going to be all right." She continued, "Being in the [school] system, I knew that blacks at Monroe did not get what they [white students] got at Albany High" in terms of the overall quality of education. In some ways students at Monroe were receiving a "second-hand education" because of the inequities in school funding, she said.

Before West came to Graves Springs, McCree Harris counseled him concerning how to act and what to say on a team in which he was one of a few black players. To his advantage, he had grown up in a segregated culture with a "special kind of understanding of the system," she said. He had developed the correct demeanor and persona in which to succeed at that time. West wasn't cocky or loud; instead, he was levelheaded and committed to being a good football player.

Former white teammate Brad Oates agreed, praising West's character and recalling that "he was a proud man." Oates himself knew something about hard work and pride on the football field: he went on to play for the Green Bay Packers. West closely followed his aunt's advice, and according to her, "We told him to be careful and watch the company you keep . . . and do your best in whatever you encounter."

While white players at Graves Springs generally welcomed West, there were blacks at Monroe who retaliated against his decision to enroll at Albany High. According to Miss Harris, there were "no problems from the white players" at Albany High, but a few of the Monroe students "did a lot of ugly things" to him. West was physically attacked, but not seriously hurt, one day as he walked through his own neighborhood. In response to this, Miss Harris and a few other adults discussed the incident with the assailant's parents in order to prevent further trouble. "At one time we thought we were going to have to pull Larry out of Albany High," she said. But they never did.

McCree Harris went to Albany High games at Hugh Mills Stadium throughout this period of racial change, but she was no stranger to the stadium. Back when the team was still all-white, her father had taken her there when she was a child. Then, blacks were made to enter the stadium through a separate gate, away from white spectators. Once inside, the two groups sat in different sections of the stadium. As the team became integrated, "We [blacks] went in with the rest of them [white fans]," she said. "And we sat in the same place."

When Larry West played, his aunt represented him at Albany High's Booster Club meetings. "At some of these meetings I may have been the only black there, but I was always well-received," she said. Coach Harold Dean Cook spoke to her regularly at the meetings about the progress of West and the other black players. She called Cook a "fine gentleman" who "gave the boys hope" as the feathers of Jim Crow were beginning to be plucked in Albany.

Miss Harris said that blacks and whites in Albany today should be thankful to Grady Caldwell, John Murphy, Ronnie Nelson, Larry West, and other minority players who helped shatter old worlds by playing football at Albany High. "It wasn't as easy as it seems" for these young men to have gone to Graves Springs. According to her, white players and their parents accepted these players not only because they conducted themselves with dignity, but also because they helped the team win. "What was important was winning," she emphasized.

When whites realized that these players could help their team win, longstanding racial prejudice began to soften. "It was a beautiful sight to see them [white and black players] out there on the field together."

\* \* \*

**Alabama**
*Oh Alabama, the devil fools with
the best laid plan.
Swing low Alabama.
You got the spare change — you got to feel strange
And now the moment is all that it meant.*

Singer/songwriter Neil Young, 1972

To McCree Harris, it was "beautiful" to watch white and black players on the same team at Mills Memorial Stadium, working for a common goal. It held for her an image of idealism not predicated on race but on character, virtue, and shared humanity. For Miss Harris and others who were working to end institutional racism and to recreate the community itself, a political event in the same stadium in 1968 indicated just how hard their task was.

Ten thousand people filled the stadium in September that year to hear a campaign speech by Alabama Governor George Wallace, presidential candidate for the Independent Party. The crowd included local and state political leaders and a sea of white faces. On hand for the event was the segregationist governor of Georgia, Lester Maddox.

Wallace himself had a well-documented political history of racial bigotry. He had won elections by attacking blacks in Alabama, but he lost an early political contest and vowed never again to be "out-niggered" by future opponents. A few years before the Albany rally, he had personally stood in a doorway at the University of Alabama to deny entrance to black students. Both men represented a Jim Crow South that Miss Harris had risked her life to change.

In his introduction of Wallace, Maddox said that the Alabama governor had been his "friend for many years." He went on to say that Wallace was the only political figure who stood by him in Maddox's efforts to operate a segregated restaurant in Atlanta. Maddox proclaimed the federal government a "gestapo" for its efforts in trying to end segregation in public places. (Both the 1964 Civil Rights Act and the 1965 Voting Rights Act became federal law in order to end public segregation and protect the voting-rights of blacks throughout the South.) "Only George Wallace had the courage to identify himself with the rights of the common people," Maddox told the crowd, igniting a great cheer. The common white man, of course.

McCree Harris was finding beauty on the very same field where others had come to celebrate the dark side of the American spirit.

* * *

# FIVE

With the end of the 1960s, as the nation was wounded by both civil rights violence and the Vietnam War, Southern collegiate football was being reborn like the country itself. Bear Bryant's boys were beaten forty-two to twenty-one by the University of Southern California in 1970. Afterwards, sportswriter Mickey Herskowitz wrote that Alabama's "skinny little white boys" were battered by Sam "the Bam" Cunningham, a bruising black fullback who scored three touchdowns during the game. Worse still was that USC halfback Clarence Davis scored two touchdowns himself. Davis was born in *Birmingham, Alabama.* Those skinny little white boys didn't sing Dixie after that game.

Before the USC game, a delegation from the NAACP met with Bryant in his office. They argued, saying it was long overdue, that black players should become part of the university's team. The Bear agreed. Herskowitz writes that Bryant had been ready to sign black athletes, but the state's regents and governor were not. Bryant showed the NAACP folks a list of fifteen names of black players who he wanted to recruit. But it didn't begin to happen until Cunningham thrashed Alabama. According to Herskowitz, who wrote the book, *The Legend of Bear Bryant,* "The line out of Tuscaloosa later was that Sam Cunningham did more to integrate Alabama in sixty minutes than Martin Luther King did in twenty years. The Bear eventually said so himself."

Bryant often spoke with USC coach John McKay during this time, providing him with names of black high school players in Alabama that he couldn't recruit, but McKay could. Following the 1970 season, the two coaches discussed Alabama's best prospect, a junior college transfer named John Mitchell, a defensive end from Mobile. Both men wanted Mitchell. The Bear got him.

That same year Bryant signed Wilbur Jackson, the first black freshman at Alabama, although at the time, freshmen couldn't play their first year. However, because Mitchell was an upcoming junior, he could play immediately. Against USC in 1971, Mitchell made the tackle in the opening kickoff, and Alabama went on to an upset victory. The following year, which was my first year at Graves Springs, Mitchell became Alabama's first black captain. And he was the first black to coach under Bear Bryant.

As a player, Mitchell roomed with Albany's Bobby Stanford, who played and lived with fellow black teammates at Graves Springs in the mid-1960s. The two became friends, and remained so after their football careers ended.

Stanford was one of the best players in the state, but as a boy race relations were far removed from his mind, which centered on playing football. "I was totally oblivious to the marches in Albany," he said. "I was twelve or thirteen. I didn't have a clue who Martin Luther King was. And I didn't care."

\* \* \*

In August 1970, five years after Graves Springs started housing integrated football teams, Willie Magwood broke the color barrier on the coaching staff. Magwood was born in 1943, one of nine children of Booker T. and Pearl Magwood in Colquitt County, Georgia. Located about forty miles southeast of Albany off U. S. Highway 319, Moultrie is the county's largest town. Still, it is a rural area where cotton and tobacco have formed the cycle of life for generations.

When Willie Magwood was eight, his father died. He and his siblings had to "crop tobacco and pick cotton" to financially help the family. During cotton-picking season in the late summer, he had to get out of bed (or be pulled out) by five-thirty in the morning. An hour later, he was picking. Pickers were "to get there [fields] while the dew's still on," Magwood said.

Some days, young Willie would pick for ten hours. "From can see to can't see" was the adage spoken by those of both races when it came to describing the hard toil in Southern fields. Willie Magwood was paid two and a-half dollars for every hundred pounds he picked, but when he finished the day with less than a hundred pounds, he paid a painful price. "I got a lot of whippins' from my mother 'cause I didn't pick a hundred pounds," he said.

Throughout his teenage years, until he left Moultrie to attend college in Albany, Magwood picked cotton each summer under the hot Georgia sun. The most money he ever made was seven dollars a day; he earned that amount in the early 1960s, when landowners started paying pickers three dollars and fifty cents per hundred pounds.

Willie hated picking cotton. Along with providing his family with money, working in the fields made Magwood realize that this kind of work was not for him. "I had a choice between picking cotton and going to college," he said. "When they opened the door [to college] I was there." He received an athletic scholarship to Albany State College, where he played both basketball and football before graduating in 1967.

Picking cotton afforded Magwood something else besides money and the desire to go to college; it was one of the few occasions growing up in which he came in contact with white people. Poor whites picked alongside poor blacks in Colquitt County and elsewhere in the South. While his mother constantly stressed the importance of education, she was also teaching her children to respect all people. But Willie was coming of age when, except for necessities, the races were separated from each other.

When Magwood was about fifteen, around 1958, he was playing basketball with a group of black friends on an outside court. A white woman in a convertible drove by during the game. She caught the attention of the players, especially the one who whistled at her.

This was a period in which a seemingly harmless gesture could turn dangerous. Breaking traditional social taboos could cost a boy his life in the South. In 1955, a fourteen-year-old black boy from Chicago, Emmitt Till, was murdered while visiting relatives in Mississippi. Emmitt Till had either whistled or said "bye baby," or possibly both, to a white woman who worked in a store. The woman's husband and half-brother became so enraged that they kidnapped Till, beat him and then shot him before tossing his body into a river.

Fortunately, this didn't happen to Magwood's teammate: Not long after the woman drove by, police officers surrounded the basketball court. According to Magwood, the boy who had whistled at the white woman was taken away and arrested, but was later released from police custody after paying a fine.

After graduating from college, Magwood worked briefly for two different high schools before being hired by Albany High's head coach, Ferrell Henry. Magwood taught physical education and coached B-team football and basketball and, by 1972, was my coach for both sports. He possessed an easy manner in the way he carried himself that made players and students easily warm up to him. He wore a short Afro, and his dark eyes evoked a sense of sincerity. It was relaxing and often comforting to be around him, especially because his style of coaching was not as hard as was Henry's and the other varsity coaches. I suspect Henry realized that about Magwood before he hired him.

Magwood soon became a favorite among athletes and the entire student body. In 1974, Magwood, one of about ten black teachers at Albany High, became the first black to receive the dedication from the *Thronateeska*, the school's yearbook. He said he was "very proud" of this recognition. "I was surprised . . . it was an all-white staff," Magwood said of those students who had made the decision to recognize him. Concerning the dedication, the annual staff wrote: "To one who has given time, thought, and effort to Albany High without counting cost . . . Whose smile has often brightened the day for all of us."

Magwood confronted none of the mean and racist reaction that awaited Grady Caldwell at Graves Springs in 1965. Coaches and players themselves received Magwood favorably. From my own experiences at Graves Springs, from 1972 through 1974, I cannot recall one incident of racial animosity toward Magwood. It was quite the opposite. "They [coaches] just treated me like one of the coaches," Magwood said. He attributes much of this to Ferrell Henry, and the other "great people" during that period who made efforts to promote racial change, even unity through the school's athletic program.

Magwood coached at Graves Springs through the 1970s, and into the following decade when the camp finally closed. He was still teaching and coaching at Albany High during the 1999-2000 school year. He has been married for twenty-seven years, and lives in Moultrie where he and his wife, Linda, have reared four children.

"I really didn't think much about it until years later. To me it was an honor to be the school's first black coach," he said. "But at that time, I was just looking for a job."

* * *

# SIX

The best athlete I ever played with at Graves Springs was Robert "Bobby" Jackson. He was a year ahead of me; but I still thought of him as a god. Jackson played college ball, and for nine years he started with the New York Jets. There were always those who said that, at five foot ten, he was too small to make it big. Gods have a way of proving mortals wrong.

Bobby Jackson was born in Albany to Robert Jackson Sr. and Donna Jackson, and he was one of seven children. Jackson grew up in a public housing complex that he and others referred to as "CME" or "Crime, Murder, and Execution." This area was near the high school, and included Residence, Tift, and Society Avenues. According to local housing officials, "CME" meant Christian Methodist Episcopal Church, which was located on Madison Avenue. Jackson said "CME" was a tough part of town where boys played ball together and often got into fistfights.

After his parent's marriage fell apart, Bobby, at about the third grade, moved in with his grandmother, Rebecca Jackson. Between his grandmother and father, there was discipline in the young boy's life. Robert Jackson, Sr., had served in the army during the Korean War, and after military service he worked with BellSouth. During the weekends, Bobby's father made extra money cleaning business offices. Bobby often helped in these cleaning jobs, learning the importance of work. He roofed houses and did other odd jobs, too. As a youngster, his grandmother ensured that Bobby would not stay out late at night, or associate with local troublemakers. She stayed "on him" about doing his best in school. He played pickup ball games in the neighborhood, but not organized sports. At Carver Junior High he played the drums, not football.

"I wanted to play football at Carver but they said I was too small," Jackson said. "I started believing what other people said about me."

Bobby Jackson was looking forward to playing the drums as a tenth grader for Monroe High . . . until he found out he had been rezoned for Albany High School. A neighborhood friend, Johnny "Mule" Coleman, had been rezoned, too. Coleman convinced Jackson to go to Graves Springs with him in August 1971.

Coleman was a linebacker who was ferocious on the field. He used to say, "Johnny Mule got ya!" after leveling a running back. It was not said in an arrogant way. Coleman was stating, in a matter-of-fact manner, what had happened on the field.

Johnny Coleman was two years ahead of me in school, and I was terrified by the way he played. When the "Mule" hit you, it sounded like a car wreck. Other than the seniors putting Atomic Bomb muscle relaxer in his athletic supporter, Jackson faced little organized hazing his first year at camp. The salt tablets the coaches made him take made him vomit, and he stopped taking them. Moreover, going to Graves Springs was the first time he had ever been away from home, but he was accustomed to hard work. As he put it, "I was used to being out in the sun."

Bobby Jackson couldn't swim and unlike most players he took showers in the varsity barracks, where he once saw a water moccasin. "I wasn't scared too much" at Graves Springs, having grown up in a tough neighborhood, Jackson said. He had found a new passion. "I never once thought about quitting," he said. "I loved playing football."

The boy who longed to play the drums developed into a hard-hitter. Jackson played defensive back and wingback or slotback, where he caught several of my passes in 1973. He ran the forty-yard dash in about four and a-half seconds. Besides his supreme athleticism, his sheer determination made him a powerful player; like a god, he was fearless on the field. College teams became interested in him, and Coach Henry began driving him to Tallahassee to watch Florida State University play. Florida State did offer a scholarship to one of our teammates, Nathaniel Henderson, a six foot, five- inch lineman. But 'Big Nate' wanted his friend Bobby Jackson to play college ball with him. Coaches at Florida State were hesitant to offer Jackson a scholarship, claiming he was too small. Big Nate said he would accept only if Jackson came with him, so the coaches gave Bobby Jackson a scholarship too.

At Tallahassee, Jackson was a four-year starter at defensive back, and after his final season he was selected All-American and finished with ten career interceptions—at that time, the school record. He kept proving people wrong wherever he went. During the 1978 National Football League draft, Jackson had expected to be a first round pick. Instead, the New York Jets selected him in the sixth round. "I was disappointed," Jackson said. "It made me hungry."

Jackson's hunger led to a starting cornerback position on the opening day of his rookie season. The Jets played the Miami Dolphins. That game was the biggest thrill of his football life. "I had a great game," he said. "I was covering Nat Moore," who was an excellent wide receiver. "I knew that people back home were watching me play."

I watched Jackson regularly on television during his professional career. He hit players so hard that once he knocked out Atlanta Falcon running back William Andrews from Thomasville, Georgia. (The same Andrews that Jackson and I played against in high school.) Twice, Bobby Jackson was selected as an alternate for the league's All-Pro game. After nine years and twenty-two career interceptions as a pro, Jackson retired from football.

Since his retirement, Jackson, who lives in Long Island New York, regularly visits Albany. One time, he went to visit his former high school teammate, Johnny Coleman. Jackson had brought with him a football, one of two he had intercepted from Miami Dolphin quarterback Dan Marino. Jackson gave the ball to Coleman and said, "I told him if it wasn't for you I wouldn't be playing football."

Not long after Jackson signed his first professional contract, he came home to see his grandmother, Rebecca Jackson, the woman who had always meant so much to him and helped him as a child. He told her that he was going to buy a house in Albany, so he would have a place to stay when he came home to visit. He asked for her advice on the houses that they saw together. She particularly liked a house on Waddell Avenue. It had a fine kitchen, and fruit trees in the backyard. It was a much nicer home, in a much nicer neighborhood, than the one she had been living in. Bobby agreed, saying he liked the house, too. He bought the house, and "I went back to see her and gave her the keys," he said. "I wanted her to have the house."

Bobby Jackson continues to come home to see those who helped him along the way. Over the years, he has helped run football camps for youngsters in and around Albany. When he comes back, he stays with Rebecca Jackson, in the house he bought for her on Waddell Avenue. Inside the house, there are several framed pictures of him, one as a Jet and others from his days at Florida State, where he graduated with a degree in criminology.

Since leaving the Jets, Bobby has worked in public relations, and in the computer industry. He has six children, two of whom are football stars at the high school and college levels, and he remains active as an alumnus with the Jets. Still, there is a passion for South Georgia football.

He went to Graves Springs expecting "some military-type camp." His father and other relatives had served in the military, and as a young boy he often thought he would become a soldier someday. The closest he ever got was Graves Springs. While the heat was awful in Tallahassee during his collegiate preseason camp, the general conditions were much better than Graves Springs. Nor was professional camp as tough as Jackson's high school experience. It was on the Muckalee Creek where Bobby Jackson's work ethic and love of the game blossomed.

"I look back and it [Graves Springs] was the happiest time in my life," he said.

There was help for Jackson when he played at Graves Springs. B-team coach Willie Magwood took Jackson "under his wing," making him work hard, building his confidence as a first-time player, Jackson said. Thirty years later, Magwood said that Jackson was the best player he ever coached. Defensive back coach Ronnie Archer also helped Jackson become an outstanding player. Archer's emotions energized "his boys" like some magic elixir.

Magwood and Archer were two at Albany High "instrumental" in the development of Bobby Jackson—the one whom others said was too small to play. Graves Springs and the coaches there followed Jackson as he moved from one level of the game to the next. Talking about his playing days after he retired, he recalled one of Coach Henry's favorite sayings at Graves Springs, "It's not the size of dog in the fight, it's the size of the fight in the dog." According to Jackson, "that saying carried me through my career."

\* \* \*

# SEVEN

**W**hite players at Graves Springs from the mid-1960s into the following decade, having been exposed to the cultural underpinnings of racism, developed a sense of athletic equality at camp. I know that some of these same players commonly used the word "nigger" when they were away from their black teammates, and even harbored some feelings of bigotry that were passed down like a family heirloom. I was only different in the sense that my own father had instilled in me a disdain for racial prejudice. But when it came to sports, my friends and later my college roommates cheered wildly for black athletes, like homerun king Henry Aaron and others. Athletics, on all levels, was one of the first arenas in which Southern white boys were beginning to accept and applaud black achievement.

\* \* \*

J. Tom Morgan grew up in Albany, and by his tenth-grade year he was attending all-white Westover High School. He played on Westover's football team, but after the first game of his junior year in 1971 (in which Westover played Albany High), Morgan was rezoned to Albany High following court-ordered integration. "Judge Wilbur Owens of Macon issued the order on the same day of our first game," said Morgan, who later became the DeKalb County (Georgia) district attorney.

Morgan and a handful of other players from Westover joined Albany's team that year and, by August 1972, he was about to get the Graves Springs treatment. "We had all heard about how Albany High School's camp was uncivilized," he said. Westover had a preseason camp, too. Players there practiced at the school and slept in an air-conditioned gym. Coaches at Westover, unlike those at Graves Springs, did not have to walk over the practice field each morning with a stick to drive away the snakes, according to Morgan. "It was the two most miserable weeks of my life," he recalled, describing life at Graves Springs, including the lack of water during the workouts. "I remember them [coaches] saying that drinking water will slow you down. We thought we were in such great shape, but we know so much more today" about conditioning athletes. Today, Morgan is a runner who competes in road races in Atlanta.

Morgan was one of several white athletes who were pitched into a world of racial diversity. "It was the first time that we had blacks and whites living and sleeping together," he said. "Looking back, but for football none of us would have had twenty-four hour integration." Albany High's 1972 varsity team included about fourteen minority players and about thirty white ones. Morgan played offensive end while finding a home at Albany High, where he became senior class president. "There was camaraderie there [at the camp]," he said. "That may sound esoteric, but we found commonality. We didn't focus on the differences."

"To their [the coaches] credit, I thought they handled the integration issue extremely well," Morgan said. "They may have said something different behind our backs" but the coaches there made real efforts to ignore race when it came to the treatment of players.

\* \* \*

By the time I arrived at Graves Springs, the same year as Morgan, Coach Henry was determined not to allow racial differences to hinder the team's drive to win. More so, Henry viewed football as something far more important than a game played by boys and coached by men. "We just didn't have any [racial] problems," he said. "I remember thinking then that football would be the ingredient to make it [integration] work. Black and white athletes working together, blocking for one another, helping one another."

I played under Henry for two years, and never did I see him treat players differently because of race; if a player worked hard, he won Henry's praise and the honor of playing Friday night games. But if any player loafed or didn't follow the rules or didn't respect the coaches, things would be unpleasant. Once, during a practice session after pre-season camp ended, a player hadn't followed the instructions of one of the assistant coaches. That same player had been verbally disrespectful. After Henry was told what was happening, he approached the player in question, who began cussing the entire coaching staff and the team in general. This same player had earlier shown signs of unwillingness to accept Henry's authority.

"I ain't puttin' up with this bull shit!" the player said, or something to that effect.

But I do recall exactly what Henry said in response: "That's about what I expect from you son . . . now get off this field and don't ever come back," instructing him to leave and turn in his uniform. The player happened to be black and of good physical ability, but he was not allowed back on the team.

One year, for a short time, there was an undercurrent of possible racial problems within the team. Players had written the phrases "white boy" and "black boy" on a poster that hung in the locker room at the stadium. The poster itself proclaimed themes like sacrifice, hard work, and team unity. Henry called a team meeting after he became aware of the graffiti. He spoke with certainty, and with the authority we had come to expect. "I don't know who started it and I don't care," he said. "But after today it's over . . . No more 'white boys' and no more 'black boys' on this team."

It was over after that meeting.

Leonard Lawless was on the team, and remembers the meeting Henry called. Lawless, himself a white player born in Iowa, still lives in Albany, where he is co-owner of a public accounting firm. He said that Henry was simply not going to tolerate race as a hindrance to what was best for the team. "We didn't have any racial problems then because Henry and his staff weren't going to allow it," Lawless said.

Lawless played fullback in the same backfield with Celious Williams, a black who, in 1973, rushed for two hundred and sixty yards in one game, at that time a region record. Williams was nicknamed "Crab" as a youngster because he was a slow runner. He grew up in Albany with ten brothers and sisters, and by the time he reached high school the only thing slow about him was his nickname. Through 1972, as a sophomore at Monroe High, he had developed into one of the fastest athletes in school. After the tenth grade, he transferred to Albany High to become a part of what he considered to be a better football program. Williams' first year at Graves Springs was 1973, when the team included about twenty black players and about thirty white players. In relation, the student body was about twenty percent black. In 1974, my senior year, there were overall fewer varsity players then there had been in previous years, of which about fifteen were black.

Williams wore his hair in a modest Afro, three to four inches extending from his head. He was quick to smile, and had a thin mustache. He was about five feet, nine inches tall, and a hundred and sixty-five pounds. All of us, coaches too, referred to him as Crab. He looked like a crab taking short, deliberate steps when walking and moving his head from side to side as if to gain a better view of whatever it was he was trying to see. Sometimes we called him "No-Neck" because his head seemed to sit on his shoulders without a neck. He had lighting feet, and the ability to quickly change directions as he ran the football, making it almost impossible for defenders to tackle him in the open field.

Crab and I were also teammates on the school's basketball team. He had a likeable personality, and the even-tempered way he lived his life meshed well with the multiple personalities of team sports. Crab never complained when things weren't going well; instead he worked harder, like all good athletes do. By the late 1990s, Williams, who at that point had been married to his high school sweetheart for twenty-five years, was employed as an electrician for Albany State University. He joined the army after high school, and had basic training at Fort Jackson in South Carolina and was ordered to Fort Benning in Columbus, Georgia before being discharged and returning to Albany. Back in Albany he enrolled in the technical school.

"It [Graves Springs] was the first time in my life I ate, slept, and lived with white guys," Williams said. "I didn't think nothin' of it." What Williams thought of was earning a position on the football team and surviving camp. "There were no racial problems when I was there," he said. "All the players were treated fair. The practices were hard on everybody." Even with the discipline demanded by the coaches, the heat, and the grind of three daily practices, Williams said he was "having fun" at Graves Springs. "It was the first time in my life I had been camping."

\* \* \*

When I was a ninth-grade football player, James Harpe, a black, was one of my teammates. Harpe attended St. Teresa's Catholic School in Albany until the eighth grade before going to Albany Junior High. He was physically a striking athlete; his body appeared to be chiseled, exemplifying the winning Greek athlete. Harpe played running back and defensive back and ran forty yards in four-and-a-half seconds.

Few black students, or for that matter white students who I knew in school, could move in and out of both racial worlds establishing friendships as Harpe did. He made a conscious decision by the time he had arrived at Albany Junior High to befriend both blacks and whites. Harpe's ninth-grade year was a "significant point" in his life, and he was determined to take a "stand" that he knew might not be popular. "I wasn't going to let others tell me what to do," he said.

Throughout high school, Harpe was criticized by a few black students who had ostracized him for socializing with whites. Harpe dated white girls in high school. It was "non-football" players, both black and white, who were bothered by his multiplicity of relationships. Football players of both races tended to be not only less critical of Harpe's wide circle of friends, but many of us had been won over by his competitive spirit and the authentic way he lived his life.

His parents had been afraid of what might happen to their only child as he was coming of age during this early period of integration. Harpe's mother, Mary Shaw Harpe, was born in 1924 in Ft. Gaines, Georgia, a rural community sixty miles west of Albany along the Chattahoochee River. The same year his father, James Autry Harpe, was born in Arlington, Georgia, some twenty miles west of Albany. His mother was a schoolteacher while his father was a civilian employee for nearly thirty years at the Marine base in Albany.

"My parents were aware of lynchings in the South," Harpe recalled. "People in the South lived in fear." His parents stressed the importance of education and they wanted their only child, who was born in Ft. Gaines, to treat all people decently.

Before moving to Albany, Harpe's family had lived in Newton, Georgia, about twenty miles south of Albany along State Highway 91. Newton is in Baker County, a place not unfamiliar with racial intolerance. In 1960, Baker County Sheriff L. Warren "Gator" Johnson arrested Charlie Ware, a black man, and shot him three times in the neck while he was handcuffed in the sheriff's official car. Three years later, an all-white jury in Columbus, Georgia acquitted Johnson of civil liability in connection with the shooting. After the trial was over, one of the jurors said the only thing Johnson had done wrong was not to have killed Ware. The jury's decision led to protest among blacks in Albany.

When Harpe was a young boy, not long after his family moved to Newton, they received a threatening telephone call from someone who identified himself as a member of the Ku Klux Klan. "I remember my father telling this guy that if anyone threatens our family he would be waiting in front of our house with a rifle," he said. The threats never materialized.

Both of Harpe's parents had died by the late 1990s, but James Autry and Mary Shaw Harpe had reared their only child with high expectations. Concerning his father, James Harpe said: "He was the only person in my life I was ever afraid of."

As Harpe came of age, he did not disappoint his parents. The thought of going to Graves Springs was a bit unnerving to Harpe because of his past experiences concerning racial issues. Race aside, he was more worried, though, about what the upperclassmen might do to him simply because he was an upcoming tenth grader at Graves Springs. "I remember being scared shitless," Harpe said. He felt a sense of "fear" about all of the horrible possibilities at Graves Springs. This anxiety came to be unfounded. "Nothing really crazy happened in terms of hazing," he said. "But there was a lot of verbal abuse from some of the seniors."

This kind of treatment was given to white and black players alike when we were at Graves Springs. It was a mild form of hazing, all part of efforts to toughen us up. "I don't remember any racial issues at camp," said Harpe, who trained there again in 1973 and 74. The coaches simply worked his "ass off," as they did all the players at camp.

Twenty-five years later, Harpe calls those days at camp "the happiest times of my life." The friendships he established and the lessons he learned there have served him well over the years. "It was a very adventurous time period for me," he said, "and after that first experience at camp, I was always looking forward," to being a part of Albany High football.

At Albany High in 1975, an overwhelmingly white faculty voted to give Harpe the McIntosh Award, the school's most coveted prize to honor a senior for exemplary citizenship and leadership. He was the first black to receive the award named after a noted local family that had begun publishing newspapers by the late 1800s.

On the page in the yearbook where there is a photograph of Harpe receiving the award, these words appear from the sixteenth-century poet Christopher Marlowe: "Honor is purchased by deeds we do . . . honor in not won, until some honorable deeds be done."

After graduating from Albany High, Harpe accepted a football scholarship at Springfield College in Massachusetts. He played football four years there, and earned a master's degree. "Graves Springs was much tougher than football camp in college," he said. Later, Harpe earned another master's from the University of Connecticut, and since leaving Albany in 1975 has lived in New England. By the late 1990s, he and his wife, Virginia and three children were living in Westville, Massachusetts.

In 1985, Harpe joined the Air National Guard and rose to the rank of major. At Barnes Air National Guard Base in Westville, he serves as chief of the military's Equal Opportunity Office. He deals with issues of race, sexual discrimination, and diversity in human relationships. Harpe routinely reflects and "falls back" on what he learned at Graves Springs in regards to his professional life today. "I think about my experiences then all the time." Harpe is employed by the Child Protection Division of the Judicial Court for the State of Connecticut.

"I think the issues of cooperating, of being one team, hard work, discipline, and the fact that nothing comes easy" are all lessons from Graves Springs that he uses today. "There are some nasty things about the South," he said. But there are "positive" things that have occurred there as well. "I was lucky, I had some good experiences in the South."

Larry Hacker was a white teammate of Harpe's who was drawn to Harpe's engaging personality. Hacker reported to camp in August 1974, his senior year, after being convinced to do so by a couple of boys who were already on the team. As a boy, he had played pick-up games in the neighborhood, not organized ball. He had asthma and was "scared to play," uncertain about his own health and ability. Growing up in Albany, Hacker had commonly heard racial slurs from adults; but going to Graves Springs and playing on the same team with Harpe and other black players caused him to develop a different view about race.

Years after he left camp, I asked Hacker what was the most important thing that Graves Springs taught him. His response was immediate: "I guess the first thing it taught me was that what my parents had been saying all these years abut race was just a bunch of crap."

"Who influenced you the most?" I asked.

Again, he didn't hesitate. "James Harpe. He definitely made an impression on me."

Harpe was a starter on offense, and at camp he sometimes would fake a minor hurt or injury during a practice session purposely so Hacker, as a receiver, would have a chance to work with the first offensive unit. Harpe befriended Hacker, and he wanted to see him have a chance to play. "I went to camp, and I was drinking after black guys and living with them," he said. After that experience at Graves Springs, Hacker was determined he "was not going to shut a blind eye to [racial prejudice] anymore." He swam and socialized with Harpe and other minority players. When practice ended he shared Gatorade from the same cooler. "All of us, black and white, dipped from the same cooler after practice."

After the season ended, Hacker's mother had told him that he could plan a team party. She eventually asked her son for a list of players he wanted to invite–but the list Larry gave her included blacks. His mother said she wouldn't allow him to invite black players. In turn, he refused to strike the names of these teammates from his list. "I didn't have the party," Hacker said. "We had a heated argument. I didn't speak to her for a few months."

Hacker said "the biggest regret in his life" is that he didn't play more organized football growing up, particularly not going to Graves Springs when he was in the tenth and eleventh grades. "If I had played earlier, I would have been a much better player."

After high school, Hacker earned a master's degree from the University of Georgia and then a Ph.D. in Agricultural Science from the University of Florida. By the late 1990s, he was part owner of Astrix Software Company based in Edison-Princeton, New Jersey. He is married and has four children, and eventually wants to return to the South, probably somewhere in Georgia. Concerning his experiences at Graves Springs, Hacker said, "I wish I could go back and do it all again."

\* \* \*

# CHAPTER THREE

# A GROUP OF HUSKY YOUNGSTERS

# ONE

Georgia State Road 91 runs north from Albany through flat and fertile land nourished by the Flint River; strip malls and subdivisions mark the same landscape today that gave birth to the Cotton Kingdom in the 1800s. Known locally as Philema Road, State Road 91 crosses Lake Chehaw before passing Chehaw Wild Animal Park. Along the road there are rows of pecan and pine trees, and at times the pines are swayed by the wind in communion with the land and its people. A small white building where black families worship called Greater United Pleasant Green Baptist Church sits several feet off the road. Not far beyond the church is Graves Springs Road, a rural but paved county road lined by houses, several with spacious lots. Alongside Graves Springs Road, there are fields where cotton still grows and cattle graze; when the sky above Graves Springs Road is blue, redtail hawks can be seen circling overhead not far from the Muckalee Creek. And if you're lucky, the sun's radiance will illuminate the predators' tails as they float high above the creek, steady and changing directions with the wind.

Graves Springs Road presses down upon the red earth, the womb that has sustained the natives and conquerors alike. Millions of years ago this land was under saltwater. Large shark teeth have been found in area waterways. Some of these teeth are on display at Darton College in Albany. It's not difficult to imagine as you drive along Graves Springs Road, knowing that the creek is nearby, Indians living here. The Muscogee—or Creek, as the whites referred to them—hunted whitetail deer, grew corn and had festivals honoring their deities to ensure bountiful harvests. By the late 1700s, they started trading with whites who were moving into the area, attracted to the land's fertility. With whites in control, the land and its people would honor another god by the following century: cotton. Blacks, first as slaves and later as sharecroppers, as well as poor whites, planted and picked cotton by hand well into the twentieth century.

Graves Springs is like hundreds of other county roads in Southwest Georgia, cutting through farmland fed by murky creeks that in turn feed the rivers. The Muckalee Creek extends north of Graves Springs into Sumter County, where Andersonville National Cemetery is located. At Andersonville during the Civil War, nearly 13,000 Union prisoners died, many starving to death, at the hands of the Confederate Army. Sumter County is also home to Koinonia Farms, an intentional religious community founded in 1942 by Southern Baptist Minister Clarence Jordan. The word "koinonia" is of Greek origin, and refers to the communal commitment of early Christians. One of the tenets of Jordan's experiment was racial equality, something most other white ministers in the Deep South were preaching against.

The Flint River passes through the heart of Albany and then flows about sixty miles to the southwest corner of the state. There, with help from the Chattahoochee River, which forms part of the Alabama/Georgia border, Lake Seminole was created. This manmade lake, known for its huge bass attracts fishermen throughout the Southeast. This lake is named after the group of Native Americans who by the 1830s had been forced out of the area by white landowners aided by the government. Beyond the lake is Florida and the Apalachicola River, which empties into the Gulf of Mexico. In earlier days along these waters, riverboats moved bales of cotton, while others offered expensive dinner-cruises for wealthy landowners, complete with music and liquor. I have fished and boated on these creeks and rivers, and have seen seven-foot-long metallic alligators that lay along the banks in the summer like creatures from a faraway world.

About an hour's drive west of Albany are the Kolomoki Indian Mounds, built hundreds of years ago not far from the Chattahoochee River. The mounds were one of the first places my parents took me not long after we moved to Albany in 1966. It was years later however, after serious reading about native peoples, that I began to appreciate the beauty of their cultures. These burial sites are a reminder of indigenous people whose world was destroyed by Europeans. It was a world in which man lived in accord with the rhythms of nature, and a world in which the unconscious is recognized as a conduit to primordial messages.

South from Albany, after receiving the waters from the Muckalee, the Flint passes near or through towns such as Newton, Camilla, Hopeful, and Bainbridge. Not far from Bainbridge is Whigham, a rural town where for years locals have conducted what they call a "Rattlesnake Roundup." During this annual event, hundreds of these vipers are caught by expert snakemen. Not in the modern world, but in primal cultures the snake is a sacred animal. Because it sheds its skin, the snake is symbolic of death, resurrection, and renewal.

\* \* \*

In the 1930s, a group of businessmen in Albany—H. E. "Yank" Davis, F. B. "Wig" Wiggins, Maurice Tift, and E. H. Kalmon—helped acquire about fifty acres of property along the Muckalee Creek, isolated in the woods just off Graves Springs Road. The land would be used as a summer football camp to prepare the Albany High School Indians for their regular seasons. The *Albany Herald* began publishing stories referring to these men, who were passionate about football, as the "Four Horsemen," a moniker of biblical origins that gained national attention when associated with the runaway gallop of the famous Notre Dame backfield. The public relations man from Notre Dame, George Strickler, was greatly affected by a 1921 movie starring Rudolph Valentino, which pictured four horsemen representing famine, pestilence, destruction, and death, riding across the big screen. He discussed the "goosebumps" he experienced during the scene with a group of sportswriters, who in turned christened the truly threatening Notre Dame backfield with the "Four Horsemen" nickname.

Albany's own "Horsemen" contributed to the importance of football in their own way, providing annual banquets to honor local football teams at the Gordon Hotel—even during the Great Depression, when many were struggling just to eat. At these banquets, outstanding players were recognized and speeches given by each of the Horsemen extolling the virtues of hard work and good citizenship acquired through football. By the early 1900s, the *Albany Herald* had published a story listing Kalmon as among "Who's Who in Albany." Kalmon was born in Griffin, Georgia, more than a hundred miles north of Albany along U. S. Highway 19. He became a partner in the Albany Produce Company, a wholesale grocery business. Over the years, the local newspaper on at least one occasion referred to the football camp off Graves Springs Road as "Camp Kalmon," but it was more commonly known simply as Graves Springs.

At the 1937 banquet given by the Horsemen, the principal speaker was Russell Lake, athletic director and head football coach at Mercer University in Macon. The *Herald's* headline in connection with the story was a quote attributed to Lake concerning Albany High's head coach Harold McNabb: "McNabb Greatest High School Coach in State."

Lake went on to say this about Albany High football:

> I think that this banquet given annually by these 'Four Horsemen' is one of the finest things I've ever seen four men do . . . I do believe that boys who play football never become a social problem to the community. They learn the creed of sportsmanship on the field and carry it with them throughout the rest of their lives.

According to the newspaper story, Lake went on to speak specifically about the exceptional qualities of local athletes:

> I like every one of your Albany boys who have come to Mercer. They're OK. They seem to have a better-than-average sense of values. No finer boy has attended Mercer than Bill Smith. Besides being one of our best athletes, he is also one of our best students.

Neal Allen and Henry "Bubber" Lawrence, two former Albany High football players, were praised by Lake for being key players at Mercer. Lake continued:

> I think you [the Indians] have made a good record this year in only losing two games . . . South Georgia football has advanced something awful . . . it is one hundred percent bet-

ter than it was ten years ago . . . to you boys not going to college, I urge you to go to work and take with you the things you learned on the football field.

Other remarks after Lake's came from members of the Albany High faculty, J. O. Allen, superintendent of schools, and Albany High Principal B. D. Lee. Finally, according the *Herald*'s story, Coach McNabb gave a short speech thanking the community and the Albany Horsemen for supporting his team.

* * *

Through interviews with players and coaches of that period and newspaper accounts and school board records, it's unclear how extensive the Horsemen's role in helping the Indians build the Graves Springs training site was. It seems likely the Horsemen, either financially, politically, or both, helped in substantial ways to secure the property in Lee County on which the camp was built, especially since the local paper at least once referred to the site as "Camp Kalmon." Today the local school board still maintains a warranty deed signed in 1948—although the Indians started using the site along the Muckalee Creek in 1934, according to former players and coaches—which states that school officials paid three thousand dollars for the land. According to the deed, "said tract contains forty-eight acres, more or less" along the creek, and was purchased from Mrs. Lula Belle Palmer. During the 1930s, the Palmer family operated a general store near the camp where players were allowed to patronize after practice. At Palmer's store, a Coke cost a dime, and players congregated and danced with the girls who came out from Albany to see them.

From Hollywood to Notre Dame to Albany, the mythical image of the apocalyptic Four Horsemen became fixated in the psyche of football fans nationwide by the 1920s; today it remains a compelling image in sports history. This image, one of death and destruction, is appropriate for Graves Springs, where for fifty years, coaches worked players unmercifully in the woods and under a broiling Georgia sun.

* * *

## TWO

By the late 1930s, with the country and Southwest Georgia struggling through the Great Depression, Coach Harold McNabb's Indians were becoming one of the best teams in the state. The *Albany Herald* more than once selected McNabb as one of the community's "Outstanding Sports Figures." After the 1938 season, the newspaper wrote this about its local sports hero: "Hard, conscientious work brought Harold McNabb, the top maestro, an undefeated season. At Graves Springs training site, he looked his prospects over, found three varsity men returning, then - with a groan - buckled down to work."

In August of that year, the *Herald* sent a photographer to Graves Springs, which had been in operation for just four years. The paper ran a photograph with this headline: "Candlelight Coaches' Session." The cutline read: "The candlelight coaches' session is a nightly feature at Graves Springs, where the Albany High Indians began this week their 1938 encampment." Pictured were McNabb, Athletic Director Hugh Mills, and coaches Rupert Langford and Hollis Stanford.

During that season Albany's victories included Sylvester, Americus, Bainbridge, Tifton, and Thomasville. The Indians tied both Valdosta and Moultrie. In post-season play, Albany tied Brunswick from the coast but because of a point-rating system, Brunswick was declared the winner.

In 1939, McNabb and his Indians again went undefeated, but this time they won the state championship outright. Jimmy Robinson's article for the *Herald* said this about McNabb after his team won the title:

Taking a group of husky youngsters to training camp at Graves Springs late last August, Coach McNabb soon drilled his charges in the fundamentals of football. So well were they drilled that the Indians went through an eleven-game season undefeated, toppled Brunswick's Glynn Academy, 27-0, to win the South Georgia Football Association's championship, then climaxed a perfect campaign by swatting the Maroons of Athens High 20-0, to annex the Georgia Class B high school grid tiara. For his work in developing his players, in instilling them with the spirit of sportsmanship and clean play, in turning out what was undeniably the greatest football team in the 25-year-old history of the game at Albany High, Coach McNabb received the staff's unanimous vote as No. 1 sports figure of the year.

Graves Springs had clearly become associated with the winning tradition at Albany High. It was there where coaches isolated their players from friends and family, and concentrated on football for two weeks. In addition, organized sports as part of public education was being locally touted as the means to instill the ideals of hard work and good citizenship into future adults.

On September 3, 1939, just two days after Nazi Germany invaded Poland igniting World War II in Europe, the *Herald* published a photograph and a story describing "Albany's Modern Junior High School Building." The outstanding features of the new school located on Jefferson Avenue included radios installed in each room "enabling classes to hear certain educational radio programs."

But the story went on to focus not so much on academics in connection with the new school, but with athletics. Above the story's lead paragraph was this sub-headline: "Offer Varied Sports Program in Albany's School System . . . Importance of Athletics Realized Here." This principal of the new school was Coach Harold McNabb.

In possibly no other city of its size in the state is there offered more varied or complete sports program than in the Albany public school system. From the high school down to the grammar schools, principals and teachers realize the importance of athletics in a well-rounded program of education, and help the students keep their minds fresh and keen with competitive spirit.

The axiom of "all work and no play makes Jack a dull boy" is well put. Therefore, all types of athletics, ranging from horseshoes, marbles and other minor events to football, basketball, tennis and other major events are open to all students. Particularly in high school, this provides enough activities that almost every student can participate in some activity if they wish.

\* \* \*

Albany High's new football camp opened five years before the above story appeared, and the camp itself was located about ten miles from downtown Albany. The Muckalee Creek and the land the camp sits on were, as they still are today, marked by thick woods of cypress, oak, and pine.

\* \* \*

Buford Collins, who was mayor pro-tem of Albany from 1960 to 1972 and worked for several years with the local Coca-Cola Bottling Company, played at Graves Springs in 1934 and 1935. I first met Collins at his home in Albany in 1999, and throughout our conversation he chewed on, but did not light, a thick cigar. His hair was white but his eyes were lit with the memory of youth and football, and he was quick to smile and laugh as he recalled his days at Graves Springs.

"Mr. Collins, people told me that I need to talk to you to learn about the history of Graves Springs," I said.

"Well, I am the only one still alive," he said removing his cigar and laughing hard.

Collins, who played quarterback at one hundred and eighteen pounds and was the 1935 team captain, played under coach Harold McNabb. "He [McNabb] would line us up to pick sandspurs off the practice field on the first day of camp." But it was impossible to completely rid the field of those irritating sandspurs. As Collins told me, "That field we practiced on grew up in sandspurs." So, at the end of each practice, Collins and his teammates picked sandspurs from one another's bodies before jumping into the creek.

Coaches gave Collins and other players quinine to help prevent them from contracting malaria, but mosquitoes were not the only animals to be mindful of at camp. The Muckalee Creek cuts through miles of swampy bottomland, home to venomous cottonmouths, rattlesnakes and alligators. There were always snakes at Graves Springs. Snakes slithered into the barracks and competed with players for swimming space in the creek, and from the base of the oak trees in which players swung from a rope into the creek, Collins and others could look upstream about fifty yards and see cottonmouths sunning themselves on a cluster of rocks in the middle of the creek. These were the same rocks I saw snakes on forty years later. The summer sun transformed the snakes into metallic, motionless coils. "I remember once when Zeke Bass caught a snake at camp and put it in Vernon Jones' bed," Collins recalled. "It scared the daylights out of Jones, and Ole' Zeke had to get his snake back or Vernon was gonna kill it."

* * *

Before Graves Springs was built, the Indians trained at Cordrays Mill in Calhoun County, twenty miles west of Albany. This was the Tribe's first out-of-town football camp. Cordays Mill opened in 1929, and was in operation until the Indians moved to Graves Springs five years later.

About two months before the 1929 stock market crash that began the Great Depression, Joe Stephens reported to Cordays Mill as part of Albany High's football team. Stephens attended the camp for three years before graduating from Albany High in 1932—the same year Franklin Roosevelt was elected president on the promise of efforts to end the nation's worst economic calamity, including that of work for all Americans. For players like Joe Stephens, there would be plenty of work on the football field.

At Cordrays Mill players slept in a hotel, swam in a swimming pool, and practiced twice daily. "We used to eat good, too," Stephens said, which was a luxury for many folks during those hard times. According to one local sportswriter, "Excellent menus have been served to the boys at regular periods. Fried chicken with plenty of hard toast is the feature dish, but there are plenty of side ones that meet the needs of the ever-increasing appetites" of the athletes. Each generation at Albany High's training camps was fed well, even during the nation's worst economic crisis.

The hotel that the players slept in was described by the local press as being "well-screened and mosquitoes have been conspicuous by their absence." Nevertheless, both Carlton Buntin and Frank Lundy, who spent the summer with the Dougherty County malaria control forces, "have been making a diligent search for the insects." Buntin and Lundy, continued the newspaper story, found few of the dangerous bugs at Cordrays Mill.

The same story addresses the issue of why coaches at Albany High, from the Great Depression until Ronald Reagan was president in the 1980s, left town with their teams for preseason training. "It [Cordrays Mill] is far removed from curious spectators and the coaches will have ample opportunity to give the boys a little inside information without being interfered with by by-standers."

A "little inside information" meant that coaches at both camps (and I know this from my own experiences as a player at Graves Springs) worked players so hard that mothers and fathers shouldn't see what their children were suffering through. The passage to manhood is laced with physical and psychological challenges.

* * *

Several years after I graduated from Albany High I was talking to my brother Jim, who played at Graves Springs in the late 1970s, about our experiences at camp. My mother overheard our conversation. She was clearly surprised to learn the details of life at Graves Springs. After listening for several minutes, Joan Lightle said: "If I had known it was that bad out there, I never would've let you two play." Coaches at both Cordrays Mill and Graves Springs wanted the seclusion that the camps provided so caring and loving mothers—like my own—couldn't see what their "babies" were enduring.

* * *

Stephens and his teammates at Cordrays Mill practiced on a field that was carved out of the woods, just like one would be later at Graves Springs. The practice field was about three-fourths of a mile from the hotel where the players slept and ate, and players usually jogged to and from the field for each practice session. Sometimes while trotting they were paced by coaches S. F. Burke and B. D. Lee, who drove their cars to practice.

Born in Albany in 1912, Stephens was one of five children of Willie and Francis Dow Stephens. The family lived for a few years on the corner of Oglethorpe Boulevard and Jackson Street until 1940, when a tornado destroyed their home. (The storm killed about twenty people.) To support his family, Willie Stephen operated a general store, worked with the postal service, and held various other jobs. Francis Stephens didn't work outside of the home but reared the children, teaching them the ideals of hard work and family commitment. The family was devastated when the stock market crashed and Willie Stephens "lost everything."

"It just broke his heart," Joe Stephens said of his father during the crash. "He never really got over it."

To help his family, Joe Stephens at one point left high school to work at Standard Baking Company on Jackson Street. As were the times he was living, work at the bakery was difficult. Young Joe worked weekends lifting many one-hundred-pound bags of flour. "During one weekend-period I lifted 87,000 pounds," said Stephens, who was in his late eighties when I interviewed him. "Back then Albany was owned and operated" by just a few families who kept wages low and all the good jobs for themselves, Stephens said.

While growing up in Albany, Stephens remembers that during weekends, Pine and Broad Avenues were bustling with blacks, some on horseback, others riding horse-pulled buggies, who came to town to socialize. It was a highly segregated society which Stephens came of age in, but poverty in Albany afflicted whites as well as blacks. Food and wood (to heat homes) were given to families by local charities, but many folks still suffered because there weren't many jobs available, Stephens said. The Depression made athletes hard and resilient, and football players were tempered by times in which simple life necessities were difficult to secure. "The boys then were tougher" than their counterparts nowadays, Stephens said.

"It was the Depression, they [athletes] didn't have automobiles. We walked to school. And the work we did was more physical" than what many teenagers do today. Stephens played fullback for the Indians and never wore a helmet. Rules then didn't require players to do so. Besides, the helmets used during Stephens' era were made of leather. To him the helmets offered little more protection than what nature afforded him. "I had a lot of hair back then," he said. Weighing two hundred and ten pounds as a player, Stephens referred to himself as "a giant back then," because most others were considerably smaller.

Stephens was such a good player that the University of Georgia offered him an athletic scholarship, but he didn't accept; instead, he stayed in Albany and worked to help his family. By 1941 he married Mildred Perry, and they had two daughters, Joan and Margaret.

During the 1930s, he accepted a dare from one of his friends to try out for the St. Louis Cardinals, the professional baseball team that kept a minor league team in Albany during that period. Stephens spent three dollars on a new pair of cleats before reporting to the local field between Society and Tift Avenues for the tryout. After it was over, the Cardinals offered him a contract, and he was to report to their Class B team in Winston Salem, North Carolina with a chance of playing in the major leagues. The pay was to be ninety-dollars a month, but Stephens didn't accept the offer.

"I was making a hundred and ten dollars with the fire department," he recalled. "I couldn't afford to lose twenty-dollars."

After working for the local fire department for some years, Stephens became chief of the fire department at the Marine Corps Supply Base in Albany in 1953. He retired thirty-one years later, and over the years did consulting work in fire safety for local companies like Bob's Candies.

As I spoke with Stephens, he was stretched out in a chair at his home on Seventh Avenue in Albany. Physically he is still imposing, and I could see how his size alone could intimidate players of his era, many weighing fifty or sixty pounds less than he did. Hanging on the wall in his house was a plaque presented to him in the mid-1960s from the Georgia High School Association in recognition of twenty-five years of officiating football games. Buford Collins, who played at Graves Springs in the 1930s, was a part of Stephens's high school referee team for several years.

Although Stephens didn't play at Graves Springs, beginning in the 1940s he regularly visited the new camp to officiate scrimmage games. While at camp, he also met with players and coaches to discuss rules, especially when changes were being implemented. "I felt free to come and go out there," said Stephens, whose younger brothers, James and Willie, both attended Graves Springs and were outstanding players like their older brother. Stephens made a point to tell me he was "free to come and go" at Graves Springs because coaches simply didn't want any visitors until Wednesday evening.

Whether at Graves Springs or Cordrays Mill, camp life did more than produce rugged players and winning teams. "It taught us to think in emergencies," Stephens said, "and it helped me a great deal when I became a captain in the fire department."

In the end, both camps served to pass down the most important lesson a boy must learn. As Stephens said, "It taught you to be self-sustaining."

* * *

# THREE

One of Buford Collins' teammates at Graves Springs was Clem Rakel, who became an outstanding running back for Albany High during the 1930s. Rakel was nine years old when the stock market bottomed, and before the crisis he had saved thirty dollars' worth of pennies in a jar. He deposited the money in a local bank, but after the Crash the bank went out of business and investors lost their money. "I lost it all," Rakel said.

Rakel grew up in Albany as the middle of five children of William and Carrie Marie Rakel. His mother didn't work outside of the home, while his father was superintendent of the Albany Laundry Company for about thirty-five years. "We never did go hungry during the Depression," he said. "We always had food on the table," but "there was no spending money" for the family.

"Growing up during the Depression you learned a lot," Rakel said. "It could make you tough." It was determination and toughness that Rakel took with him to Graves Springs in August 1934, and for the next three years. With few job opportunities and little money for college, Rakel purposely didn't take enough courses one year at Albany High so he could repeat a grade. By 1937 he developed into one of the team's finest players, and the local press published a photograph of Rakel touting him as the "Shifty Indian Runner." Further, the *Herald* said:

"Running with characteristic Indian speed and elusiveness, Clem Rakel, regular halfback of the 1937 Tribe, has distinguished himself this year with performances that have made him a dreaded figure among the Braves' opponents this season."

When Rakel was in the sixth or seventh grade, Coach Harold McNabb took a special interest in him and other young, promising athletes. McNabb typically scouted younger players and encouraged them to work hard and attend Graves Springs when they reached high school. According to Rakel, McNabb took him and a few younger boys to practice and talk football at a country field in Northwest Albany.

"He was the only head coach I knew - he was the greatest," Rakel said. "He could get more out of you than anyone. He didn't fuss or cuss, he just looked at you" when a mistake was made or when a player wasn't doing his best.

During practice, McNabb sometimes scrimmaged with the team. Once, he ran the ball during an offensive play, but the defensive players ran him out of bounds instead of tackling him. McNabb was furious with his team for not tackling him. According to Rackel, "he called us pansies or something like that." McNabb then told the defense he was running the same play again and they had better tackle him hard this time or they would all be punished by doing extra tackling drills. Every player, Rackel recalled, feared the wrath of McNabb.

"He ran the same play and eleven players hit him," Rakel said.

Rakel, who broke a vertebra in his neck during a high school football game, joined the U. S. Navy just a few days before the Japanese bombed Pearl Harbor on December 7, 1941. He spent most of the war years in Brazil, returned to Albany after the war, and worked for more than forty years in the insurance business before retiring.

\* \* \*

By the early 1830s, Connecticut businessman Nelson Tift had begun planning the founding of Albany along the west bank of the Flint River and at the south fork of the Muckalee Creek. Planters and businessmen from other parts of the United States realized that if they removed the Indians from Southwest Georgia and cleared the land, the area would be productive for growing cotton and other crops. And they were right. In 1836, with the final defeat of the Native Americans at Chickasawhatchee Swamp, Albany was incorporated.

In an effort to help prevent white domination of Southwest Georgia, Shawnee leader Tecumseh traveled from the Ohio River Valley to unite the Indians in the South. Tecumseh said this to Indians of Southwest Georgia: "Oh, Muscogees! Brethren of my mother! Brush from your eyelids the sleep of slavery, and strike for vengeance and our country! The red men have fallen as the leaves now fall. I hear their voices in those aged pines. Their tears drop from weeping sky . . . " Nowhere were native peoples able to stop white encroachment.

Before whites moved into the region, the Creek or Muscogee Indians dominated the landscape. Prior to their forcible removal, the Creeks' largest settlement near Albany was called Aumuckalee, which was situated along the Muckalee Creek in present-day Lee County, not too far from Graves Springs. By the early 1800s, Aumuckalee included about one hundred and fifty men, and probably an equal number of women and children. It was just one of the many Indian villages that existed along the creeks and both the Flint and Chattahoochee Rivers.

In Creek religious life, as is the case with other Native Americans, there are constant themes of mankind harmonizing with the spiritual forces that exist in all forms of the natural world, especially rivers and creeks. The creative energy of the universe comes from animals, rivers, and creeks. The Indians who once lived on the Muckalee Creek, where football players would spend a great deal of time by the 1930s, taught that the Great Spirit or "Hisagitaimmisee" was the "Master-of- Breath" of all life. According to Creek mythology, Master-of-Breath lives and moves among all animals in and around the creeks of Southwest Georgia, giving life to the life forms that sustained the Creek Indians themselves.

Creek religious stories were sacred accounts of how water, animal life, and all aspects of the natural world were divine. It was through the telling of these stories that adults in Creek society sought to rear their children in accord with the ideals of their culture.

When football players began living along the Muckalee for two weeks each August, the coaches at camp were instilling in teenagers the ideals of a different culture. Players were not necessarily learning how to harmonize their minds and bodies with the forces of nature as the Indians had done before them. What they were learning and would continue to do so for nearly five decades at Graves Springs was that personal sacrifice, self-discipline, and unity with others for a common purpose are noble traits as one passes into adulthood. Of course, all of this was done to win football games, one of the South's highest callings by the mid-twentieth century. Creek children heard stories from their parents, fasted, and sought direction through visions and dreams—all in efforts to achieve the discipline and guidance needed to live as an adult. While teenagers at football camp were getting the discipline and guidance from coaches like Harold McNabb, who according to his players, "turned boys into men" at Graves Springs.

During high school and when I was at Graves Springs, I listened to a song called "Indian Sunset" by Elton John:

> Now there seems no reason why I should carry on, in this land
> that once was my land, I can't find a home.
> It's lonely and it's quiet and the horse soldiers are coming,
> and I think it's time I strung my bow and ceased my senseless running.
> For soon I'll follow the yellow moon, along with my loved ones.
> Where the buffalo graze in clover fields without the sound of guns.

I played that song over and over in my dad's car using an eight-track tape player. The words were sung in a haunting way, evoking a sense of suffering and loss. But it was not until years later that I began to read about Native American history through books like *Bury My Heart at Wounded Knee* by Dee Brown. Through researching federal government documents, Brown wrote of how the western tribes were defeated after the Civil War by means of starvation, slaughter, and forced removal from their native lands. As an adult, I came to understand just how tragic and real are the words from "Indian Sunset."

\* \* \*

J. P. Champion graduated from Albany High School in 1937, played football for one year and attended Graves Springs. A self-described mediocre player, Champion weighed one hundred and thirty five pounds and played offensive end. "I was the worst pass catcher there ever was," he said. "I made a touchdown against Thomasville High School, it was my one catch all year. The fellow [quarterback] threw it so hard I couldn't let go."

His father, a school board member during the 1930s, believed football camp at Graves Springs would help the younger Champion learn some of life's hard lessons. When Champion was at camp, the coaches awoke the players each morning at six o'clock, and for about forty-five minutes they had calisthenics. Players then had breakfast, rested, and had a two-hour practice session. By late afternoon, the team took the field again for another two-hour session. After each practice, Champion said he picked "sandspurs out of my knees, butt, and everywhere else."

"There wasn't much free time," he said. "And we were all so dang tired after each practice . . . Plus, it was just hot as hell out there." It's always hot as hell at Graves Springs.

After high school, Champion served five years in the U.S. Air Force before he began working in his family's warehouse business. Champion said, "It [Graves Springs] taught me how to take orders and get along with people with different backgrounds."

# FOUR

By August of 1938, Albany High hired a new assistant football coach, Paul Robertson, who had recently graduated from South Georgia Teachers' College in Statesboro. The college today is a university. Robertson was born in Bulloch County Georgia, played sports in college, and in 1935 was catching in Savannah during an exhibition baseball game in which major league baseball's homerun king, Babe Ruth, hit two home runs. Of the two home runs Ruth hit that day, Robertson said, "They started out like a ball but ended up like peas."

For almost fifty years Robertson was employed by the local school system in various capacities. Often addressed simply as "Mr. Rob," he served as the superintendent of Dougherty County Schools from 1971 until his retirement in 1986. Throughout his tenure as superintendent, Robertson was a strong supporter of the camp, and remained convinced that it helped change boys into men. His own son, Paul, whose nickname was "Red Rob" because of his flaming red hair, attended Graves Springs in the early 1970s when I was there.

When Mr. Rob arrived in Southwest Georgia in the summer of 1938 to teach and prepare players for the upcoming football season, he found himself in the remoteness of the woods along the Muckalee Creek. He was totally unprepared for the Spartan life at Graves Springs.

At camp, Robertson and the other coaches no longer slept in the same barracks with the players. Coaches began sleeping in the dining hall, the second of three buildings that were built on the site. They laid mattresses on top of the same tables they ate from. There were other changes, too. By the early 1940s, the original practice field was vacated and a new one was built closer to camp, about a hundred yards or so from the barracks. This was the same field I practiced on thirty years later. The new field shared the most dreaded feature of the old one—sandspurs.

Generally, about forty players attended camp each year during this period. Even though they worked hard during each practice session, some nights the players walked a short distance from camp to a store owned by Noah Palmer. Although the store had been torn down by the time I went to Graves Springs, Robertson said when he coached there the store included a pavilion where music was played and girls and boys gathered to dance and drink Cokes, which cost a dime. Players, who were awakened by the sound of the whistle before daybreak for their first practice, were supposed to be in the barracks each night by nine. Robertson and other coaches conducted bed checks to make sure that the boys returned from the store before curfew. Players liked to slip off to "Uncle Noah's" hoping for a dance and maybe a kiss from the pretty girls, Robertson said. Sometimes the boys missed curfew and "we would wait up and make them run wind sprints," Robertson recalled with a grin. "We used to give them players fits."

Coaches during every era at Graves Springs gave players "fits." The philosophy of the coaches, according to Robertson, continued to be one of isolation; keep the players away from their families and girlfriends, and they could concentrate on football and build a sense of camaraderie. The physical demands the players endured had the coaches convinced that their team was in superior condition to that of the opposition. "Listen, our boys were in shape when we came back to town," Robertson said. "We could whip somebody." Whip somebody they did, winning a state championship in 1939.

\* \* \*

Sam Yarborough played on the 1939 team as well as the teams the following two years; before the start of each of those seasons he went to Graves Springs. At five feet, eight inches and one hundred and sixty-five pounds, Yarborough, whose son attended the camp in the 1960s, played quarterback. "I don't know how we did it out there," Yarborough said. "We had players that had heat exhaustion, but nobody ever died.

But there were times you thought you were going to die." Players of every era always longed for water.

After graduating from high school, Yarborough served in World War II fighting the Japanese. For Yarborough, Graves Springs was tougher than the basic training the government put him through before he entered the war. His experiences at camp, and the coaches he played under, established the foundation needed to endure the war years and later to be successful in his business and family life.

"Graves Springs taught you more about becoming a man out of boyhood," he said. "It instilled in you the will and urge to succeed." Following the war, he earned a degree from Georgia Tech and returned to Albany, where he worked for more than thirty years in the steel and construction businesses.

Like many of the players and coaches who attended Graves Springs, Yarborough recalled the friendships, the episodes of laughter, and foolish behavior.

"I remember once, one of our managers was giving a player a rubdown one afternoon in the barracks," Yarborough said. The player was naked on top of a table in the barracks as the manager rubbed a hot muscle relaxer over the player's aching body.

"About that time another player walked through the door, grabbed the muscle relaxer and rubbed on the boy's bottom," he said.

The player, who was naked on the table and whose rear was now on fire, jumped up from the table and chased the manager out of the barracks.

"That boy, and I can't recall his name, was literally so hot that he ran straight through the door and broke it down trying to catch the kid that burned his bottom," Yarborough said. "The rest of us had a good laugh watching that naked boy run through camp."

There were times to laugh and play practical jokes at Graves Springs, but not when Coach Harold McNabb was conducting practice. Yarborough described McNabb as someone who worked hard on the field making "men out of boys." McNabb's way was that when someone didn't block or tackle properly, he personally used his thick-muscled body to show the player the proper technique. "When he hit you, he hit you hard," Yarborough said. There was only one way and that was McNabb's way, but the other coaches who followed him at Graves Springs were just as uncompromising in how they worked and disciplined their players.

Yarborough, who survived combat, graduated from college, and had achieved considerable success in his business and family life, said of Graves Springs, "It is one of the most memorable - nothing but fond memories - experiences that I ever had. It was a life experience."

\* \* \*

Carlton Bullock, who graduated from Albany High in 1943, played one year of football during the 1942 season, and attended Graves Springs that year. He weighed one hundred and sixty-three pounds and was considered "big but not huge." There was one two hundred pound player on the team, said Bullock, who over the years in Albany has made his living as a professional photographer taking wedding pictures, as he did for Susan and me when we were married in 1986.

"It [camp] would either kill you or cure you" by getting you into top physical shape while establishing a sense of togetherness and pride among players, he said. "I don't remember anybody getting seriously ill from the heat," Bullock said. "We might have had players to fall out from the heat, but they would eventually come to."

For this generation of Albany boys, spending two weeks at Graves Springs was the first time in their lives they were away from home for an extended period. "It [camp] was the first time in my life I had been away from home," Bullock said. "Most people didn't travel in the 1940s the way they do today."

Unless they went to war.

Nine months after the United States entered World War II, the Indians opened their encampment on August 31, 1942. The season's schedule was shortened from the regular eleven games to nine. In order to save fuel as a part of the nationwide war effort, the team canceled some of their away games. Other schools in South Georgia could not even field football teams because so many young men were serving in the military.

On September 9, 1942 the *Albany Herald* reported this from Graves Springs: "The year's first scrimmage was held on the steaming sod Tuesday with only a sprinkling of onlookers, direct result of the tire and gasoline rationing which has cut civilian attendance at the camp about 99 percent."

Albany's team that year included only thirty-five players, the smallest in its "modern history." Locally, there were constant reminders about war, death, and rationing. The *Herald* carried advertisements like those for the Trutred Tire Company announcing that everyone is "working together to save rubber."

At least one year during the war, 1944, the Indians did not go to Graves Springs for preseason training. Probably attributed to the rationing of fuel and rubber, the team stayed in Albany and had its summer camp at Mills Memorial Stadium. After the war ended, Graves Springs would again be the site of the Tribe's encampment for the next forty years.

# FIVE

By the late 1940s, Frank Orgel was a third grader whose family moved to Albany from Columbus, Georgia, about a hundred miles northwest of Albany. He began playing football in Albany as a young boy, and remained intimately involved with the sport for the next fifty years. Orgel's passion for football grew when he and some other youngsters played a football game in Jacksonville, Florida before a crowd of several thousand who were awaiting the start of the Gator Bowl.

As Orgel was approaching his eighth-grade year, his father contacted the coaches at Albany High School asking if his son could attend Graves Springs even though he wasn't an upcoming high schooler. During that time ninth graders were the youngest to attend Graves Springs, but the coaches agreed to allow young Frank to come to camp. At the practice sessions Orgel went through the conditioning drills, but wasn't directly involved in the physical contact among the older and stronger players. Orgel also held blocking and tackling dummies as the varsity worked on fundamentals. He was subjected to the same rites of initiation and hazing that the freshmen endured. Orgel was "scared the whole time" at Graves Springs.

During that August in 1951, the upperclassmen at Graves Springs devised a game in which all freshmen, including Orgel, were made to spit in a small hole in the floor of the barracks. Any boy who didn't hit the mark with spit was immediately whacked on the ass by a varsity player swinging a solid wooden board. These big senior linemen were mighty strong. "I remember staying up all night practicing" by spitting at the hole, Orgel said. However, during the initiation game the upperclassmen positioned a fan, directly over the hole in the floor, that blew air aimed to misdirect the spit being fired at the target. Although he practiced at night trying to perfect his spitting, Orgel got hit with the board several times because his spit missed the mark.

"Let's see if this Orgel boy can hit the hole!" a senior exclaimed.

"Yeah, let's get the young boy! Let's tear his ass up!" said another.

This spitting competition was conducted in the evening after the day's final practice, and not long before the coaches ordered lights out. There were times when Orgel's spit landed in the hole in the floor, but the instances when he missed, he was struck with the board by a hard-swinging varsity player. "When an upperclassman hit you - he hit you hard," Orgel remembered.

After Orgel's first week of camp, he went home Friday afternoon, as did the other players, to spend the weekend with his family. He was supposed to report back to camp the following Sunday afternoon. "I didn't want to go back after that first week," he said. "I told my dad that, but he made me go back." Orgel complained of the heat, the three daily practices, and the hazing from the older players who scared and taunted him. "It was even forbidden to drink water during practice."

He wanted no more football.

But Orgel's father made him go back for the second week of camp, and he played at Graves Springs for the next four years, becoming a standout player at Albany High before graduating in 1956. Orgel probably attended Graves Springs longer than any other player. He played offensive end at one hundred and seventy-five pounds, and was good enough that the University of Georgia offered him an athletic scholarship. He accepted and became a standout player for the university as well.

After graduating from college, he spent two years in the military before signing a professional contract with the Buffalo Bills. While playing, he suffered a broken leg and left the game for good as a player after two seasons.

For thirty years, beginning in the 1960s, Orgel coached at the high school and college levels. His collegiate coaching career included stints with Clemson University, Auburn University, and the University of Georgia. Along the way, he was inducted into Albany's Sports Hall of Fame. By 1996, he returned to Albany to accept the job as Athletic

Director for the Dougherty County Schools, a job previously held by one of my former coaches, Ferrell Henry. Orgel's office overlooks Hugh Mills Stadium next to Albany High School.

Having attended training camp at both the collegiate and professional levels, no camp was as demanding as Graves Springs, Orgel said. At the professional level, and to a lesser degree during college, the camps were more instructional and not necessarily designed to either "make or break" players. Orgel saw players come to Graves Springs but leave before camp ended because they were unable to endure the rigorous treatment from the coaches, the unforgiving heat, and the hazing from upperclassmen.

"When you go out there [Graves Springs] and stay two weeks, you were really something," Orgel said, describing the "prestige" associated with anyone who was able to survive the camp and play for Albany High. "It's a place you can't talk about to a whole lot of people," he said. "If they weren't there they wouldn't believe it."

\* \* \*

In 1957, Albany High School hired a new assistant coach, Gordon Dixon, who was born in nearby Mitchell County just south of Albany. Having recently graduated from Florida State University where he played on the school's basketball team, Dixon taught and coached for Albany schools until 1994. From the 1950s until the early 1970s, he went to Graves Springs as an assistant—probably one of the longest tenures for any coach at camp.

During some of Dixon's time there, the hazing continued and the upperclassmen took the freshmen into the woods and "beat them with a board," he said. It was during this period when some freshman slept in what was called the "Freshmen Inn." Dixon describes this as a "shack" big enough to accommodate just a few boys. The shack was located a short walk up the creek, away from the two barracks and mess hall. I had never heard of the "Freshmen Inn" by the time I arrived at Graves Springs in 1972. It was years later, when I spoke with Dixon and other former coaches, that I found out about it.

Dixon saw the rites of passage or the hazing that so many boys feared. On the first day of camp, each senior selected a freshmen to act as a body servant for the next two weeks. The freshmen were made to wash the uniforms of the seniors, which meant beating the uniforms against the rocks in the middle of the creek then hanging them out to dry. The servants gave the varsity rubdowns, cleaned up around their bunks, and generally carried out any other duties the upperclassmen demanded.

Harold Dean Cook, who played at Graves Springs in the 1950s and was a coach there the following decade, recalled that through this indentured servitude freshmen were even made to fight fellow freshmen. When Cook was in the ninth grade there was an outhouse at Graves Springs. He was told by a senior, who went to relieve himself, to make sure no one bothered him while he was in the outhouse. As Cook was doing his duty as the outhouse lookout, another senior approached with his freshman servant. The other freshman was ordered to fight Cook, and they "tussled" on the ground next to the outhouse.

"Neither one of us got hurt during the fight," he said. "We always did whatever they [seniors] told us to do. We were scared of them."

Gordon Dixon saw lots of boys fight at camp. "Our kids were tough," said Dixon, who was coaching when the team won the 1959 state championship.

Players at Graves Springs dreaded its mental and physical rigors, and nearly everyone thought about quitting. Others left during camp, only to be brought back by their fathers, like Jimmy Ussery and Tom Giddens in 1972. Others who were expected by the coaches to report to Graves Springs didn't show up at all. Dixon recalled one instance when a key player during the early 1960s, Gene "Big Daddy" Watson, didn't report to camp. "Big Daddy" was a senior who weighed well over two hundred pounds and a key player for the Tribe; Dixon was determined to find him and bring him to Graves Springs.

"I drove my truck to Big Daddy's house to bring him to camp," said Dixon. "I talked to his daddy, who said that Big Daddy was already at camp."

"Mr. Watson your son is not at camp . . . and I need to find him and get him there," Dixon told his father, who said his son left for Graves Springs earlier in the day. But Dixon was adamant, saying that he and the other coaches had not seen "Big Daddy." The two men eventually found Big Daddy hiding under his bed, refusing to go to camp. "I put Big Daddy in the back of my truck and took him to Graves Springs," Dixon said.

By the early 1970s, Dixon was named head basketball coach at Albany High School, and he no longer coached football. I played basketball under him during that period. While coaching and teaching over the years, he built a successful local insurance business. His office walls today are lined with pictures of both basketball and football players he coached at Albany High. "It [Graves Springs] was tough on the coaches," Dixon said. "You stayed hot, you stayed nasty, and you got sandspurs in your hands" when you showed players the proper techniques of tackling and blocking. Dixon told me he probably spent more time at Graves Springs that any other previous coach. "I was just happy not to go back," he said.

\* \* \*

# SIX

When I was growing up in Albany, my family's home was on Gary Avenue. Bob Fowler lived just around the corner. By then, Fowler was employed as the purchasing agent for Dougherty County Schools, but earlier he coached at Graves Springs. Born in 1932 in Albany, Fowler was the youngest of five boys, and one of his older brothers, Jim Fowler, was regularly appearing on a national television program called *Mutual Of Omaha's Wild Kingdom*. On the program, Jim Fowler traveled all over the world learning about animals. I watched that show Sunday evenings regularly with my family. I remember as a boy visiting Bob Fowler's house when Jim was there. Jim had brought a cheetah to his brother's house that scared the hell out of my little black dog that followed me around the neighborhood.

The Fowlers' father had been a scientist who was born in the Midwest but was directed by the U.S. Department of Agriculture to do soil research in Albany. His job was to survey land in connection with pecan production. The elder Fowler became attracted to the region's warm climate and purchased a farm outside of Albany. The family still owns several hundred acres of land there today.

"My dad first came down here after World War I," Bob Fowler said. "It took him thirty hours to drive from Indianapolis to Albany," about seven hundred miles.

When Fowler was a boy, his father was transferred by the federal government to Falls Church, Virginia. Fowler attended high school in Philadelphia and then on to Indiana where he enrolled at Earlham College in Richmond, a Quaker school that included about fifteen hundred students. Fowler, at six feet, eight inches and two hundred and sixty pounds, earned fifteen varsity athletic letters before graduating in 1954. After leaving Earlham he returned to Albany, where he planned to farm his family's land. Then sports got in the way.

By 1955 he met and began playing recreational basketball with some of the local coaches, including Albany High School's head football coach Bernie Reid. That year Fowler accepted a job to teach at Albany Junior High School and coach at the high school. In August 1955, Fowler reported to Graves Springs, and would do so through August of 1961.

As with earlier decades, the local paper continued to send photographers to Graves Springs when Fowler was there so that football fans—which were nearly everybody—could follow the team's progress. One such photograph includes the head coach, Bernie Reid, and Fowler, Pat Field, Graham Lowe, and John Tillitski, the assistants. Bob Fowler is in the background, but he's not standing. He has his hands on his knees, and still appears as tall as some of the other men. I can hear those men today as they were getting ready for their picture to be taken: "*Fowler, don't show us up! You're just too damn tall!*"

Fowler said, "They [coaches] told me how tough it was," concerning the living conditions at Graves Springs. "It was tough, rugged, bare bone. But in a sense, it was the highlight of the year—it was just primitive."

Coming from college in Indiana, where basketball was a unifying force in most Hoosier communities, Fowler quickly learned it was football, not basketball, which galvanized Albany and South Georgia. Football games themselves were social events that attracted thousands of people, and local businesses helped support the team. But it was Graves Springs that ignited this annual passion. "Graves Springs was identified with success in football," he recalled. "And it was a badge of honor for the players who survived."

There was always much excitement during the first day of camp. On that Sunday, families and girlfriends would accompany the players to camp in the afternoon, since the start of camp symbolized the preparation needed in order for players to win football games while energizing local folks. There was generally so much emotion during that first night of camp that players often found it difficult to go to sleep, Fowler said. Because of the rowdiness in the barracks throughout the night, coaches called a "midnight practice" in order to calm the vociferous spirits. "We would always get them up at one or two in the morning for calisthenics," Fowler recalled.

During the first practice on Monday morning, there were always some players who became sick because of the strenuous workout; especially those who had done little training over the summer. Players, according to Fowler, eagerly anticipated the traditional Wednesday evening visitation when they could see their girlfriends and family members. Local businesses such as First State Bank provided the evening meal of barbecued chicken, ice cream, and cold Coca-Colas.

Throughout the late 1950s, hazing did continue at camp, although coaches stopped it when they found out about it, Fowler said. There were times when the coaches—who were the ones swinging the belts—made some of the seniors go through the "belt-line" *themselves* in order to punish them for hazing the younger boys.

Fowler's imposing physical presence at camp signaled a challenge to some of the tough, cocky players. He was involved in wrestling matches. At one point on the practice field, "four or five players" jumped on him trying to pin him to the ground. Seeing that the giant had been weakened, others joined the fray. "I was handling four or five, but so many more jumped on me I thought I was going to be squashed," he remembered. In another effort to subdue the biggest person at Graves Springs, a group of players managed to throw Fowler into the Muckalee Creek. They tried repeatedly, but were unable to dunk him under the water. "I was taller than any of the players and they just couldn't do it," he said.

These were successful years for Albany High football; while being undefeated and state champions in 1959, during the next two seasons, according to Fowler, the team recorded eighteen consecutive wins. Graves Springs instilled the physical and mental toughness needed to win, and in doing so "there was a spirit out there that brought the team together," he said.

By 1961, Fowler left coaching and Graves Springs to become purchasing agent for the local school system. He later served fourteen years as assistant school superintendent in Albany. Throughout this period he continued to be involved in athletics by filming Albany High's football games in order for players and coaches to study game films. After retiring from the school system, he became vice-president for the Dougherty County Credit Union, which serves local teachers.

In his mid-sixties, Fowler remained active by playing racquetball regularly at the local YMCA. Over the years I have played basketball with him in various leagues in and around Albany. Once in the late 1970s, while I was an undergraduate student at Georgia Southwestern College in Americus, Fowler joined me and a few other players to form a basketball team. We entered a tournament in Americus, Georgia sponsored by my fraternity. Most of our players were like me in that they were about twenty-years old, while Fowler was twenty years older than the rest of the team and our opponents. With only five players in the championship game, our team was barely beaten by a team from Macon, Georgia. Fowler had to play the entire game, scoring about fifteen points and having as many rebounds. Fowler wasn't just big; he had a beautiful soft touch when he shot the ball, and had great instincts for the game.

"Damn, Lightle, how old is that guy?" my fraternity brothers asked in disbelief after the final game as Fowler came off the court exhausted but satisfied.

Someone else said, "Hell, he's older than my daddy!"

\* \* \*

On September 26, 1963, the *Albany Herald* ran this headline in its sports page in bold, red letters: "Indians Bring 8,000 To Their Feet In 7-0 Thriller." The night before the story appeared, Albany had defeated Columbus High School seven to nothing at Hugh Mills Memorial Stadium.

Playing in that "Thriller" against Columbus was junior lineman Carl Williams, who spent three seasons at Graves Springs. Williams graduated from Albany High in 1965 and then from Georgia Southwestern College, and was hired as an assistant coach at Albany High in 1974. By August 1999, Williams remained a teacher and football coach in the local public schools. He grew up with a mythological image of Albany High football.

"I loved running out on the field on Friday nights with the band playing and people cheering . . . you feel like a gladiator, like a warrior," he said. "It's the greatest feeling in the world." In the Arthurian legends, Sir Gawain accepts the quest for the Holy Grail and leads a life of chivalry; Carl Williams had undertaken his own quest at Graves Springs.

Williams heard the "horror stories" about camp as he finished his freshman year, and was mentally preparing himself for Graves Springs before the start of the 1962 season. There were rattlesnakes and cottonmouth, the oppressive heat, and coaches who were impossible to please. Worse were the varsity, who Williams feared would do unspeakable and humiliating things to him and other sophomores.

Williams came to camp one Sunday in August 1962, and he began to settle in for the night and talk to some of his teammates about what they were confronted with. One of the seniors that year was Sambo Arnold, a defensive lineman who was a hard hitter; coaches expected much from him on the field. That Sunday night before the first practice, Sambo ate about a dozen Jimmy's Hot Dogs, and drank four or five bottles of Coke. (For years Jimmy's Hot-Dogs has been a local favorite, specializing in fast service and spicy chili.)

Before sunrise Monday, the coaches woke up Williams and the other players, who began the zombielike walk to the practice field as the stars were fading from the morning sky. There, coaches put the players through a series of grass drills; players were required to bellyflop on the ground, roll over, stand up, and hit the ground again while quickly moving their legs up and down. During the first few minutes of the drill—*"Faster! Faster! I said Faster!"* Assistant Coach Harold Dean Cook screamed—players were gasping for breath and already covered with sandspurs.

Throughout the course of the drill, Williams saw Sambo Arnold doing something strange. "He started throwing up," Williams said. "All those hot dogs started coming up during the grass drills."

Coach Cook, who himself had been a player at Graves Springs, noticed that Sambo was vomiting on the field. Cook rushed over where Sambo was throwing up and started yelling at him. "Arnold, you're supposed to be a leader!" Cook said berating Arnold, who had eaten all those hotdogs the night before. "You're a senior, look at you, you're supposed to be a man. You're pitiful." he continued.

Cook wanted to embarrass his senior lineman in front of younger players like Williams, but Sambo was determined to redeem himself in front of his teammates and coaches.

"I'll show you I'm a man, Coach! I'll show you I'm man! Coach Cook, I'm a leader!" Sambo said.

"Sambo then reached down on the ground and started picking up the hot dogs that he had just puked up," Williams said. "Then he crammed hot dogs, dirt, pieces of grass, and whatever else he picked up, into his mouth," Williams said. "And he didn't even take his helmet off."

That was Williams' first day of practice at Graves Springs. Afterwards, he realized that those "horror stories" he heard about camp were true. "These people are crazy," Williams said. "I thought to myself 'God these guys are animals out here. And if you're going to survive with the animals, you're going to have be one of them.'"

Williams learned that Graves Springs could make a player do some outrageous things, just like Sambo Arnold.

At Graves Springs there were three practices daily, but the midday practice lasted about an hour and a-half, and it focused only on the kicking and passing games. Players during this session were required to wear only shorts and helmets, not their full uniforms.

Carl Williams was a good defensive lineman, not very tall but stout. He wasn't fast. Because of his lack of speed, he knew he wouldn't be a part of the punting or kicking teams that were given special attention during the noon practices. One year at camp, Williams trotted on the field with the kicking team as he had done previously, but this time he received special attention from his teammates.

"Carl, you sure look good today!" one player hollered.

"You look sweet, Carl!" another said. "I hope you come to my bunk tonight."

Except for shoes and socks and his helmet, Carl Williams was naked.

Coach Harold Dean Cook wasn't laughing. "Williams, what are you doing?" he bellowed. "You make me sick, Williams. I thought you were a leader."

"But Coach, you said helmets and shorts. I got my shorts on," Williams said. He grabbed a piece of his shorts, which were sticking out from underneath his helmet. Unorthodox as it was, he had placed his shorts on top of this head, under his helmet, thereby meeting Cook's dress requirements for the noon practice.

"I hated the noon practices, and I knew I wasn't going to be on the kicking team," Williams recalled. "I was too fat. I remember telling my friends I was going out naked."

For coming to practice naked, Cook punished Williams by not

allowing him to have lunch that day. Williams was made to run extra wind sprints. Later, Cook told Williams that he got one helluva of a laugh out of seeing him running naked on the practice field; nevertheless, he had to punish Williams for not following the rules. Players may relax and joke off the field, but not on the field. The code would be obeyed.

Sometimes players practiced more than the regular three daily sessions. "Midnight practices" were as common as sandspurs, and they were equally hated. If there was loud talking and rowdiness among players in the barracks beyond ten, the time that lights were supposed to be out and players asleep, coaches would call a special session to help the boys settle down.

During Williams' first night at camp in his senior year, some of the players wouldn't stop talking. They started throwing pieces of food in the barracks late at night. "Somebody would throw a banana or plum and you would hear it smack against the wall," he recalled. "We just wouldn't stop laughing even after the coaches had warned us once to be quiet."

Around midnight, Cook and the other coaches had enough of the rowdiness. They blew their whistles and told players to put on their full uniforms and report to the practice field. Vehicles were then parked on the field, and headlights used to provide light so the coaches could see well enough to conduct practice. For the next thirty minutes, the players did grass drills. "But we still wouldn't stop laughing," Williams said.

Cook then told the team to take off running toward the dirt road that leads to Graves Springs Road. This particular road led to a cemetery a mile or so from camp. One player, Seaborn Curry, was running ahead of the rest of the team and off the road and into the weeds. Williams and other players could hear Curry's distant laughter, as if he was having such a wonderful time being made to run and practice at midnight.

As Curry was about to reach the cemetery, he stopped and slowly retraced his steps and ran up to Cook. "Please, Coach, don't make me go through that cemetery," Curry insisted. "I'm afraid of ghosts."

The coaches called off the practice and sent all the players back to the barracks. Williams and his teammates slept well afterwards . . . but they had to get up in four hours for practice.

Williams came to Graves Springs as an assistant coach in August of 1974, the beginning of my senior year. He was as fiery as his red hair, and loved the orange and green of Albany High football. Williams remained a coach and teacher in Albany for thirty years, but Graves Springs changed his life. It allowed him to prove his own worthiness, his own sense of self-discipline. Teammates like Sambo Arnold, Seaborn Curry, and others remain forever fixed on what they meant to Williams.

"You can talk all you want about survival, but I really feel like what Graves Springs taught me was what true friends are all about," he said. "You got hurt out there and you got hit real hard. But there were so many good friends to help you."

\* \* \*

# SEVEN

In the summer of 1963, *Albany Herald* sports editor Gary Phillips wrote a column praising Graves Springs for turning boys into football players:

Football Fever In Air

In two weeks Albany High School's varsity football candidates will be making the journey to Camp Kalmon at Graves Springs for two grueling weeks of practice, getting in shape for the football opener in Savannah with Benedictine on Sept. 7.
This is where the football team is made, the techniques of blocking and tackling emphasized and the spirit of each individual boy made or broken. Beginning Aug. 12 high schools throughout Georgia begin intensive training, some teams opening the season as early as Aug. 31.
Still, the hot summer sun can slow down even the most aggressive guard or tackle, the snappiest pass catchers and the hardest runners. Overcoming the weather is just about as big as teaching a player to overcome a tendency to move before the ball is snapped, to hit the right hole, to block with the proper shoulder and to lock his arms when making a tackle.

The following paragraph in the same column written by Phillips appeared in bold print:

We firmly believe a team is made or broken in summer

camp and in spring practice. These two periods are the most time coaches have to work on fundamentals before getting down to the actual job of trying to set up a winning record. It's the only time they have to devote to an intense practice on fundamentals of the game, which often prove to be the difference in a winning team and an average team.

* * *

"Made or broken." That is exactly what Graves Springs and the coaches there set out to do. To make a player, for example, was to take one who was shorter and weighed less than his opponents and put him through a myriad of physical and mental challenges at Graves Springs. If that player endured, his game performance might well surpass his own perceived limitations. Through sport, as the ancient Greeks had begun to understand centuries ago, a participant may realize the full potential of one's physical, mental, and emotional powers. The meshing of these three qualities can become metaphorical of what the late writer and teacher Joseph Campbell, who was also a track star for Columbia University in the 1920s, called "a peak life experience." Athletic competition is perhaps one of life's opportunities in which these three powers can be realized in full accord.

* * *

Before the opening game of the 1964 season, with Northside High School of Warner Robins, another sportswriter for the *Albany Herald*, Vic Smith, described the toughness of Albany High's team after training two weeks at Graves Springs. Portions of Smith's column appeared in bold print.

> . . . For this is an Albany High School Football team dedicated to the principle that the best team wins and willing to battle anybody to prove it. At least, that is the way these boys impress me.
> **It seems they like their youthful head coach, Harold Dean Cook; they want to give their utmost at all times; they want to be remembered as a team somebody else has got to beat, if**

they are beaten. All opponents they face will have to climb over them - they'll never walk over them. They will never remain prostrate and get trampled. They will not give up and take anything lying down.

They will beat you - unless you can prove without any question of doubt that you are better than they are, and this is going to take some sort of proving. If you prove it, you will have to know that you have been down the hard road - that only "after the fight" did you subdue these kids.

. . . And after these boys finish with Northside, if you can conscientiously lodge a complaint against them or their coaching staff, I will stand quietly at parade rest and let you belt me with all you've got.

Which won't be much.

* * *

Albany High went on to defeat Northside nine to nothing, and despite strong winds and rain from Hurricane Dora, about three thousand—seven thousand fewer than usual—fans saw the opening game at Albany's Hugh Mills Stadium that year.

To Smith, whose columns frequently referred to Graves Springs, players offered their "sweat, blood, and tears" as a rite of passage, a quest for transformational powers. Football is a hard, violent game. Players got hurt and bones were broken. Those players who have been worked the hardest, however, will be the ones who win. "Fundamental for a successful football player is conditioning," wrote Smith, and it was the test-of-fire that the coaches created at Graves Springs to ensure that their warriors were prepared for conquest. Smith continued:

Further, let me tell you: When you come through that two weeks you are ready for anything anybody can throw at you. Further preparation for the season itself will be rugged enough, but by the time the sheep are separated from the goats and when the first game finally arrives all the butting that had gone before will make the counting competition almost like a breather.

Smith was right. Any player who survived Graves Springs realized that the rest of the season was a stroll along the Muckalee Creek with your girlfriend.

\* \* \*

Coach Harold Dean Cook knew how to get every ounce of toughness out of his players, including sophomore Glenn Smith, who came to Graves Springs in August 1965. Smith played two more seasons before graduating in 1968. Smith was born in Albany, where he played youth football. His older brother, Vern, attended Graves Springs in the early 1960s. Their father, Vern Smith Sr., worked for more than two decades with Albany's Recreation Department. I remember the senior Smith from the early 1970s when I coached sandlot baseball for the recreation department. He helped coordinate the program while delivering lunches to the children at playgrounds throughout Albany.

During Glenn Smith's junior year at camp, he became dehydrated at one of the practice sessions. "I don't remember a whole lot about it [the incident], but it was hot as the devil," he said. "The coaches gave me some water and threw me in the creek." Smith recovered, and didn't miss any practices at Graves Springs that year.

Smith was such a good linebacker that he played varsity, not the traditional B-team during his tenth-grade season. He recalled minor incidents of hazing at camp, specifically comedy skits that the young players performed for the upperclassmen. At night, if players weren't quiet when the lights were turned off at ten o'clock, coaches smacked the rowdy players with a wooden paddle or a thick leather strap. The whippings helped players settle down and go to sleep, Glenn Smith said.

Smith was offered a football scholarship at Murray State in Kentucky, but chose instead to marry his high school sweetheart, Romana Patrick, and remain in Albany. I met Smith at Rubo's Grocery Store in Leesburg, Georgia, ten miles north of Albany. Rubo's is one of Smith's twelve family-owned grocery stores throughout South Georgia. He wore a butcher's apron stained with blood while waiting on customers at the meat counter. Our conversation was interrupted for a few minutes when a young man stopped to talk to Smith about deer hunting.

Smith loves to hunt and as I was finishing my interview, I asked if he had any final thing he wanted to say about Graves Springs and Albany High football. He paused for a few moments and then continued.

Sometime near Christmas, after Smith had completed his senior football season, he and two other athletes went rabbit hunting one night. It was after midnight when the three hunters returned from the woods and were driving down Slappey Boulevard in Albany. Slappey Boulevard was popular among teenagers who cruised up and down in their cars, sometimes stopping to congregate in adjacent parking lots.

"It was maybe one-thirty in the morning and we decided to have a smokeout," Smith recalled. A "smokeout," according to Smith, is competition among those inside a vehicle who roll up the widows and light cigars. The object is to determine who will lose by succumbing to the smoke and become the first to roll down a window.

Smith and his fellow hunters continued down Slappey. Finally, they stopped at a traffic light and rolled down the windows after being overcome by the smoke. "When we rolled down the windows - smoke was everywhere - we were parked right next to Harold Dean," Smith remembered.

Coach Harold Dean Cook jumped out of his car and threw his hat down on the road, disgusted by what he saw. Smith and his fellow hunters sped away, but worried that their coach had seen them.

"We knew he was mad," Smith said.

Although Smith's playing days under Cook were over, when Smith returned to school his coach punished him anyway for the smokeout. "I got licks from Harold Dean and he made me run. That's just the way he was," Smith said. There was a way players behaved for Cook— even when they were no longer his players.

\* \* \*

Phil Franklin was born in Nashville, Georgia about sixty-five miles southeast of Albany. Nashville, in Berrien County, is a rural farm community just off Interstate 75, which runs through the center of Georgia and further South carrying millions of tourists annually into Florida. Franklin's father, Vinson, grew up in this area during the Great Depression, and because of those hard economic times, as a boy had little free time for organized sports.

When Phil Franklin was six, his father was transferred to Albany as an employee with Harvey's, a chain of grocery stores in South Georgia. Three years later, Phil—unlike his father before him—was playing organized midget football in Albany.

"He [Father] never pressured me to play," Franklin said. "He always said 'do your best.'"

After playing at Albany Junior High, Franklin reported to Graves Springs as a sophomore in August 1964. He went to camp for three years, and was a premier quarterback and defensive back for the Tribe. At one hundred and forty pounds, he earned a starting defensive position with the varsity his first year at camp. During the regular season that year, Albany beat Valdosta. These were two of the best teams then in Georgia, and the game was played at Valdosta where the Indians secured victory in the final seconds.

Earlier in the contest, though, the Valdosta quarterback was injured and left the game after being hit illegally by an Indian defender. Albany was penalized for the late hit, but Valdosta lost a key player. Valdosta fans became irate because of the illegal hit, and at the end of game they started "cussing us, throwing ice, and hitting us with belts as we left the field," Franklin recalled.

Albany's coach, Harold Dean Cook, was worried about the safety of his team and instructed his players to immediately board the buses for the two-hour ride north to Albany. "We didn't shower, we didn't change our clothes," Franklin said. "Harold Dean told us to keep our helmets on and get on the bus."

Franklin played on winning teams that established their work ethic at Graves Springs. The best was in 1966, when the Indians finished with eight wins, a tie, and one loss. Included in that record was a six-to-nothing win over Valdosta, that year's state champion. Franklin's teammate, Bobby Stanford, who later became a starting linebacker for the University of Alabama, called that game against Valdosta "the hardest hitting game I ever played in and that includes college."

At camp, Cook established the tone for work and sacrifice among his players. Cook himself would get "a bloody nose or lip" while physically demonstrating the proper way to block or tackle, Franklin said. Cook and the Graves Springs regiment aimed to make players tougher than they ever thought they could be. "You better be looking at that man in the eyes when you're talking to him," said Franklin, indicating the respect that Cook expected, indeed earned from his players.

Once, while the team was practicing its kicking game, Franklin forearmed a teammate. On the next play, the player he had just hit clipped or hit Franklin in the back. Following that retaliation, the two started slugging one another with their fists. Cook stopped the fight and made both players to get in the "Bull-in-the-Ring." This was a drill used by coaches, and one which I despised, to develop a player's meanness on the football field, not designed to teach a specific fundamental. Before the drill begins, the team forms a circle and within it the two players hit another until the whistle blows. As the players are going after each other, their teammates yelled out: *Hit 'em! Knock his head off!*

"Cook put us in the Bull-in-the-Ring and we went at it until we couldn't stand up," Franklin said. "You're not going to get hurt unless you take your helmet off." As a quarterback, I was rarely made to get inside the Bull-in-the-Ring. Generally, that was for players who regularly blocked and tackled.

During another instance, Franklin became so overwhelmed on the football field that something unexplainable happened to him. He refused to come out of a scrimmage game after Cook told him to do so.

"During my senior year something happened to me," Franklin said. "I was crazed during one practice. I even jumped down to play tackle and Harold Dean kept saying, 'What are you doin'? Come off the field, Franklin!'"

"I wouldn't come off the field," he continued. "I still can't understand what happened then."

\* \* \*

Dr. Carl Jung, who wrote extensively on the collective unconscious, theorized that all modern humans share some of the same emotions with their primal ancestors. While most moderns are taught not listen to the subconscious, primal man lived in accord with his. Jung lived among and studied traditional cultures. He had this to say about experiences of the subconscious:

> So you see, when you have lived in primitive conditions, in the primeval forest among primitive people, you know that phenomenon. You are seized by a spell, and then you do some-

thing that is unexpected. Several times when I was in Africa I got into such situations and afterwards I was amazed. One day I was in the Sudan, and it was really a very dangerous situation which I didn't recognize at that moment at all. But I was seized by a spell, and I did something I wouldn't have expected, I couldn't have invented it. The archetype is a force. It has an autonomy and it can suddenly seize you. It is like a seizure. Falling in love at first sight is something like that.

\* \* \*

Graves Springs was hard on Franklin but there were moments of laughter and frivolity that he'll forever remember. "We all walked around naked except when we ate," Franklin said.

One year, as naked players were casually strolling around Graves Springs in between practices trying to stay cool, a car was driven down the dirt road that leads to camp. There were girls in the car, but their faces were covered with paper bags. The car sped between the barracks, stopped and turned around in a cloud of dust and headed back down the dirt road away from camp. The girls, no doubt laughing and screaming all the while, saw several naked players. "Hey, baby come back," the boys shouted as the car sped away. "Please come back and see us." But they didn't.

"To this day I don't know who was in that car," Franklin said.

When his playing days were over at Albany High, the local newspaper bemoaned his absence in August 1967. One columnist said this in describing the team: "There is yet a quarterback in the class of Phil Franklin, the complete player who could pass and run with the best at his position and was a deadly defensive man."

After high school graduation, Franklin had scholarship offers from two small colleges in South Carolina. He chose instead to try out for the University of Georgia's team in Athens. He played freshman ball there before returning to Albany, and by 1971 he earned a degree from Georgia Southwestern College in Americus, not far from Albany. He then began working for a local bank. Having remained in the banking business since, by 1999 Franklin became a vice-president for Bank America. His office is in downtown Albany near the Flint River.

I met Franklin in the early 1980s, as we were regularly playing pick-up basketball games at the YMCA. He was a tough competitor on the court, and over the years I have followed closely his success in the banking business and his involvement in community projects like Chehaw Wild Animal Park, just a few miles from Graves Springs.

"Graves Springs and football taught me tenacity," said Franklin. "It carried over to the business world."

* * *

# EIGHT

Tommy Aldridge, who graduated from Albany High in 1967, spent three seasons at Graves Springs and was one of Franklin's teammates. Aldridge and his family moved to Albany from nearby Sylvester when he was in the second grade. He went to Albany Junior High, and played football there while winning the admiration of Franklin and other teammates.

"Tommy was one of the most determined athletes I knew," Franklin said. "He won a sit-up contest in junior high . . . I think he did six hundred."

"I don't remember exactly how many I did," Aldridge said. "It was several hundred. I did so many that I rubbed blisters on my back."

Playing offensive guard at one hundred and seventy-five pounds, Graves Springs toughened players like Aldridge, who would have to block much bigger opponents. "The things we did at camp were tough," he said. " . . . practicing when it's a hundred degrees, hitting one another all the time. The drill I hated the most was when you had to stand still and let somebody run up and tackle you."

Those who played sacrificed a great deal. That was simply "the price you paid" to be on the team, Aldridge recalled.

He grew up one of three children in a family that taught him early lessons about hard work and sacrifice. The examples were set by his parents, Henry and Lucille Aldridge. His mother worked at a local factory, and his father was a butcher. They didn't push him into sports, but they were there to support him. "They were great providers," he said. "My parents sacrificed a lot . . . I thought everybody had parents like mine."

While playing for the Indians he had two operations, one on an ankle and the other on a knee. Since high school, that same knee has had four additional operations. Once an avid runner, Aldridge is unable to do so now because of the damage done to his knee.

Aldridge has been married to his high school sweetheart for thirty years. They have three daughters, and since leaving high school he has earned both a degree from Georgia Tech and a master's from Valdosta State University. After working for BellSouth for twenty years, he founded his own company in Albany, Select-Tel. The company deals with network integration and computer hardware.

Of Graves Springs, he said: It taught that "you can do a lot of things you didn't think you could."

\* \* \*

During the 1960s, few players who went to Graves Springs were tougher than Bobby Stanford. He was a linebacker who, although he had knee surgery in high school, went on to a promising career under Coach Paul "Bear" Bryant at the University of Alabama. Sports ran thick, like the Bear's Southern accent, in the Stanford family.

Bobby's father, Hollis Stanford, was an outstanding basketball player at Mercer University in Macon, Georgia. After Hollis Stanford graduated from Mercer, he started teaching and coaching. By the late 1930s, he was Albany High's head basketball coach and assistant football coach, and during this period he coached at Graves Springs.

The Stanford family even found romance among the sports they played. Hollis met his future wife and his children's mother, Francis Weatherly, at a basketball game in which she was playing.

Bobby Stanford grew up playing sports and hoping to make it big someday. His father encouraged him and his older brother, Johnny, to play hard, and he guided them along the way. Hollis wasn't pushy with the boys when it came to sports, not overbearing like some fathers might be, especially the ones who want their children to become the athletes they failed to be.

"We were never pressured to play," Bobby Stanford said. "All Daddy required us to do was our best."

Bobby Stanford always did his best on the football field. Hollis Stanford left coaching for a job with Bobs Candies, and would serve on the board of education. During this time he filmed Albany High's football games so coaches and players could learn about the good and bad that happened on the field. Hollis had earlier coached with Harold McNabb, and the two men developed a close friendship over the years. For instance, Stanford and McNabb slept at Graves Springs during the weekends to ensure that the players' belongings were secure when they went home to see their families between the two weeks camp was in session.

Harold McNabb became Bobby Stanford's godfather. Young Bobby Stanford was becoming enamored by men like his father and godfather. These were men who worked harder than anyone else to become better than the rest. This was the generation tempered by the Depression and world wars: "Sacrifice son . . . you've got to work hard. No one gives you anything in this world . . . keep working hard, always do your best."

When Bobby was a boy, and not yet in high school, he visited Graves Springs regularly to see his father and McNabb, and he saw the big boys working hard under an unforgiving sun. Three practices a day for two weeks? Of course these boys can handle that. They better be able to endure; their fathers could do that and much more. Besides, out here at Graves Springs these boys would soon be men. Growing up, Bobby came to believe, and the community supported it, that there was something mythical about football. He wanted it, and one day he would have his chance.

By August 1965, at less than a hundred and forty pounds, Stanford began his first week as a sophomore at Graves Springs. "I was scared to death," he recalled. He was scared like every boy who went to Graves Springs for the first time, including myself.

Unlike my own experience, when Bobby Stanford went to camp the varsity had its own special way of welcoming the new boys. He and other sophomores performed skits to appease the upperclassmen, and they were systematically paddled hard on their backsides by big, strong seniors using wooden boards. But when it was over "it wasn't so bad," Stanford said. That was simply what he had to endure to be on the team he had been dreaming about for so long. To Bobby Stanford, the boy who was determined to fulfill his dreams, the hazing from older players and merciless coaches couldn't run him away from Graves Springs. He played under Harold Dean Cook, who coached hard like baked Georgia clay. The game was brutal, so the coaches were too. Bobby Stanford was willing to make the sacrifice, and he respected Cook.

The work at camp was so demanding and the conditions so primitive, players experienced dehydration because the coaches wouldn't give them water during practice. Of this, Bobby Stanford said, "It's a miracle that somebody didn't die out there."

Bobby Stanford went to camp for three years. By the time his senior year began, he was sixty pounds heavier and one of the most feared linebackers in the state. In his last two years at Albany High, the Tribe won sixteen games, losing only three. In 1966 the Indians beat Valdosta, a state powerhouse, in a game which Stanford called "the hardest hitting game" he had ever played in, including college. Big-time college recruiters came calling, and Stanford eventually signed with the University of Alabama.

By the time Stanford was a freshman at Tuscaloosa in 1968, Paul Bryant had coached for more than twenty years. He was well known nationally, and idolized in the South. Bryant had already won three national championships, and had gone undefeated in 1966. Stanford had been recruited by others schools, but the Bear won out.

Despite his knee injuries from high school, Bobby was making his mark early in Tuscaloosa. After one freshman game, the *Birmingham News* reported that "Bobby Stanford of Albany, Georgia made several jarring tackles" leading the Crimson Tide defensive charge. That news was no surprise to folks back home in Albany, who had watched Bobby Stanford play ball.

Bobby loved the "Bear," who was quickly realizing he had made the right choice in signing Stanford. The following year, Stanford earned a starting linebacker position with the varsity. Nothing is bigger in the South than Alabama football. To those in Alabama and for many throughout the South, Coach Bryant was no mere man, but lived in the mythological realm of heroes and gods. Now Bobby had become a part of all this. All of Bobby Stanford's hard work and his struggles at Graves Spring had come to fruition.

In the opening games of the 1969 season, Stanford had seven tackles against Virginia Tech. But after that year it was never the same for Bobby Stanford; a series of knee operations forced him to miss the next two seasons.

Because of the severity of these injuries, he never regained the physical form that earlier allowed him to play with so much drive and promise. Yet he didn't quit, even through all the physical pain and the anguish of not being able to play like he once had. During the 1972 season, as a sign of respect, he was selected as a team captain against Southern Mississippi. He was able to play tackle in that game, but not linebacker.

On October 26, 1972, after I had finished my first year at Graves Springs, the *Tuscaloosa News* attributed this quote to Stanford concerning that game: "I just got tired of watching from the stands and asked Coach Bryant if he was willing for me to try to play in the offensive line. He agreed only if I got my doctor's permission. I'm happy to play as much as I do."

There's no denying through his words that the love of football then transcended the visible and invisible worlds of Bobby Stanford. In the face of great physical pain, he was willing to do almost anything to play again. His collegiate career ended in 1972, with Alabama going ten and two. The following year the Crimson Tide was again national champions, posting an eleven-and-one record.

It was serious injuries that likely kept Bobby Stanford from becoming then one of the best linebackers in the Southeastern Conference. It certainly was not heart or lack of desire, both of which burned deep inside of him as they do in every remarkable athlete.

\* \* \*

Stanford played at Graves Springs when it was going through desegregation. He was no different from other white boys in Albany, going to segregated schools and living in segregated worlds. But at Graves Springs, 1965 saw the arrival of Grady Caldwell, the team's first black. Other blacks followed when Stanford was at camp, including John Murphy, the first black to play football at Albany Junior High. Stanford called Murphy a "fine man" whom he got to know well.

"Athletics evens things out," Stanford said in regards to race and other personal differences. "It doesn't matter who your daddy is." What matters is how hard you hit and run.

Bobby Stanford was at the University of Alabama when Coach

Bryant broke a longstanding tradition by recruiting black players. One of the first blacks to play for the Crimson Tide was John Mitchell, who became Stanford's roommate. When I spoke with Stanford not long ago, he showed me a photograph that was taken at a reunion with his former Alabama teammates. Mitchell was the only black in the picture along with Stanford and a few other white players.

As a boy, Stanford said that he was "totally oblivious" to the civil rights marches in Albany. Moreover, he "didn't have a clue who Martin Luther King was . . . and didn't care." But by the time he had gotten to the University of Alabama, Bobby Stanford was a part of something bigger than just football.

After my senior season in 1974, my team had its annual banquet at Albany Junior College, which is today called Darton College. The guest speaker was John Mitchell, Stanford's former teammate at Alabama. Stanford gave the introduction for Mitchell, but I don't remember a word either one of them said. I was so nervous that night, especially when I got up to speak for a few moments about Head Coach Cardon Dalley and our team. I stumbled out a few words, shaking through each syllable.

Today, Bobby Stanford lives in Albany, not far from Albany High School. He helps manage a local greenhouse, and remains an active Alabama alumnus by scouting high school players in South Georgia for the university. Over the years, he has worked to promote Albany's Sports Hall of Fame. I was speaking with Stanford in his office at a local landscaping company when I noticed a black-and-white framed photograph hanging from one of the walls near his desk. The picture was taken at a hunting club in Green County, Georgia in the early 1980s. It included two people: Coach Bryant and former Auburn University coach Pat Dye. The Bear didn't live much longer after the picture was taken. In the photograph, the Bear looks dignified and confident. They're sitting around a table relaxing and no doubt talking about hunting and those glory days along the sidelines.

Bryant knew that if his players had total determination like Bobby Stanford, that kind of character would serve them well no matter what they did with their lives. "When you're thirty-five and you got the ranch mortgaged and your children need clothes and the banker turns you down, and you drive home and your wife has run off with a drummer . . . by God, you better know how to fight by then!" Bryant once said.

"He was not going to sacrifice principle to win," Stanford said.

Stanford took to the University of Alabama in 1968 the same flaming desire that he had developed three years earlier at Graves Springs. Of the camp on the Muckalee, he said, "It teaches you not to quit."

\* \* \*

# NINE

Paul Duffy, whose first year at Graves Springs was 1968, weighed about one hundred and seventy pounds while playing defensive back and occasionally quarterback. Duffy's father, Ed, was from Lynn, Massachusetts. His ancestors were Irish immigrants. While stationed at Turner Air Force Base in Albany, Ed married Janie Sheffield, from Colquitt, Georgia. Paul grew up in Albany playing youth football, always a tough hitter, and was coached by his father who constantly encouraged his son to play hard. Harold Dean Cook said that Duffy "loved to hit people," giving him one of the highest accolades a coach could afford a Graves Springs player. His aggressiveness on the field came to epitomize the Irish saying, 'Is this a private fight or can anyone get in it?'

Approaching the first night of camp in August of that year, Paul Duffy begin to have some frightening thoughts based on what older players had told him about Graves Springs. Like those before him and those after, he was just plain scared.

"My first night in that son-of-a-bitch, I was scared to death," Duffy recalled. "I had this gut feeling that we were going to get it."

As it turned out, Duffy and the other sophomores did get it.

On Sunday evening, Duffy's first day at camp, upperclassmen made the sophomores get naked and form a line in the varsity barracks. The tenth graders were walked in a single-file procession as upperclassmen used a long stick to rub "Atomic Bomb," a muscle relaxer that elicits a concentration of heat, on their testicles. After this warm-up, the initiation rites continued when varsity players smeared the underclassmen with ketchup, mustard, fruit, and other foods.

Other welcoming activities included the "white elephant." This event occurred when an upperclassman would take some white athletic tape, stick it to the nose of one sophomore and then take the other end of the tape, two to three feet long, and stick that to the naked ass of another tenth grader. Then the two, who were now connected by tape, crawled around in the dirt together for as long as the seniors required them to do so. In order to complete the "white elephant," the tape must not come undone before one of the seniors makes them stop.

Next, some of the tenth graders were forced to swallow tobacco juice while others performed comedy routines or skits while they were naked. If the seniors didn't respond with laughter as they watched the skits, they made the naked comedians continue their acting until it evoked laughter. All of this in the name of Graves Springs football.

Duffy even suffered through the belt-line. "They [the varsity players] would pop the shit out of you with those belts," Duffy said.

Duffy and the other sophomores were marched naked up to the practice field, where varsity players poured down their backsides an ointment normally used to treat sick horses, and according Duffy, "It burned like hell."

Finally, the players were instructed to walk single-file to the creek and jump in. The baptism, with the varsity players acting as high priests, concluded the ritual.

Welcome to Graves Springs.

* * *

David "Tex" Wall, a rising junior who played linebacker, was watching Duffy and the other sophomores catching it from the seniors. He couldn't believe what he was seeing. Wall was born and grew up in North Carolina, but had recently moved with his family to Albany from Texas, where he lived for the previous two years. "When I got to Albany everybody just called me 'Tex,' " he said.

Wall played football in Irving, Texas, but experienced nothing remotely comparable to Graves Springs. Initiation-night at Graves Springs in 1968 was something Tex will never forget. "I thought the seniors might get me because I was new. But they didn't," he recalled. The seniors wanted Duffy and all the other tenth graders.

Wall didn't participate, but he watched this "terrible thing" unfold that Sunday evening. He saw a group of seniors chasing a "big heavy kid who was naked" through the camp and toward the creek. "The kid tripped and disappeared from sight," Wall said. "It was like a comic event." He saw some sophomores hiding in the showers and others—who were naked—being chased all over the camp. "I saw one guy hiding behind a toilet and I remember seeing him and saying 'this was out of control.'" The initiations "just terrified some of these guys like Duffy," Wall said.

Wall went to Graves Springs his senior year, but didn't confront any of the extreme hazing that occurred in 1968. He was a standout player for the Indians for two years, and signed a scholarship with the University of North Carolina at Chapel Hill. He played for only one year before quitting after a teammate collapsed on the practice field and eventually died because of being overworked and not given any water. After that player's death, Coach Bill Dooley gave the team water during practice. "They treated us like a commodity and football was no longer fun," he said. But Graves Springs and Albany High was different. "I remember it [Graves Springs] as being fun. It was a bunch of guys playing a game . . . that's fun."

Wall earned a journalism degree from Chapel Hill in 1974, then spent about ten years in New York City working as an actor. During this time he had some small parts in Hollywood movies including *All That Jazz*, *The Jazz Singer*, and *Kramer Vs. Kramer*. From New York he moved to Seattle, where he operated a bar for a couple of years before working in the newspaper business. By the early 1990s, he had moved to Lenoir, North Carolina, where he and his wife, Elizabeth Bruce, bought an advertising agency called E. B. Wall and Associates. In 1990, David Wall published a novel, *One Cried Murder*, which sold about two thousand copies. He continues to write, and hopes to have more of his work published. "I still hold the view that I can tell a good story."

Wall returned to Albany only a few times since he graduated from Albany High in 1970, but his two years at Graves Springs, located "in the middle of bumf—," are fond memories of boys being on a team, swimming naked in the creek, and having fun. "I don't remember talking to anyone in football that had that experience," Wall said. "It was unique to my experiences and still is."

\* \* \*

Ferrell Henry was born in Miller County, Georgia, not far from Albany, and graduated from Florida State University in 1964, where he was a tough defensive football player. In that year, as part of his student teaching duties, he helped coach Albany High's traditional spring practice in preparation for the upcoming fall season. By that summer, Henry had accepted a position as an assistant coach at the school.

Up to that point in Henry's life, he had played a lot of football and had a passion for the game. But he was unprepared for Graves Springs. "I was totally amazed at it," he recalled. "It was the most controlled and concentrated" and "mentally challenging" form of football that he had ever been exposed to. The isolation, the heat, and the general living and playing conditions at Graves Springs were much more demanding then what he had experienced as a high school and collegiate player.

Henry coached at Albany High for the next two years, left to take a coaching job in Florida, then returned to Albany High in 1968 as an assistant coach under Harold Dean Cook. By 1970, after Cook accepted a job as headmaster for a private school, Henry became Albany High's head coach. He had the job for the next four years until resigning to accept the head coaching position at Crisp County High School. Henry returned to Albany in 1984 and became director of athletics for the entire Dougherty County School System, where he worked until his retirement in 1996. During the summer of 1999, he was inducted to Albany's Sports Hall Fame in recognition of his contributions over the years in athletics.

Philosophically, much has changed concerning the coaching strategy at Graves Springs compared with that of yesterday. "We thought giving water during practice was for sissies," Henry said. "That was just the sacrifice you made to be an athlete then." Henry sounded almost apologetic as we talked about the way in which the camp was operated, fully realizing today just how dangerous it was.

One year at Graves Springs when Henry was an assistant coach, one of the players because of the heat and lack of water went into a "spasm," but later recovered. "We were lucky then" that throughout the history of Graves Springs no one died, Henry said. The whole concept of training has changed today "for the better." Players today are generally given generous water breaks to replace the body's fluids that are lost during practices. He said this about Graves Springs:

> I had some real good kids, who worked hard out there. And they came from good families. At Graves Springs they learned discipline and mental toughness and a lot of my players have gone on to do good things with their lives. What they learned at Graves Springs has helped them in whatever they've done with their lives.

\* \* \*

One of Henry's players, Brad Oates, learned things at Graves Springs that carried over into college football, and then on to professional teams as well. Oates graduated from Albany High in 1971, and accepted a scholarship from Brigham Young University. He was a defensive lineman. He then played professionally from 1976 to 1984. In addition to the Green Bay Packers, he played with the St. Louis Cardinals and Detroit Lions. Oates' younger brother Bart, who attended Graves Springs in the late 1970s, played for the New York Giants.

Brad Oates, meanwhile, played football at Westover High School in Albany in the late 1960s. He went to football camp there, which was conducted at the school where players slept in the air-conditioned gym. After Brad's junior year, he was rezoned to attend Albany High School. Before summer camp began at Graves Springs in August 1970, Coach Henry visited Brad at his house and welcomed him to the team. Brad was apprehensive about leaving Westover for Albany High during his senior year. The six foot five, two hundred and fifteen pound upcoming senior was going to be even more apprehensive when he reported to Graves Springs.

"I was completely shocked by the conditions at Graves Springs," Oates remembered. "Frankly, after Graves Springs there wasn't anything in college or pro ball that I experienced that even comes close. You never think you're going to make it at camp," he continued. "I remember as a player out there praying for little things, like practice to end early."

At Graves Springs, Oates found himself quite a ways from the air-conditioned gym and indoor plumbing of Westover High School's football camp. During my first conversation with Oates about his experiences at camp, more than once he used the word "isolated" in reference to Graves Springs being in the thick of the South Georgia woods.

"Everybody thought about quitting," Oates said. "The problem was you were so far out. How were you going to get back home?" Players could either swim for miles or walk for miles to get back to Albany. "It was just two weeks of absolute hell," he recalled.

Oates, who was inducted into Albany's Sports Hall of Fame, was working as a bank executive in Dallas, Texas by the late 1990s. Some years back, he traveled to Albany with his brothers, Bart and Barry, who both attended Graves Springs. They set out to find the camp, but were unable to because there are several dirt roads that intersect with Graves Springs Road and no markings or signs to indicate which one leads to the sight.

Oates called it "barbaric" when describing the fact that coaches didn't allow players to drink water during practice, and that "clearly we had players with heat exhaustion that continued to be pushed, but you learn to go through anything, and I think you walk away with a sense of pride when you survive Grave Springs."

\* \* \*

## CONCLUSION

## SHOOT MAN, THAT CAT WAS TOUGH

One Sunday in the summer of 1999, I took my children to visit Graves Springs, but I couldn't find it. I wanted to show David, ten, and Dylan, six, the camp because they had heard me talk about it so much during the last few years. During the fall and winter we frequently drive down Graves Springs Road on our way to a site on the Muckalee Creek, not far from the camp, where we built campfires and slept out with friends. Each time we traveled the road, I'd say to them, "Over there's where Daddy went to football camp," as I would point toward the camp. They were never too impressed.

There are no markings today along Graves Springs Road to indicate which dirt road to turn onto to reach the old camp. That Sunday with my children, I turned down the wrong dirt road and was unable to locate the camp. It was as miserably hot as it was when I practiced at Graves Springs, so we went home and I told them we'd try another day to find it.

Even if I located the right spot along the Muckalee Creek I wasn't certain if the three buildings, on the site when I played there, remained standing. A few days later, I telephoned Harold Dean Cook, the former Graves Springs' player and coach, and asked if he knew how to get to the camp. Cook said yes and agreed to take me there, then told me he had visited the site recently himself.

I picked Cook up at his house, and we drove in my van along Graves Springs Road; he pointed out the correct dirt road that leads to the camp. The road runs less than a quarter mile past a vacant field, and shrinks to a footpath near a thicket of oak and pine trees. "We just have to walk a bit up this trail, then we'll be there," Cook said.

We cut through high weeds, and I looked closely at the ground, concerned about the cottonmouths and rattlesnakes. The land was unchanged with its dense underbrush and the sounds of crickets and other small animals. The sky was cloudless, and the sun as mean and unforgiving as it was for every practice twenty-five years earlier.

As we got closer, I could see the varsity barracks, the "fancy one" with indoor plumbing and made from cinder-blocks, and as the trail turned right several yards from the creek, the two wooden buildings—the sophomore barracks and the mess hall—came into full view. Built during the Great Depression, these two structures had fallen down and were piles of rotting wood and tin. I remembered the punishing flood that hit South Georgia in 1994, when people were killed and hundreds of homes destroyed while the creeks and rivers rose to unimaginable levels. The two piles of debris where I once ate and slept came to rest along the line of trees on the bank of the creek. If not for being stopped by the trees, pieces of the fallen barracks would've been swept downstream, far away from camp.

I stared hard at the dark pieces of wood, shattered pieces of cement-block steps, and sheets of tin, all of which lay mangled together. On the wood there were red, blue, and white markings where players, covering five decades, had written their names. I couldn't clearly read any names, only an occasional letter or two. Looking at the pile, I remembered the coaches complaining because we used to relieve ourselves next to the backdoor of the barracks. We were too tired to walk to the woods to go to the bathroom.

Cook and I walked from the tumbled-down barracks to the creek, and we stood next to the oak tree where for years a rope was tied to a large branch and players swung out onto the water after each practice. Cook looked straight up the tree in the hot, glaring sun and said. "We used to swing out from this tree on a rope," he said.

"Coach, we did the same thing," I said, looking up the tree and then out over the quiet, murky water. I looked upstream about fifty yards and saw a cluster of rocks in the middle of the creek, the water gently sliding over them like a song, eternal and soothing. I saw no snakes atop the rocks like I did when I played at Graves Springs, even though it was a perfect day for the cold-blooded cottonmouths to be out sunning themselves. It was on those rocks were I stood with my teammates and beat our dirty uniforms and dipped them into the creek.

"Hey, hey who are we! The One-Eyed Pirates of the Muckalee!" We sang it loud with jock straps over our heads. Naked, clean, and happy, we walked and sang our way back to the barracks, soon to practice again.

We then walked from the creek into the varsity barracks. The faded white paint on the barracks still revealed names and jersey numbers written by players wanting to leave their marks at Graves Springs. Inside, mattresses and the bunks we slept on and played poker on were scattered about. Dirt and thick dust covered everything inside. The smell was of musty sweat, the same that covered my uniform after the first day at camp. The camp hadn't been used in about fifteen years; at the front door of the barracks were charcoal remains of a small campfire, maybe lit by young boys spending the day along the creek, fishing and laughing and talking about girls. The wooden beams of the barracks remain covered with names of players and the years they attended Graves Springs. There were names of a few girls, and short stories about how much they were liked. I saw my brother's name written in bold, black letters: "**JIM LIGHTLE CLASS OF 79.**" I saw other names from other years, including Paul Duffy, Wes Westbrook, David McClung, and Ricky Spence. I thought about walking up to the practice field that day, but I didn't because it was so hot. Instead, after a few minutes of looking and talking in the barracks, Cook and I went home.

* * *

Not long after Coach Cook took me to Graves Springs, I telephoned Leonard Lawless and asked him if he wanted to visit the camp. "Man, I've been trying to find the camp!" Lawless said. Over the years, he had driven down Graves Springs Road a few times trying to find it but could not.

When we got to camp, Lawless looked intently at the pieces of old wood and twisted metal that was once our tenth-grade barracks. We walked near the creek and into the varsity barracks. "I can still hear the music out here," he said. *You must been down in the Texas town 'bout that shack outside of LaGrange.* "We always listened to ZZ Top out here," he continued. "Don't you remember?"

"Yeah, man, the music was everywhere," I said.

Lawless looked at the names on the walls of the varsity barracks as if he was a famous archeologist on the verge of a monumental discovery. "You remember that time Ferrell ran our asses off at midnight for raisin' hell in the barracks?" he said. He was referring to the night in 1973, when Coach Ferrell Henry made the team run wind sprints at midnight because a few players were talking loud, laughing, and throwing food in the barracks when they should've been asleep.

Lawless was excited to be at Graves Springs, more so than he was when he arrived there as a player in 1972. That was a time of dread and uncertainty, and the memories were racing through him, as hard as he used to run the football.

"Hell, yeah, I remember that," I said. "I thought we were gonna die that night."

"We could've died any time out here," he replied.

We walked up the trail that leads to the practice field; it was awfully hot that day, like it always was at camp. About half of the field was overgrown with pine trees, most about twenty feet tall. At one end of the field, which was thick with trees, there used to be a metal sign that coaches made us touch as we ran laps during practice. "I'm gonna find that sign," Lawless said, disappearing into the trees. He came out about ten minutes later, unable to find the sign.

"Man, let's get out of here," I said. "It's too damn hot."

"Yeah, it reminds me of practice," Lawless said.

As we were walking to my van, Lawless saw something in the weeds not far from where the mess hall used to be. I saw him walk cautiously, looking down with each step to make sure he didn't step on a snake. He picked up a plastic plate, like the kind we ate our meals on at Graves Springs. He was excited when he picked it up and said, "I'm taking this home with me."

No longer the famous archeologist, but he was now a seven-year-old boy full of excitement on Christmas morning. He held the plate firmly and hit one end of it against the ground to shake off the dirt and bugs that covered it. The plate broke into two pieces. "So much for that," Lawless said as he threw both pieces of the plate into the weeds.

\* \* \*

Before the summer ended, I finally drove my children out to Graves Springs.

"You really got up at six o'clock to practice?" asked David, who was in the fifth grade.

"Every morning, son," I said.

"Where did you sleep?" David said.

"Right there one year," I pointed to the pile of wood that was once a barracks. "And for two years over there," I said pointing toward the varsity barracks.

"Daddy, I'm hot!" Dylan said. We stayed a few more minutes, and then drove home.

\* \* \*

Sometime before Christmas in 1999, I went back to Albany High to talk with Willie Magwood, who was still teaching and coaching. Magwood had never left since 1970, when he became the school's first black coach. I found Magwood around noon in the cafeteria, eating with a few of the custodians. As I walked toward the table where he was sitting, he looked up and his eyes were bright and sincere, the same as they were when I played for him in 1972.

"Hey, Coach Magwood," I said, reaching out to shake his hand.

We shook hands, and then he raised his right arm as if he was throwing a pass and said, "Lightle, can you still throw it?"

"Coach Magwood, I can still throw it some," I replied. I told him that during the previous fall I played on an intramural football team at Darton College, where I was teaching.

We walked from the cafeteria to the gym to sit and talk on the bleachers; Magwood talked about growing up and picking cotton all day and being determined to go to college so he wouldn't have to pick cotton. He talked a lot about how proud he was to have been the first black coach at Albany High. He sounded and looked the same except for his hair, which was dotted with gray.

We talked about Graves Springs and football players he coached over the years. "If a kid could go out there for two weeks," Magwood said, "he's a special kid." He remembered that a player once, but couldn't recall his name, left Graves Springs one morning on the back of a milk truck that made morning deliveries to the camp. For some, Graves Springs was too tough.

He specifically recalled my former teammate, David McClung, who played every game his senior year with a broken hand. "Shoot man, that cat was tough," he said. "You can't get football players to do that today."

Maybe Magwood's right about having fewer real tough players today like David McClung and other boys he coached at Graves Springs. He's been coaching high school football for thirty years, so he should know something about character. Or maybe it's just the nostalgia that all of us have for days gone by, the days of our youth.

What's certain though, is that Magwood saw plenty of boys along the Muckalee endure hell to be with their friends and earn a position on the team. Graves Springs "built character" he said, teaching boys the ideals of determination in the face of pain. "Every school needs a Graves Springs," Magwood said.

Cardon Dalley was the head coach my senior year. He coached at Albany High from 1974 to 1979. "Coach, what do you remember about some of the players you coached at Graves Springs?" I asked him years after he had retired.

"David McClung will always have a special place in my heart," he said. "He played that whole year [1974] with a broken hand."

\* \* \*

Graves Springs opened in 1934 as a place to make boys tough and mean enough to play football, a game becoming very popular in Southern culture. These boys were coached by men who weren't pampered as children, and damn sure weren't going to pamper and baby their players. Coaches like Harold McNabb, Hollis Sanford, and later Harold Dean Cook and Ferrell Henry, all would be out of place on some popular talk show today discussing the need to be sensitive and understanding in dealing with teenage boys. We don't want to hurt their feelings, do we?

Graves Springs hurt your feelings and your body. These coaches were tempered by traumatic events where great suffering occurred. World wars and the Great Depression weren't sensitive to a person's emotions. Albany and South Georgia, furthermore, has historically been a poor, hardscrabble area for many people since whites began pushing into the area by the 1800s. A few of them would come to control most of the land and wealth, but most people here, both white and black, were poor as was typical throughout the Deep South. Many here farmed, and others worked in textile mills, where the conditions were poor and the pay little. What a hard life it was for those enslaved, and for most of those who weren't, who toiled the fields and did hard physical labor.

\* \* \*

By 1965, with the arrival of Grady Caldwell, the first black to play at Graves Springs, the camp must now be viewed in a more significant social and even political context—one lone black boy living and practicing in the woods with sixty white boys during a time of racial change and even violence used to thwart that change. Some of the other black players at Graves Springs, like Ronnie Nelson, John Murphy, and James Harpe, knew that lynchings had occurred throughout Georgia. They were from the race of Americans who had historically been deemed inferior by whites and victimized through such evil things as slavery and lynchings.

Caldwell, too, knew the possible dangers of integrating Graves Springs; there were white players there who called him "nigger" in an effort to force him to leave to camp. But he endured, paving the way for other blacks. Coaches like Harold Dean Cook and Ferrell Henry, Southern whites who had a passion for football and who influenced the lives of hundreds of boys, probably did as well anyone could have in terms of guiding the camp and the team through the volatile period of integration.

Even Harold McNabb, the first head coach when Graves Springs opened in 1934 and later principal of Albany High during the 1960s, was said to be "very helpful" to black students and players, according to Leola Caldwell, Grady's mother. Both Cook and Henry, and other coaches, too, reached out to black players during this period.

I spoke to several former black players who came through Graves Springs, and every one of them commended Cook and Henry for how they treated black players themselves at camp. Ronnie Nelson, who was a fine black running back, called Cook his "dream man." Robert Jackson, who went on to have a remarkable professional career, was helped in many ways by Ferrell Henry, especially in being exposed to college scouts. My own life was enriched by being on the same team at Graves Springs with blacks such as James Harpe, Dewitt Williams, Celious "Crab" Williams, Al Steele, Robert Jackson, Nathaniel "Big Nate" Henderson, Johnny "Mule" Coleman, and others. They were examples of courage and decency that I never would've experienced had the team and the culture remained segregated.

We suffered together at Graves Springs, and shared a desire to be a part of the same team. Any differences were cast aside for the team, and we had no choice playing under Ferrell Henry, who made it clear that effort mattered, not race.

In 1972, my first year at Graves Springs, the Big Ten Conference in the Midwest, which at that time was one of the most racially tolerant intercollegiate conferences, issued a report saying, "The pattern of racial discrimination both overt and covert, institutional and individual, found in larger society are reflected in and perpetuated in athletics in the United States."

Of course this was apparent to anyone willing to look honestly at American culture. Some white players, like Larry Hacker, told me that because of Graves Springs they were beginning to change their views concerning race. All their lives they heard racist dogma at home and from adults. Black boys, too, were changing. Grady Caldwell said that before seeing how hard some of the white boy played, he had thought blacks to be "superior" athletes, but this supposition was disproved at Graves Springs.

It seems foolish today, but as a historian I realize that because white domination of blacks in American culture was founded upon economic lust and cultural superiority, what was happening at Graves Springs between the races took so long to occur. When the impulses of wealth and political power are involved, history often turns oppressive and violent. Slavery and lynchings support this argument. It would not be true to suggest that Graves Springs manifested immediate and remarkably better relations between the races in Albany. What is more accurate is that sports in general represent the prevailing social beliefs in regards to race. Of course, for centuries that belief was one of superiority and segregation fostered by whites. High school, collegiate, and professional sports, like American culture itself, has a history of racism. Graves Springs did promote better relations between blacks and whites at exactly the same time Albany and the South was undergoing a metamorphosis in race relations.

The camp provided a means for white and black boys, probably for the first time ever in Albany, to live and work together for a common cause—win football games. Team sports represents one of the purest forms of democratic principles, because participation and results are so easily measured. As Bobby Stanford said, who played at the University of Alabama and was one of Albany High's great players of the 1960s, "athletics evens things out, it doesn't matter who your daddy is." It also doesn't matter what color you are, and you can clearly tell in sports who tries hard, who runs fast, who never gives up, who doesn't complain when things don't go well, and how one handles himself in victory and in defeat. Plus, it's easy to discern whether a player thinks and acts more for himself then his team.

All of our lives are enriched by beauty, and it must be recognized daily to validate our own life experiences. Sports is captivating because it represents the beauty of those working in concert, teammates committed and sacrificing as we did at Graves Springs, which is one of the highest ideals of human relationships. McCree Harris, that wonderful woman of Albany who worked for human dignity and promoting racial change, said simply but poignantly that it was "a beautiful sight" as she watched, for the first time, black and white players on the same Albany High team.

\* \* \*

Unlike some of the other players and coaches who attended Graves Springs, I never lived through a time remotely comparable to the Great Depression, nor was I in the military like Sam Yarborough, Clem Rakel, Frank Orgel, Celious Williams and others who went on to serve after leaving the football camp. I have read a lot, furthermore, about the brotherhood of soldiers and in particular, Stephen Ambrose's books *D-Day: The Climatic Battle of World War II* and *A Band of Brothers,* spectacular narratives of bravery among soldiers who invaded Western Europe on June 6, 1944. Soldiers who trained together, laughed together, and got drunk with one another—some went to their deaths to save the world. Graves Springs, in that sense, is far removed from a soldier's life. We weren't asked to kill, even though many times at Graves Springs we thought the coaches were trying to kill us.

The voices of all those who ever went to Graves Springs are heard today as the Muckalee Creek is in harmony with every sound I heard when walking past the tumbled-down barracks, mess hall, and the varsity barracks, then up to the field now overgrown with pine trees. The noiseless heat of summer and the still of the Spanish moss echoes with the music and the laughter, and the struggles we shared at camp.

Bill Lightle<br>
Albany, Georgia 2002

## AUTHOR'S NOTE

As this book was being edited, Grady Caldwell, the first black to play at Graves Springs, was released from prison. By 2002 Grady was living in Hampton, Georgia, and working as a counselor in a drug abuse program; and he is a part-time minister at Zion Baptist Church. Caldwell told me by phone that he had gotten "my life back on track." I wish you the best, Grady.

In addition, McCree Harris has died. She had been a retired teacher, civil rights activist, and a kind and compassionate person that I was fortunate to meet. Ms. Harris encouraged players like Caldwell and other blacks during the mid-1960s to attend Graves Springs to help crack segregation. With her passing, Albany lost one of its finest citizens.

Carlton Bullock, who attended Graves Springs in the 1940s, has also died. Bullock was a professional photographer who I always saw in the spring when he took the pictures of my children and many others who played little league baseball in Albany.

Former teammate and boyhood friend, Brent Brock, is now the head football coach at Jackson County (Georgia) High School. He has worked with many young players over the years instilling in them the values of hard work and sacrifice that he learned at Graves Springs. Good luck Brent.

Bill Lightle<br>
May 2002

LaVergne, TN USA
31 March 2011
222349LV00001B/53/A